Books by

Historical Western Romance Series

MacLarens of Fire Mountain

Tougher than the Rest, Book One
Faster than the Rest, Book Two
Harder than the Rest, Book Three
Stronger than the Rest, Book Four
Deadlier than the Rest, Book Five
Wilder than the Rest, Book Six

Redemption Mountain

Redemption's Edge, Book One
Wildfire Creek, Book Two
Sunrise Ridge, Book Three
Dixie Moon, Book Four
Survivor Pass, Book Five
Promise Trail, Book Six
Deep River, Book Seven
Courage Canyon, Book Eight, Releasing 2017

MacLarens of Boundary Mountain

Colin's Quest, Book One,

The best way to stay in touch is to subscribe to my newsletter. Go to *www.shirleendavies.com* and subscribe in the box at the top of the right column that asks for your email. You'll be notified of new books before they are released, have chances to win great prizes, and receive other subscriber-only specials.

Sam's Legacy

MacLarens of Boundary Mountain

Historical Western Romance Series

SHIRLEEN DAVIES

Book Four in the MacLarens of Boundary Mountain

Historical Western Romance Series

For permission requests, contact the publisher.

Avalanche Ranch Press, LLC
PO Box 12618
Prescott, AZ 86304

Sam's Legacy is a work of fiction. Names,
characters, places, and incidents are either
products of the author's imagination or used
fictitiously. Any resemblance to actual events,
locales, or persons, living or dead, is wholly
coincidental.

Book conversions by Joseph Murray at
3rdplanetpublishing.com

Cover design by Kim Killion, The Killion Group

ISBN: 978-1-941786-46-8

I care about quality, so if you find something in error, please contact me via email at shirleen@shirleendavies.com

Description

Sam's Legacy, Book Four, MacLarens of Boundary Mountain Historical Western Romance Series

Samuel Covington, ex-Pinkerton agent and deputy in the frontier town of Conviction, has come a long way from his upbringing in Baltimore. His job, and a particular woman, occupy his time and thoughts. His future is assured—until a message from home tears it all apart.

Jinny MacLaren loves the ranch, her family, and one particular deputy. Even though Sam's never said the words, she's certain of his feelings, envisioning a future as his wife—until the day he announces he's leaving without a promise to return.

His future no longer belongs to him. Sam never anticipated the news awaiting him, or the consequences of a past he'd left far behind.

Shoving painful thoughts of Sam aside, Jinny focuses on a life without him, allowing a friendship to grow with someone else. He's handsome, smart, and caring, yet in Jinny's heart, he'll never be Sam.

As both face an uncertain future without the other, neither anticipates the dangers stalking them.

Protecting what's his is Sam's calling. Reclaiming what he left behind may prove to be the biggest challenge of his life.

Sam's Legacy, book four in the MacLarens of Boundary Mountain historical western Romance Series, is a stand-alone, full-length novel with an HEA and no cliffhanger.

Visit my website for a list of characters for each series.
http://www.shirleendavies.com/character-list.html

Acknowledgements

Many thanks to my husband, Richard, for always being by my side during this wonderful adventure. Your support, insights, and suggestions are greatly appreciated.

As always, many thanks to my editor, Kim Young, proofreader, Alicia Carmical, Joseph Murray who is superb at formatting my books for print and electronic versions, and my cover designer, Kim Killion.

Sam's Legacy

Chapter One

Sheriff Brodie MacLaren walked around the newly built structure, bending to inspect the drop sections in the platform. It had been designed to hang three people simultaneously. Straightening, his somber expression didn't change as he joined his deputy, Sam Covington, and Stein Tharaldson, the man in charge of building the gallows.

"What else do you need to do, Stein?" Brodie looked up at the sky, the morning sun beginning to wash the town in light. By noon, they'd be dismantling the structure, hoping to never use it again.

"My work is done, Brodie." He set his tools aside. "I've tested it with bags of sand and rocks. It will do the job. You'll need two men to knock out the supports, and I'd suggest all your deputies be present."

"I'm surprised the judge sentenced all three to death. At most, I thought he'd send them off to San Quentin." Sam thought of the prisoners. None were older than twenty when they rode into

1

town, poured glass after glass of whiskey down their throats, then rode out as rowdy drunks, shooting wildly into the air. There'd been one casualty. Bob Belford, a local rancher, had been strolling down the boardwalk with his wife, collapsing when a bullet ripped through him.

"A death is a death, Sam, whether an accident or not. At least, that's what I tell myself when I start believing the sentence is too harsh." Brodie swallowed the bile in his throat.

The jury had been made up of Belford's neighbors and friends, people who'd already convicted the three before the trial started. People who had rallied around his widow, doing what they could to help. Doc Vickery's testimony that Belford was dying of cancer and didn't have more than a couple months left didn't sway the men who'd found them guilty. The fate of the three cowboys had been sealed when the judge, known for doling out harsh sentences, slammed the gavel down a final time before leaving town.

"I can't argue with you, Brodie."

Sam Covington had come to Conviction on an assignment through his employer, the Pinkerton Detective Agency. Through a series of events, he'd left Pinkerton, taking a job as a deputy for six months. After almost a year, Sam still wore the badge.

"Sorry, Sheriff. I overslept." Jack Perkins, another deputy, hurried up beside them, looking as if he'd just crawled out of bed.

Brodie looked behind him toward the hotel. "Have you seen Nate?"

"No sir, Sheriff. Not since last night. Want me to go back to the Gold Dust and roust him?"

"I'll go." Sam didn't wait for Brodie to comment before his long strides took him toward the hotel and up to Nate's room. "Nate?" When his first knock went unanswered, he pounded harder. "Nate. Are you in there?" He could hear deep grumbling before what sounded like a body hitting the floor. A moment later, the door drew open, a bleary-eyed Nate staring at him.

Rubbing his red-rimmed eyes, he coughed, clearing his throat. "What time is it?"

Sam walked past him and into the room, looking around. "Time for you to toss water on your face and get down to the street." Turning toward Nate, he studied him, not liking what he saw. "What's going on with you?"

His brows furrowed. "I don't know what you mean."

Sam gestured around the room. "Look at this place. It's a mess, and so are you." Crossing his arms, he glared at Nate, his impatience with his fellow deputy obvious.

Raking a hand through his hair, Nate shook his head. "Give me a few minutes and I'll be down."

Sam didn't like the way Nate ignored his question, but they didn't have time to argue about it now. "Tonight, we're going for a drink, and you *will* tell me what's going on."

Nate cringed. He had no intention of sharing his private pain with anyone, especially Sam or Brodie, men he respected. They wouldn't understand, and he didn't know how to change the path he'd chosen.

Splashing water on his face, he grabbed a towel, glancing at himself in the mirror. He almost didn't recognize the man staring back at him. Over a few short months, he'd changed from someone of purpose, showing little weakness, to a man obsessed with relieving the excruciating pain from the amputation of his left arm below the elbow.

Tossing down the towel in disgust, he struggled to dress, strapping on his gunbelt before heading outside. The grumbling of his stomach almost had him pausing outside the restaurant, but coffee and breakfast would have to wait. He'd already held up the others long enough. Shoving his hand into his pocket, he crossed the street, strolling up to the menacing structure.

"Stein did a good job."

Brodie turned at Nate's voice, his gaze narrowing at the man's puffy face and red eyes. Chastising himself for not having a conversation with him months ago, he nodded, vowing to sit down with him after the hanging.

"Aye, he did."

Sam stepped next to Nate. "What do you want us to do, Brodie?"

"I'm not expecting trouble, but we've never had a hanging before. No telling how many of our good people will come out to watch."

"You think they really want to watch something so gruesome, Sheriff?" Jack let out a disgusted breath. "I sure wouldn't be here if it wasn't my job."

"I witnessed a hanging on my way through Denver. More than half the town showed up." Nate glanced over his shoulder, noticing a few people already standing on the boardwalk, gawking at the gallows. "More than a few lost their breakfast."

"I've never seen a hanging, and I'm not looking forward to this one. Colin has spread the word to keep the MacLarens at Circle M today." Someone from Brodie's family rode to town several times a week for supplies, to check for mail, or send a telegram.

At the mention of the MacLarens, Sam's thoughts turned to Jinny, Brodie's younger sister. The vivacious blonde-haired young woman had intrigued him from the first moment they met. Not beautiful in the way of the society women he knew back east, but beautiful in her own way. Her deep blue eyes always seemed to dance with mischief. Her fair skin, with a smattering of freckles, gave her a wholesome appearance he'd call pretty or cute, although he expected she wouldn't like either description. Sam knew she considered herself a grown woman, and at almost twenty, as much as he wanted to deny it, she was right.

Not long ago, her closest friend, Emma Pearce, married Quinn MacLaren, Jinny's cousin. Seeing her at the wedding, Sam had found it impossible not to stare or think about what a future with her in his life would be like. There were two problems with the dream. First, her brother was his boss. Courting her would add complications to her life and his. Second, he'd already tried love and failed. He wasn't anxious to repeat the mistake.

"Sam, I'd like you and Nate to find a few men who'd be willing to stand under the scaffolding. They'll be responsible for knocking out the two supports."

"We can do it, Brodie."

"Nae, Sam. I want you and Nate to keep watch on the crowd, make sure there aren't any wee ones running loose who might see it. At the trial, none of the boys spoke of kin or what brought them to Conviction, so it's doubtful we'll be faced with grieving widows or mothers."

"Where do you want us?"

"You'll be on the main street up near my house, Nate. Sam, I want you at the other end, toward the river. Jack, you'll be helping me bring the prisoners from the jail and up the platform. Their hands will already be bound. When we get them in place, I'll put hoods over each of their heads. No sense having the crowd watch that part."

Sam's gaze wandered up and down the structure, a shiver running through him. "Who's releasing the drop sections?"

"I'm the sheriff, so it's up to me." The dread in his voice told them how much he didn't look forward to this part of the job. Executing cold-blooded killers was one thing. Hanging three young men who'd made a horrendous mistake was something else, an action Brodie would remember for the rest of his life. "For now, get yourselves some coffee, then meet me at the jail."

Sam turned to Nate. "Let's go to the Gold Dust. I'll buy breakfast."

Walking alongside his friend, Nate knew it wouldn't be a simple meal. His fellow deputy would ask questions, try to figure out what had happened over the last few months. How could he explain it to Sam when *he* didn't understand the way his body betrayed him? After such a long time, he thought the pain would've receded. Instead, it had intensified to the point he could hardly sleep and didn't care about food, his work, or much else.

Taking a seat across from Sam, Nate took off his hat, placing it on the seat next to him. They ordered breakfast and coffee, then sat in silence until Sam spoke.

"You want to tell me what's going on?"

Nate scrubbed a hand down his face, not meeting Sam's intense stare. "It's nothing I can't handle."

"Let me rephrase it. You look like you've been dragged by a spooked horse. You've lost weight, your eyes are bloodshot, and you forget simple stuff, like your work." Leaning forward, Sam rested his arms on the table. "You want to try again?"

The place where Nate's left hand should've been throbbed. If he didn't get it taken care of soon, he'd be no good to anybody. Neither alcohol nor laudanum, which used to deaden the pain, worked. He'd found just one remedy, and it wasn't found in Doc Vickery's clinic.

Thanking the server as she placed their food down, he dug in, feigning interest in the eggs and bacon. Picking up his cup, he took a swallow, still avoiding Sam's questioning gaze.

"Brodie isn't going to be able to dismiss what's happening to you for much longer. He's already mentioned his concern, and it wouldn't surprise me if he's the next one to ask questions."

Nate stopped chewing, set down his fork, and sat back. "I've been doing my job."

"Sure, if one of us makes sure you're out of bed. Do you have any idea how many times Jack, Brodie, or I have had to almost break into your room to make sure you were all right?" Seeing the blank expression on Nate's face, he let out a sigh. "Six or seven times...at least. Before whatever is going on started, we never worried about you showing up on time, with a full stomach, ready to do your job. Now..." Sam shook his head, glancing out the window to see Brodie emerge from the jail. Shifting his attention back to Nate, he pushed away his plate. "I'd like to help if you'll let me."

Nate considered confiding in Sam, seeking help from a man he trusted. The sound of Brodie's voice stopped him.

"It's time. The crowd is growing, more people riding in. Jack is in the jail with the prisoners, as is Reverend Andrews."

Sam's eyes widened as he stood. "The reverend, huh?"

"The lads asked for him." Brodie shook his head. "Nothing about this feels right to me. I know they killed Bob and we're doing our job. Still, it doesn't sit right. Nothing to do now but get it over with."

All three sets of eyes scanned the street as they stepped out of the Gold Dust and onto the boardwalk.

Sam's face stilled when his gaze settled on a group of riders, Colin and Quinn in the lead. "I thought you told your family to stay away."

Brodie's head whipped in the direction Sam stared. Cursing under his breath, he moved toward the group, Sam right beside him. "Nate, stay at this end of town," he called over his shoulder as they made their way through the already crowded boardwalk. Reaching his family, Brodie and Sam stood in the street, blocking their progress. "What are you doing here?" His cousins didn't miss his stern expression and hard voice.

Colin sighed, glancing over his shoulder at several members of the MacLaren family, including Jinny. "They were determined to come, with or without Quinn and me."

Sam moved past the men, heading straight for Jinny. Gripping the reins of her horse, he glared up at her. "You shouldn't be here. This isn't a party, and certainly not a place for ladies."

She sat up straight in the saddle, doing her best to hide her surprise at Sam seeking her out. "I have every right to be here, Deputy Covington, as do the others."

He moved toward her, not letting go of the reins, his voice calm. "Why, Jinny? This isn't something you want burned into your memory."

Letting out a breath, she leaned down. "We aren't here to watch. August Fielder filed an appeal and sent a request to the governor for a stay of execution. We're hoping to convince Brodie to delay the execution for a few days." She nodded behind Sam. Quinn and Colin had dismounted, having a heated discussion with their cousin.

Sam turned, seeing Brodie's face redden as the debate continued. He calmed when Fielder stepped up beside him, placing a hand on the sheriff's shoulder. Sam let go of the reins. "You should've told Brodie your intentions, Jinny. This isn't the way to work with your brother."

She opened her mouth to speak, then shut it, biting her lower lip. Glancing at Sam, she sighed. "I'm sure you're right. It wasn't our intention to leave him out of it, but it all happened so fast..."

Her voice trailed off, pain flashing across her face when she saw Brodie turn to look at her, his disappointment evident. "All I can say is we did what we thought was right."

"I need to find out what's happening." Sam turned away, striding toward Brodie, not bothering to look back at Jinny. His hands fisted at his sides as he approached the group of men. He agreed with the motives and reasons for the action, but not the way Brodie and his deputies had been left out. Stopping, he looked at the sheriff. "What do you want us to do?"

A muscle in Brodie's jaw twitched as he looked from one man to the next. "Disperse the crowd. I've agreed to put off the hanging for forty-eight hours."

"I'll let Nate and Jack know." Sam glanced at Colin and Quinn, seeing strained expressions, not the looks of relief he expected. Walking down the street, he called out to the spectators. "There's nothing to see today. We're asking for you to go back inside your shops or return to your homes." He repeated it several times before spotting Nate.

"What's happening?"

"Fielder has filed an appeal and contacted the governor about staying the hanging. Brodie has agreed to wait forty-eight hours."

Nate nodded. "Can't say as I'm sorry about it."

"Me, either. I don't think Brodie's too pleased with the way it came down. Well, let's get the people out of the streets. I'll talk with Jack. Brodie should be the one to tell the prisoners."

As he crossed the street, Sam's gaze landed on a group of men sitting atop their horses. He didn't recognize a single one. Disturbed by their grim expressions, the way their hands rested on the butt of their guns, he committed the faces to memory. A tug in his gut told him he'd be seeing them again.

"Deputy. Hold up." Clarence Maloney, owner of the general store and Conviction's postmaster, held out a letter. "This came for you. I heard the execution is postponed. That right?"

Sam opened the letter, nodding absently at Clarence as he began to read the contents. Initial confusion was replaced by his jaw hardening, anger surging through him. Shifting his stance, he released a silent curse.

"You all right, Deputy?"

Letting out a frustrated breath, he nodded, gritting his teeth. "I'm fine. I'll be in the store later to post my own letter."

"I'll head back then." Clarence hurried back down the street, his gaze once again locking on the scaffolding before disappearing inside Maloney's.

Sam watched him leave, his thoughts fixed on the contents of the letter. He hadn't seen this coming, never even considered it. It had been years since he'd heard from her, anticipating they'd never be in contact again.

Lifting his head, Sam spotted Jinny down the street. His stomach roiled at how this could change his life and the future he planned. Taking a deep breath, he slid the letter into a pocket, resigned to deal with what had just become a priority in his life.

Chapter Two

"I'm sorry, Brodie. We would've said something sooner, but Mr. Fielder made the decision to move forward when he visited the ranch yesterday. Colin and Quinn wanted to ride into town last night to forewarn you." Jinny sighed, looking at the stoic face of her brother. "I'm afraid Emma, Sarah, and I talked them out of it. We thought you'd understand."

"I do understand, lass. Still, you shouldn't have stopped them from coming to talk with me. I'm the sheriff. I should've known you and Fielder were doing this." Brodie was also angry with town leader and attorney, August Fielder, the man who'd convinced him to take the job as sheriff.

He'd already told the three prisoners what Fielder had done, the hope on their faces moving him in a way he couldn't describe. They were the age of his younger cousins, who also took their turns releasing stress by drinking too much, unaware of the damage their actions could cause.

"Sheriff MacLaren?" A familiar voice captured his attention.

"Mrs. Belford. I believe you know my sister, Jinny."

"Yes. Hello, Jinny."

She stepped up, touching the woman's arm. "How are you doing, Mrs. Belford?"

"I've been better." The older woman glanced at the structure, a shudder running through her. "I wonder if I could have a word with you, Sheriff."

"Of course. We can go into the jail."

Her eyes widened. "Oh, no. I'd rather stay out here. Jinny is welcome to hear what I have to say."

"Let's at least sit down." Brodie took her elbow, escorting her to a nearby bench. He sat on one side, Jinny taking a seat on the other side of Bob Belford's widow. "What may I do for you?"

"I heard August Fielder filed an appeal and has contacted the governor."

Brodie nodded. "Aye, he has. I'm sorry if his actions upset you."

"No, Sheriff. You misunderstand." She gripped her hands in her lap. "My husband would not have wanted those boys to hang. I think what Mr. Fielder has done is right, and I'm certain Bob would agree."

A whoosh of air escaped Brodie's lips. "What makes you so sure?"

Staring down at her hands, she sucked in a shaky breath. "Bob was dying of cancer. Doc Vickery gave him a few months to live, but we knew he was being optimistic." She glanced up, her eyes welling with tears. "I don't believe Bob would've lasted another week. The pain never let up, the laudanum had stopped working, and whiskey did nothing. He couldn't sleep or eat. My husband was wasting away before my eyes." She opened her reticule, pulling out a worn piece of paper. "I found this in Bob's desk after he died."

Taking the paper, he unfolded it, reading the scribbled words of a man who knew he had little time left. Shaking his head, Brodie looked up. "Does this mean what I think?"

"Unfortunately, I believe it does. He planned to ride out and never come back. I can't say for certain, but I'm convinced Bob meant to end his life the day after the shooting. What those boys did was wrong. Should they die for it? I don't believe so." She swiped at the tears on her cheeks. "I can't have their deaths on my conscience."

"Aye, ma'am. I understand. Have you spoken to Mr. Fielder?"

"Not yet. I wanted to let you know I've sent my own telegram to the governor, asking him to commute their sentences." The corners of her mouth tipped up slightly. "I gave the governor my suggestions."

Chuckling, Brodie glanced at a surprised Jinny, then set a comforting hand over Mrs.

Belford's. "Thank you for telling me. You'll have my support, whatever is decided."

"Thank you, Sheriff. I knew you'd understand." Rising, she smiled at Jinny. "It was good to see you again, young lady. You have a good brother in Brodie."

Jinny and Brodie stood, her face reddening, guilt washing over her. Bob Belford's widow had handled the request for clemency better than the MacLarens.

Nodding, her gaze moved to Brodie, then quickly away. "Aye. He's a wonderful man."

"I need to get back to the ranch. Please pray for a good outcome."

Tipping his hat to her, Brodie placed an arm around his sister's shoulders. "Aye, ma'am. We will."

Leaning up, Jinny placed a kiss on his cheek. "You've made quite an impression on Mrs. Belford."

Brodie chuckled, dropping his arm to his side. "Perhaps, lass. Say nothing to our family, or anyone else, about the letter Bob wrote to his wife."

"I understand. It's a private message. Still, I'm glad she shared his intentions with you." Hoping for a glimpse of Sam, she scanned the people still milling about.

"I saw him go into the jail before Mrs. Belford walked up."

Shooting a look at Brodie, she shook her head. "I don't know who you're talking about."

A smile curved the corners of his mouth. "I'm sure you don't, lass."

"Well, I suppose it's time to join the others for the ride back to the ranch."

"Maggie and I will see you at Sunday supper."

"You aren't angry with us for not getting word to you sooner?"

Turning toward her, he gripped her shoulders. "I'm disappointed, but not angry, lass. I've already had words with Colin and Quinn. The lads know how I feel. It's doubtful this will happen again." Seeing Sam come out of the jail, he nudged Jinny. "Now is your chance to talk to him."

Her chest squeezed as she wondered if the entire family knew her feelings toward Brodie's deputy. "How would you feel if Sam wanted to court me?"

Brodie's gaze narrowed. It had bothered him when he first realized his sister had feelings for Sam. When he discovered his deputy might feel the same, he'd come to accept the possible outcome. He loved Jinny and would never stand in her way. Sam was a man he respected, had

19

already learned much from him. Brodie could see no reason to stand in their way, doubting their father, Ewan, would object.

His face sobered. "It's between you and Sam. He's a good man, but not good enough for you."

She laughed. "You'd say that about any man who wanted to court me."

Brodie smiled. "Aye. It's my job as your brother." He stepped forward as Sam approached. "Is Jack still in the jail?"

Sam glanced at Jinny, his features grim, then turned to look at Brodie. "He and Nate are both there. If you don't need me for a while, I have some business to attend to. It won't take long."

"Do what you have to. I'll be at the jail when you've finished." Brodie bent to kiss Jinny's cheek. "Let him know what Mrs. Belford did."

Jinny watched Brodie walk away.

"What did he mean for you to tell me what Mrs. Belford did?"

Sam's strained features softened as she explained the widow's decision, mentioning the letter, but omitting the part about what her husband intended to do.

"What do you think, Sam?"

"She acted on her conscience. I don't blame her. It would be hard knowing you could have stopped someone from dying when you had reasons to prevent it."

Sam's gaze moved over her, desire growing. His heart squeezed when he saw the same look in her eyes.

Until he'd received the letter, Sam had every intention of approaching Brodie, getting his approval to court Jinny. In the span of a couple minutes, his plans had changed. Too bad his feelings for the woman before him hadn't. Sam wanted her as much as always, didn't foresee a time when he wouldn't, which made what he had to do that much harder. Drawing in a deep breath, he touched her elbow.

"Walk with me, Jinny."

Swallowing the excitement at his invitation, she allowed him to escort her down the street and into a small restaurant. Taking a table in a quiet corner, he pulled out her chair.

"I hope this is all right."

Smiling, she nodded. "Aye, this is perfect."

A young man walked up, pointing to a menu on the wall. "Hello, Deputy. What would you like today?"

Sam looked at Jinny. "Are you hungry?" When her stomach growled, he chuckled. "I believe you are. Two of your specials, please."

Jinny's face flushed as she removed the hand settled on her disruptive stomach. "Thank you for inviting me to lunch."

Sam shifted in his seat, knowing she might not feel the same after he told her the reason for wanting to see her. Pushing aside his personal feelings, he leaned forward. "Jinny, I—"

"Here you are. Two specials." Placing plates before them, the waiter left to see to another table.

"This smells wonderful." Picking up her fork, she took a bite. "Mmm."

"Seems this restaurant was a good choice. I eat here a few times a week." His appetite had vanished. Still, he forked a bite, chewing slowly.

"You started to say something before the food arrived." Glancing up at him, Sam couldn't miss the enthusiasm on her face. He knew what she expected him to say. It wasn't to be.

Setting down his fork, he swallowed the dread he felt. "I'm leaving Conviction, Jinny."

Her hand stilled partway to her mouth, her hopeful expression dissolving. "Leaving?"

"There is business I must attend to back home."

"But you'll return, right?" Her stomach clenched at the distress on his face.

Sam shook his head. "I don't know."

Sucking in a shaky breath, Jinny set down her fork, no longer hungry. "I see."

"I wouldn't be leaving if I didn't have to."

She nodded, then looked away, his words barely registering. Her brain had shut down, as if protecting her from the pain closing around her.

"Jinny..."

Focusing on Sam once again, she straightened her spine, doing what she could to hide the devastation raging inside her. "I don't know what to say." To her disgust, her voice broke. Setting the napkin on the table, she pushed back the chair and stood. "Thank you for lunch, Sam." Turning, she rushed off before he had a chance to stop her.

"Jinny, wait."

She didn't respond, pushing through the door and dashing down the street. Frustrated at the tears pooling in her eyes, Jinny tried to remember where she'd left her horse. A hand gripping her arm had her stopping. "Let me go."

"Jinny, let me explain." Sam tried to turn her toward him, feeling her resist. "There are reasons I must go."

She refused to look at him, let him see how much his leaving hurt. She'd been a fool to dream about Sam, hoping someday he'd feel the same. "I'm certain there are, and I respect that you believe you must leave."

Looking around, he eased her between two buildings, out of the range of prying eyes and ears. Placing his hands on her shoulders, he held steady, even as she twisted to leave.

"Look at me, Jinny." He waited until she stopped squirming, her reluctant gaze meeting his. "I don't *want* to leave. It's something I *have* to do. You were the reason I stayed beyond the time I'd agreed to with Brodie."

Her eyes widened. "I don't understand. Why must you go now?"

Letting his hands slip from Jinny's shoulders to stroke her arms, he felt her shiver, his own body tightening. A life with her was what he wanted. He'd thought of little else the last few months, yet it may now be out of his control.

His resolve began to slip as she moved closer, her feelings for him clear on her face. Even as his hands moved to her back, he knew it was a mistake. Drawing her to him, he leaned down, brushing a soft kiss across her lips. Seeing the intensity in her eyes, feeling her hands tighten on his arms, he took her mouth again, letting passion take control.

A thrill rushed through him as he realized she knew little of what was happening. He doubted she'd been kissed before, yet her response was immediate. Moving his lips across her jaw, trailing kisses down her neck, he felt a shudder rush through her.

"Sam..."

Her soft plea brought an unwelcome flash of sanity. Placing one more kiss on her lips, he pulled Jinny close, tucking her head below his chin.

"There are things you don't know about me. I wish it could be different. You know I'd stay if I could."

Her body stiffened at his whispered words. Moving her hands to his chest, she pushed away. Clearing her throat, Jinny took another step back. "I should go."

"I'll walk with you."

"Nae. It would be better if I go alone." Taking a few hesitant steps, she stopped. "When will you be leaving?"

His throat worked as he sucked in a slow breath. "As soon as a decision has been made on the prisoners. I can't leave Brodie with just two deputies."

"A few days then." Her voice was devoid of all emotion. "Then I won't see you again." She tried to smile, but couldn't manage it. "I wish you the best, Sam. Always the best." Without waiting for him to respond, she hurried away, leaving him feeling a loss greater than he'd ever known.

Chapter Three

As the miles passed, Sam stared out the train window, seeing nothing. He'd left his saddle and horse, Pirate, with Stein Tharaldson. One bag, holding everything else he owned, had been stowed near his seat. Sam would get word to Stein to sell Pirate back to the MacLarens if returning to Conviction became impossible. Leaving his horse gave him a measure of hope he'd return.

The last few days had been spent in solitude, daydreaming of the woman he had to leave behind. He needed to concentrate on the reason for returning to Maryland and his parents' home in Baltimore, not on Jinny and a kiss he couldn't scrub from his mind.

Brodie accepted his resignation without asking questions, telling Sam he could have his job back anytime. Once the governor's decision to change the sentence on the three boys had been received, he'd made plans to leave. After sending a reply to the man who'd contacted him, he mailed a short letter to his parents, letting them know of his return.

It angered him how he'd just learned of what happened, of obligations never considered. It had been years with no word, then a detailed letter changed his life.

"May we join you?"

Sam continued to stare out the window, not hearing the woman's voice until she repeated it, louder this time.

"Sir, may we join you?"

Shifting in his seat, he stood, removing his hat. "Please." He looked at the woman and the young boy, who couldn't be more than seven. Glancing outside, he saw the station. So lost in his own thoughts, he hadn't even noticed the train had stopped.

"Thank you. We almost lost hope of finding two seats together."

When they were settled across from him, Sam sat down. "I'm Sam Covington. Where are you headed?"

"I'm Minnie Ritter, and this is my son, Harry. We're traveling to Baltimore. Have you been there?"

"Yes, ma'am. I was born there. It's where I'm headed."

"Wonderful. Then we'll be sharing the entire trip with you, won't we, Harry?"

"Yes, Mama." He didn't look at his mother, staying focused on the canvas-covered ball in his hand.

"How old are you, Harry?"

When he didn't answer, Minnie spoke for him. "Five. He'll be six next month. It's why we're going to visit his grandparents in Baltimore. They've never met him."

"Your parents?" Sam asked, watching the boy toss the ball from one hand to the other.

"No. They're my late husband's parents. He died soon after the war started." Minnie glanced at Harry. "He never had a chance to meet his son. When I received word of his death, we moved from Pennsylvania to live with my parents in St. Louis. Do you have children, Mr. Covington?"

"No, ma'am. I'm not married." He saw no need to elaborate.

She laughed. "I don't suppose that matters much anymore. I know of at least a dozen women in St. Louis who have children and never married. The war, I guess. People make poor decisions when faced with possible death." She reached over and stroked Harry's head.

"Mama," he protested, moving away.

"He thinks he's a man and doesn't need me much anymore." Minnie placed her hands in her lap and glanced out the window as the train began to move. After a while, she reached into her bag, pulling out yarn and needles. "You don't mind if I knit, do you?"

"No, ma'am. I hope you don't mind if I take a nap."

"You go right ahead, Mr. Covington."

Closing his eyes, Sam crossed his arms, stretching out his long legs as best as he could without disturbing the Ritters. Within minutes, he'd fallen asleep, images of Jinny filling his dreams.

Circle M Ranch

"It must have been very important or he wouldn't have left, Jinny." Emma MacLaren, Quinn's wife, sat beside her closest friend on the porch swing after supper.

"Aye, I'm sure it was." She lifted her gaze to meet Emma's. "At least, that's what I keep telling myself. I thought he might try to see me again before he left."

Sam had been gone for over a week—ten days since he'd held her in his arms. She'd never been kissed before, never been held so close. Remembering broke her heart.

"Brodie said Sam left right after the governor changed the sentences of the three prisoners. He didn't even wait until the following morning."

"I heard." Jinny glanced out at a clear sky covered with stars. "He's not coming back."

Emma squeezed her hand, then let go. "I know, honey. At least he didn't give you hope. Now you're free to meet someone else."

Jinny shook her head, then looked at Emma. "Sam's who I love. Remember how you were when Quinn told you there'd never be a future with him?"

Emma nodded, still feeling the pain of his words months after they'd married.

"Even then, you weren't interested in anyone else. You waited until the eejit found some sense."

Emma laughed. "True, but *my* eejit lived here. Yours is thousands of miles away."

Jinny's eyes widened. "You know where he went?"

"Well, yes. Didn't he tell you? According to Quinn, he left to go home...to Maryland."

Jinny's throat tightened. "A country between us. No wonder he won't be coming back."

"I'm so sorry. I wish there was something I could do for you. Brodie and your parents are beginning to worry."

Jinny glanced toward the barn. She'd done all her chores, been to every meal, done her best to participate in conversations. "I didn't realize it was so obvious."

"It isn't to most of the family. I told Brodie you needed time, the same as he did when Maggie left."

"Tell me I'm not as bad as he was."

Emma grimaced. "Well..."

Burying her face in her hands, Jinny groaned.

"Give yourself time. When you're ready, we'll go into town, buy some fabric, and make you a new dress."

Dropping her hands, she tilted her head. "Why would I be needing a new dress?"

"For the community dance, of course. It's the one we go to every year. The whole family is going, and that includes you."

Even with her passion for dresses, Jinny had no interest in a new one or in attending the dance. If her family was concerned, she'd force herself to go.

"I suppose it's time to accept Sam is truly gone. I've no interest in meeting someone else, so don't push any of the lads on me." She watched Emma's face brighten. "Ach, I mean it. I'll not be having you parade people in front of me. Promise me, or I won't go."

"Fine. At least you'll be there with me."

Jinny smiled, although it didn't quite reach her eyes. "You forget, you'll be with Quinn."

"Who'll tire of me wanting to dance. Don't worry. You and I will have plenty of time together." Yawning, Emma stood. "It's time I found Quinn and went to bed. I'll see you in the morning."

Walking down the front steps, she headed for the barn, knowing the men would be in there, telling lies while trying to hide the bottle of whiskey she'd seen Quinn's brother, Bram, stash in a pocket.

Standing, Jinny stretched her arms above her head. Stepping into the house, she headed up the stairs to her bedroom, closing the door behind her. Somehow, she had to put Sam behind her, and it needed to start soon. She didn't need anyone wasting time worrying about her.

Tomorrow would be a new day. A day Jinny would use to start over and forget about what couldn't be changed.

Conviction

"One more stop, Emma. I'm in need of a new saddle." Jinny held her packages against her chest as she crossed the street, dodging wagons and riders as she headed toward Ferguson Harness and Saddlery.

"I didn't realize anything was wrong with the one you have now." Holding her skirt to avoid the muddy ruts from last night's storm, Emma followed Jinny's path, bounding up the steps to the saddlery. "Quinn told me Mr. Ferguson hired someone. Maybe we'll get to meet him."

"It doesn't matter who takes the order, as long as the work is done right." She pushed through the door, glancing around the shop, her gaze halting on a tall, good-looking young man standing behind the counter. "Oh my," she breathed out, watching him finish with a customer.

"He must be the new help Quinn mentioned."

"Aye." Jinny cleared her throat, doing her best to show disinterest as he walked toward them.

"What may I do for you ladies?"

Emma glanced at Jinny, nudging her when she didn't answer. "I, um...need a new saddle."

"Then this is the right place." His gaze locked on Jinny, a broad smile enhancing his already handsome face.

Squaring her shoulders, she glanced at the saddles on display. "Something similar to the one against the wall."

"Good choice, Miss..."

"Jinny MacLaren, and this is my cousin, Emma MacLaren. And you are?"

"Deke Arrington. I'm Rube Ferguson's nephew. It's a pleasure to meet both of you." He glanced behind him. "You've good taste. If what you want is anything like the one over there, you'll be the envy of all your relatives."

Jinny's eyes widened. "You know of my family?"

His deep, easygoing chuckle warmed her. "I've met several members of your family, including the sheriff, who I'm told is your brother."

"Brodie mentioned me to you?"

"Not quite. Uncle Rube spent several hours telling me about the town and his most prominent customers, including the MacLarens. Don't worry, though. All I know are names. It's nice to put a face to yours. So, about your saddle, why don't you tell me exactly what you'd like."

"I'm so pleased Deke showed an interest in attending the community dance, aren't you?"

Unable to garner much interest in the dance, Jinny glanced at Emma as they walked toward their horses. As attractive as she found him, Deke didn't stir her blood, make her heart pound the same way Sam did.

"I suppose."

"It will be a perfect way for him to meet single women," Emma prodded.

"Aye, there are quite a number in Conviction. I'm certain a man such as Deke won't lack for attention."

"You found him attractive, didn't you?"

Sighing, she nodded. "Aye, he is quite handsome." Stopping next to their horses, she turned toward Emma. "He's also charming and smart. The problem is, he isn't Sam."

"I'm not asking you to do anything more than accept a dance if he asks and introduce him to others. It's better than sitting alone at the house, wishing Sam hadn't left."

Securing the package of fabric to the back of her saddle, Jinny grabbed the reins and swung into it with a graceful ease. She didn't fault Emma for encouraging her to get out and forget what could've been.

The two rode at a slow pace out of town, Jinny pondering Emma's words. She couldn't deny how much his leaving hurt, but pining over Sam wouldn't help. And it didn't bring her any closer to forgetting about him. "I understand you worry about me, Emma, but there's no need. Sam's gone and that's the end of it." Sucking in a breath, she settled into the saddle for the ride back to the ranch. "We'll make our dresses, and I'll go with you and Quinn to the dance."

"That's wonderful. I'll let—"

Jinny cut her off before Emma could get carried away. "But...do *not* push any of the lads toward me. If you do, I'll not be going with you to another dance for a long time."

Baltimore, Maryland

As he had for the last ten minutes, Sam stood outside the front door of a house he hadn't thought about in years. Coming here had been required, part of a responsibility he refused to shirk. It didn't mean he liked it.

He'd gone home, explained to his parents what little he knew, then began his own investigation. It took over two weeks to gather the information he needed. He hadn't been happy with the results, nor the data that forced him to do what he was doing now. Standing outside the house owned by his ex-lover's parents, he remembered the woman he thought he loved, planned to marry—until she destroyed all they had with a few short sentences.

After meeting Jinny, Sam knew his feelings for another young woman years ago didn't compare to the desire he felt for her. He found himself wondering how he could be attracted to two such different women. One sweet, trusting, and naïve. The other world-weary at a young age, a lie rolling off her tongue with an ease he'd never anticipated. Not until it was too late.

Knowing he could wait no longer, Sam lifted his hand, knocking three times, then standing back. In less than a minute, a large colored man answered the door, nodding congenially, then stepping aside when the homeowner came up behind him. Arthur Foster offered his hand.

"Samuel Covington. We've been expecting you. Please, come in."

Sam stared at the outstretched hand, deciding his best course was to be gracious about the elder Foster's summons. Stepping inside, he felt a moment of extreme unease pass through him. It had been years since he stood in this foyer, watching a beautiful, vivacious young woman glide down the stairs. He could almost feel her presence now, years after she'd died.

Foster, an elderly man with thinning gray hair, stopped in front of a set of closed doors, his expression bleak. "My wife is waiting for us in the drawing room. She is not in good health and tires easily." His eyes had a wistful, faraway look. "I'm afraid she won't be with me much longer." Opening the door, he ushered Sam inside. "Ethel, Mr. Covington is here."

Dressed in all black, her pale skin and haunted expression had Sam rooted in place. "Good morning, Mrs. Foster."

"Sam?"

He moved toward her, not wanting to seem too aggressive. "Yes, ma'am."

"Oh, I don't believe Vera is expecting a caller." She glanced at her husband. "Arthur, would you let Vera know Sam is here?"

Sam's confused expression shot to Arthur. "I'm afraid my wife lives in the past. Most days, she is unaware of Vera's passing." He glanced at Ethel. "I'm afraid Vera is out right now. Perhaps we can entertain Sam until she returns."

Nodding, she stood. "Of course. May I get you some tea?"

"Uh..."

Arthur sat down. "Please accept, Sam. It gives her something to do while we talk."

Taking a seat in the chair Arthur indicated, he glanced at Ethel. "Tea would be fine. Thank you."

As she walked from the room, Arthur turned toward Sam. "You must know we wouldn't have contacted you if the need weren't critical. I take it you thought the information in our letter important enough to bring you back from California."

"How old is he?"

"Ah, right to the point. I always liked that about you, Sam." Arthur leaned forward, resting his arms on his legs. "Four. His name is Robert Samuel Foster Covington. We call him Robbie, and I'm afraid he's quite precocious. Some days, he doesn't stop talking."

Sam's jaw clenched. All the letter had said was he had a child. The more he learned, the more real it became. "Where is he?"

"With his nanny at the park. I didn't believe it wise to have him meet you until we had talked."

He didn't trust Foster, not after all the deceit of the past. "Why would I believe he's my son?"

Chuckling, Arthur sat back, resting his hands in his lap. "When you see Robbie, you'll have no doubt. Before she died, Vera swore you were the father."

Snorting, Sam crossed one leg over the other. "You and I both know your daughter was a consummate liar."

Pain flickered in Arthur's eyes. "No matter Vera's shortcomings, she would not have lied about the parentage of her son. She listed herself as your wife and you as Robbie's father on the birth certificate."

Sam grimaced. "My wife?"

"Vera had no intention of letting Robbie suffer for her actions or the fact you refused to marry her."

Anger at the intended accusation rushed through Sam. Standing, he paced away, trying to rein in the words he wanted to say. Targeting his fury at Arthur would accomplish nothing. Gaining control of his emotions, Sam turned, his voice calm.

"The facts didn't lie. Vera was a subversive for the Confederacy, a traitor to the country she professed to love. She meant to turn me over to her superiors in Lee's army. If I hadn't intercepted her missive, I wouldn't be standing before you now."

"I understand how her betrayal must have felt to you. Her change in allegiance devastated Ethel and me. Still, Vera was our daughter, and Robbie is our grandson. Your son, Sam. Now, you can choose not to accept him and walk away. I wouldn't blame you if you did. However, as much as you grew to hate Vera, I believe you will grow to love your son. He's been blessed with the best parts of both of you." A knock on the door had them turning. "That will be Robbie and his nanny. Shall I ask them in?"

Pushing aside whatever doubt Sam had, he nodded.

"Enter." Arthur stood at the sound of laughter in the foyer.

Heart pounding, stomach churning, Sam watched as the door opened and a young boy ran inside, his face filled with excitement.

"Grandpapa, I saw so many animals today." Robbie reached up to grab Arthur's hand. "Come with me and I'll show you." Tugging at his grandfather's hand, he spotted Sam. Dropping his hold, he took a few tentative steps toward him. "Are you a friend of Grandpapa's?"

Sam's gaze shot to Arthur, then back to the small boy staring up at him. Dropping to a knee, he studied Robbie's features. Arthur had been right. The boy was his. "Yes, I am. My name is Samuel Covington."

Whipping around to stare at his grandfather, he smiled. "That's my name, too, isn't it, Grandpapa?"

Sighing, Arthur nodded. "Almost, my dear boy. Your name is Robert Samuel." He gestured to Sam. "As I recall, my friend's name is Samuel Robert. Now, young man, where are your manners?"

Turning back to Sam, Robbie stuck out his hand. "It is a pleasure to meet you, sir."

His breath hitching, throat tightening, Sam clasped his much larger hand around Robbie's. "Believe me, young Robbie, the pleasure is mine."

Chapter Four

Circle M Ranch

"I didn't realize the change in their sentence meant they would be working at the Belford ranch." Jinny finished pinning the hem of Emma's dress as they discussed the news from town. Colin and Quinn took turns fetching supplies and picking up mail. Their trips generally included having lunch with Brodie.

"Quinn said the governor stayed their execution, providing their new sentence a few days ago. Brodie told them Mrs. Belford insisted she wanted the three at her place where they could be watched. If they don't do as instructed or hurt anyone else, they'll be headed to San Quentin." Emma looked at herself in the mirror. Even though she much preferred pants, she was pleased with what she saw. "Brodie tried to talk her out of it. August Fielder had offered to have them work for him, but Mrs. Belford insisted, since her husband had been the victim, they needed to work off their sentence on her ranch."

Jinny stood up, stretching her arms above her head. "That should do it." She walked around Emma, then nodded, seeing nothing amiss. "She's always been a strong woman. If anyone can make those lads toe the line, it will be her. Mr. Fielder is a taskmaster, but—"

A soft knock on Jinny's bedroom door interrupted what she planned to say next. Pulling it open, she gasped at the sight of her cousin, Heather, standing in the hall, a garment slung over her arm.

"Is that a *dress*?" Jinny's smile broadened. Heather was worse than Emma when it came to wearing dresses. Of all the MacLaren women, she never attended dances, didn't know how to sew, and seldom cooked beyond heating up a can of beans. For several months, she'd worked at a neighboring ranch owned by Widow Evanston. She'd never been happy working as a ranch hand for her family. Working somewhere else seemed to give her what she needed, although none of the family could ever quite figure out what that was.

Her face reddened as she walked into the room. "Aye, it is. I, uh...I wondered if one of you might have time to help me alter it."

Jinny cocked her head. "Are you planning to go to the community dance?"

Heather pursed her lips, nodding. "I'd thought of it. Mrs. Evanston is going and insisted I ride along with her." Sighing, she sagged down on the edge of the bed, staring at the floor. "It's probably a daft idea. I don't even know how to dance."

Emma glanced at Jinny. "We can teach you."

Heather looked up, surprised at the offer. "You would do that for me?"

"Of course. You're family. We MacLaren women must stick together." Although Emma hadn't been an official MacLaren for long, she'd always felt like part of the family.

"First, let's look at your dress." Jinny plucked it off Heather's arm and held it up. "Where did you get this?"

Heather winced. "From Ma. It's one she wore a few years ago. Is it all right? I mean, will it make me appear an eejit?"

Jinny studied her cousin. She'd never seen Heather concerned about her appearance, wanting to make a good impression. Sitting down, she folded the dress and placed it in her lap.

"How do you want to look, Heather?"

"I don't know what you mean." She bit her lower lip, her gaze looking away, then returning to Jinny, letting out a breath. "Aye, maybe I do. There's someone going, and, well..."

Jinny's jaw dropped. "You're interested in a lad?"

Swallowing, Heather nodded. "Aye." Sitting up straighter, she hardened her voice, features indignant. "Don't be asking me who, though, as I won't be telling you."

Jinny looked away, trying not to smile. This was the Heather she knew. Proud, easily annoyed, and closed. A woman who could shoot, rope, and ride better than most men, and wasn't afraid to tell them so.

"All right then. I won't be asking. What I will say is you can't wear this dress. We have to make you a new one or alter one of mine. What do you think, Emma?"

"I'm not as good at fashion as you are. The dance is Saturday. Do we have time to buy fabric and make a new one?"

"I don't think so." Jinny dashed to her wardrobe, rifling through her dresses, tossing four on a nearby chair. "You're taller than me, Heather, and a little more, well...rounded."

Heather snickered. "You mean my bust and rump are bigger than yours."

Emma laughed at her sister-in-law's honesty. "If anyone can adjust a dress for you, it's Jinny."

"Let's hope I live up to your expectations. It's time to get to work."

Baltimore, Maryland

"Good morning, Arthur. I hope this isn't too early for you." Sam fingered the hat in his hands, signaling how nervous he felt. He'd met with Robbie and his grandparents two more times. As yet, Robbie hadn't been told about their relationship. Today, he'd made arrangements to take his son riding, an activity the boy had been begging his grandparents to do.

"Not at all. Robbie has been up and dressed for hours. I'm afraid I've been lax in providing him with opportunities normal for boys his age. Please, come inside."

"Grandpapa, is he here?" Robbie came bounding down the stairs, his face a picture of excitement.

"He is. And I believe Mr. Covington is ready to take you on your little excursion."

Robbie could barely contain his excitement, jumping up and down, clapping his hands.

"Robert, you may want to settle down a little before Mr. Covington changes his mind."

The little boy's face fell at Arthur's words. "You won't change your mind, will you?"

Sam knelt before him. "No, I won't change my mind. In fact, my horse and yours are out front. Would you like to see them?"

"Yes." Running to the door, Robbie didn't wait for Sam before dashing outside and down the steps.

Smiling, Sam turned to Arthur. "Has he ridden at all?"

"Very little. He was a baby when Vera..." Arthur's voice broke.

"He'll be safe with me. With your permission, I'd like to keep him through supper."

"He's your son, Sam. All I ask is for Ethel and me to be present when he learns you're his father."

Nodding, Sam settled his hat on his head before heading toward Robbie. As yet, he still wore his wide-brimmed western hat, preferring it to the smaller bowlers and top hats worn by men in the eastern states. If all went as planned, he'd have one made for his son.

"Robbie, I want you to listen to what I tell you and do what I say. Is that understood?"

The boy's face went from excited to somber in an instant. "Yes, sir."

Sam kept the smile from creeping across his face. "Good. This is the horse you'll be riding." Robbie reached out, then drew his hand back. "It's all right. You can touch him. Let me lift you up." Slipping his hands under Robbie's arms, he held him close to the horse's neck. "Go ahead and stroke him."

Robbie's small hand reached out, touched the horse, then pulled back. An instant later, he did the same again, letting it move down the animal's neck several times. A nicker had him snatching his hand back.

"It's all right. He's saying hello to you."

Robbie shifted, wrapping his arms around Sam's neck. "Do you think Grandpapa will let me have a horse one day?"

His breath caught as a strong protective feeling flashed through him, making him shudder. "I can promise you will have a horse one day." He'd almost slipped, calling Robbie *son*. The thought had come so naturally, it scared him.

It hadn't taken long, mere seconds for Sam to see the striking resemblance, admitting Robbie was indeed his. At least Vera hadn't lied about that. By putting Sam's name on the birth certificate, she'd made his ability to claim him simple. In fact, if he thought it best for Robbie, he could book two train tickets and be gone by morning.

Sam had seldom been around children, except for those in the MacLaren family. He knew Jinny loved children, wanted several of her own. A flash of pain gripped his chest, wondering if she'd ever be able to accept his son.

Thinking of Jinny and what could've been seemed pointless. They were thousands of miles apart.

Over two months had passed since he'd seen Jinny, held her in his arms, spoken to her. The emptiness he felt receded a small amount each day. Sam doubted the loss could be filled by making a life for him and his son, yet he had no choice but to try.

The Baltimore police chief had offered him a position as a detective, Sam knew Allan Pinkerton would hire him back, and his father offered him a high-level job in his company. Three good opportunities, and not one appealed to him. A decision had to be made soon. Within days, he intended to claim his son, set up a house, and build a new life. Sam couldn't rely on his savings and modest trust left to him by his grandmother to last forever.

When he closed his eyes at night, one picture captured his thoughts, as if to remind him he could still achieve his own dreams. The strongest image, the one he fell asleep to and woke up with each morning, gave him hope. A man, woman, and small boy rode across an open plain, each one laughing as they dropped over a hill and out of sight.

"Did you have a good time today, Robbie?" Sam reached up, helping his son to the ground after returning to Arthur and Ethel's house after supper. It had been a long, wonderful day. One Sam hoped to repeat over and over.

"Oh yes. Can we do it again?"

He ruffled the hair on Robbie's head. "I believe it can be arranged."

Taking his son's hand, they walked toward the front door, Sam lifting him into his arms when Robbie's steps began to falter. Resting his head on Sam's shoulder, he'd fallen asleep before the front door opened.

"Ah, you've returned." Arthur stood aside, a look Sam couldn't quite describe on his face. "Is he asleep?"

"He dropped off in the last few seconds. Shall I take him to his room?"

"Please. Up the stairs, first door on the right. Ethel is already in bed, but I doubt you'll disturb her."

Making his way up the stairs, Sam felt Arthur's gaze on his back. The Fosters didn't want to give their grandson up, but poor health and age worked against them. Ethel may not last the year, and Arthur's doctor had given him the somber news his own heart had begun to fail. If they'd been younger, having more strength, Sam might never have known about his son.

Removing Robbie's shoes and pants, he settled him in the bed, drawing up the covers. He didn't hesitate to lean down and place a kiss on his forehead. Standing, Sam stared down at his sleeping son, his heart squeezing. With a sigh, he closed the door and walked down the stairs.

"I'm in the drawing room, Sam. Would you like a brandy?"

"Whiskey, if you have it."

Reaching into the back of his liquor cabinet, Arthur pulled out a bottle. Opening it, he poured two glasses, handing one to Sam. "Whiskey sounds better than the weaker stuff the doctor recommends."

Sam rolled the glass in his hand, studying the amber liquid. "I'd like to talk to you about taking Robbie home with me."

Arthur's shoulders slumped. "He's your son, Sam. You can take him whenever you want."

"I have the legal right, but it's important to do it in a way that's best for Robbie, and for you. I know he means a great deal to you and Ethel, and his leaving will cut deep."

Lowering himself into a large leather chair, Arthur stared out the window at the black night. "Yes, we will miss him. It gives us both comfort knowing he'll be with his father. Where do you plan to live?"

"With my parents until I've purchased a house."

"So you've decided to stay in Baltimore. Ethel and I wondered if you might take the boy west."

Downing the whiskey, he set the glass on a table. "I've thought about it, and maybe I will someday. For now, I think it best he stay close to those he already knows."

Arthur glanced away, lost in thought, before his gaze returned to Sam. "I know you're trying to do what's best for Robbie. If you'll permit me, I'd like to offer my opinion."

Sam's jaw tensed. He hoped Arthur didn't try to talk him out of taking Robbie home. "Of course."

"Do what's right for you, not because you believe it's the best decision for Robbie. We haven't spent a great deal of time together, Sam, yet I sense you miss the life you had in California. If that's true, don't build one here and then uproot Robbie later. Go now, while he's young and everything is an adventure."

Sam's brows furrowed. "I thought it would be best to keep him close to you and Ethel."

"The boy needs his father, not two doddering grandparents who aren't able to give him the life he deserves. And I'm not talking about money. I know you were a deputy in a frontier town."

Sam nodded. "Conviction. It's growing rapidly. I'd been looking at a parcel of land east of town, hoping to build a house, maybe raise some cattle." Jinny's image flashed across his mind, but he shook it off. He couldn't go back and expect her to want him now with his changed circumstances. Besides, they hadn't spoken of love or commitment. She might have even moved on, met someone else while he'd been attending to his responsibilities in Baltimore. The thought of not having her in his life made it difficult to breathe.

"From what I've heard, there's opportunity out there. Are there families?"

Sam chuckled. "Yes, there are many families. Strong ones with good values. My boss, the sheriff, is part of one of the largest families in the area. His sister..." Sam caught himself before he said too much.

Arthur's eyes flashed. "His sister interests you?"

Sam didn't want to say more, knowing Arthur and Ethel still grieved the loss of their daughter.

"It's all right if you have feelings for another woman. Robbie needs a mother. There are fine women in Baltimore, from good families, who want nothing more than to marry well and have a family. In fact, our neighbor's daughter—"

Chuckling, Sam held up his hand. "That's enough. I understand your point and promise I'll consider what you've said." Standing, he walked toward Arthur, extending his hand. "Don't get up. I'll show myself out. Thank you for the drink and the sage advice."

Clasping the outstretched hand, his face relaxed. "You'll make a good decision and be a wonderful father, Sam. When do you plan to take Robbie to your parents' house?"

"Saturday morning."

Chapter Five

Conviction

Quinn strolled into the community dance, a broad smile on his face. Decked out in his finest, he had his wife, Emma, on one arm, his cousin, Jinny, on the other.

Hearing the music, Emma couldn't contain her excitement. "This is going to be a wonderful night."

Chuckling, Quinn tugged her close. "So far, I'm the luckiest man at the dance. I'm arriving with two beautiful women. It's a fine start to the night."

Walking in behind him, Colin escorted his wife, Sarah, and mother, Audrey. "You're no luckier than I am, lad."

Glancing over his shoulder, Quinn chuckled. "Aye. You've a handful, as well."

A procession of MacLarens followed them inside, selecting a group of empty tables near the band. Almost everyone from the family came, including Caleb Stewart, who'd been on the wagon train with them when they'd traveled across country to begin their new lives.

Quinn looked at Emma and Jinny. "Caleb and I will get you ladies some punch."

"Oh my. Look who's here." Emma's gaze focused on two women walking inside. Standing, she motioned them over.

Caleb's jaw slackened at the beauty coming toward them. Heather MacLaren turned heads as she strolled across the dance floor, unaware of the stir her presence caused. He'd never seen her in a dress, light brown hair twisted into an intricate knot and highlighted with flowers, curled strands falling to her shoulders. He exhaled, the slow breath calming his racing heart. Without thought, his steps led him to meet her.

"Good evening, Heather." The slight catch in his voice surprised him.

"Good evening, Caleb. I believe you've met Mrs. Evanston."

"Mrs. Evanston. You look beautiful tonight." He bowed at the waist, eliciting a chuckle from the older woman.

"Enough of that, young man. It's Heather who's beautiful."

Caleb swallowed the knot in his throat. "Yes, ma'am." He glanced at Heather, who averted her eyes, looking toward Emma and Jinny. "Please, let me escort you to our table." Standing between them, he placed his hands on his waist, waiting as they slipped their arms through his for the short walk to the table.

"Heather, you look wonderful." Emma walked up, giving her a hug as the band began to play.

"Hello, Mrs. Evanston. It's nice to see you." Jinny turned toward Heather. "Ah, you are very bonny tonight." She took her arm. "Come, sit next to me." Showing her to two empty seats, Jinny sat down, leaning to whisper against Heather's ear. "Did you see Caleb's face when you walked in?"

Her spine straightened, a look of surprise crossing her face before she concealed it. "Ach, Caleb Stewart appreciates all women."

"Don't be daft. The lad can't stop looking at you. Is he the reason you're here tonight?"

Sucking in a breath, Heather shook her head. "Nae. I came because Mrs. Evanston asked me to accompany her and for no other reason."

"Ah..." Jinny bit her lip, doing her best to hide a smile.

"Miss MacLaren. May I have this dance?"

The women turned to see Deke Arrington standing across the table, his gaze fixed on Jinny.

"I believe he's speaking to you," Heather whispered, smiling.

"Thank you, Mr. Arrington. I'd be pleased to dance with you."

Stepping around the table, he pulled out her chair, extending his hand. Walking her to the center of the floor, he led her into a waltz. "I'm glad you invited me."

"I believe you would've heard about it on your own."

He looked down at her. "Perhaps. But now I have an excuse to spend time with you."

Jinny's heart skittered, although it wasn't the jolt she always felt around Sam. Nor did the feel of her hand in his send shivers down her spine. They came to a slow stop as the song ended.

"May I ask for another dance tonight, Miss MacLaren?" Escorting her back to the table, he pulled out her chair.

"Aye, Mr. Arrington." She smiled at him as he nodded and walked to the other side of the room.

Emma grinned. "I believe you have an admirer, Jinny."

"He is quite handsome. Who is he?" Heather watched Deke walk away, working to keep her eyes from straying to Caleb, who danced with a petite redhead she didn't recognize.

Jinny followed her gaze. "Deke Arrington. His uncle is Rube Ferguson."

"I did hear something about a new man at the saddlery."

Gripping Heather's arm, Jinny started to rise. "Let me introduce you."

Groaning, she shook her head. "Nae. You know I'm not good at talking with men the way you and Emma are. I'd rather sit here and watch. Actually, I'd rather not be here at all."

"Well, you're here and ought to make the most of all the time spent getting ready. I'm so glad Mrs. Evanston asked you to come."

Heather's face scrunched into a frown. "You'll not be fooling me, Jinny. The widow *forced* me to come. She said I spent too much time alone...as if I don't have a huge enough family."

"Who you rarely see."

"Ach. I'm there for Sunday supper." Heather looked at her mother, Audrey, who sat at another table with Kyla, Colin's mother. She felt a rush of guilt. Audrey would never voice it out loud, yet Heather knew she'd let her mother, and the rest of the family, down when she took the job with Widow Evanston.

At first, she'd enjoyed being away from the boisterous, often overbearing MacLaren clan. After more than a year, it surprised her how much she missed her family and those they'd brought into the fold, such as Caleb. As much as she wished it wasn't so, she missed his superior attitude, much like her brothers and male cousins. She also missed the smoldering glances he tried to hide.

Jinny linked an arm through hers. "You need to come home more, Heather. Everyone misses you."

Her gaze wandered again to Caleb, who hadn't left the dance floor. By her count, this was his third dance with the redhead. "Who is Caleb dancing with?"

"From what I've heard, she's related to August Fielder. Her family is visiting from back east. I can't remember her name, but I'm sure Caleb can tell you once he comes back to the table." Jinny's voice held enough humor to let Heather know she wasn't fooling her cousin. "The lad's been an eejit about you since traveling here from Oregon. You'll dance with him if he asks, won't you?"

Always one to know her own mind, and all too quick to voice her thoughts, Heather hesitated, insecurity clear on her face as she bit her lower lip. "I'd hoped *no one* would ask me."

Slapping a hand over her mouth, Jinny held back a laugh. "Then why get all dressed up, lass? You must've known the lads would be asking you for a dance."

Shaking her head, Heather straightened. She couldn't let anyone think of her as weak or unsure. "I came as a duty to the widow. The rest wasn't important."

Jinny didn't believe a word of it. "How long since you've been to a dance?"

Heather's shoulders slumped a slight bit, enough for Jinny to notice. "Not since I was a lassie."

"Then I have just the fix for you." Standing, Jinny marched to the other side of the room. Getting Deke's attention, she whispered in his ear, then slipped her arm through his, walking back to the table. "Heather, I'd like to introduce Mr. Deke Arrington, Mr. Ferguson's nephew. Mr. Arrington, this is my cousin, Miss Heather MacLaren."

Deke bowed slightly. "It's a pleasure, Miss MacLaren."

Her gaze moved between Jinny and Deke before she nodded. "The same, Mr. Arrington."

Deke held out his hand. "May I have the pleasure of this dance?" When he saw the panic on her face, he leaned closer. "We'll take it slow. I promise not to embarrass you."

Heaving a sigh, Heather took his hand and stood. "You've no idea what you've let yourself in for, Mr. Arrington."

"How bad can it be?" Deke smiled, escorting her to the dance floor.

"Who's Heather dancing with?" Caleb stood between Brodie and Quinn, one hand in his pocket, the other holding a glass of fortified punch.

"Deke Arrington." Brodie explained about him working at the saddlery for his uncle. "Why don't you ask her to dance?"

Caleb choked out a laugh. "You know as well as I do she'd turn me down."

Quinn clasped him on the shoulder. "Is that all that's stopping you? Where's your spirit, lad?"

"About where yours was when you were trying to stay away from Emma."

Brodie threw his head back and laughed. "He has you there, Quinn."

"True." Quinn touched the rim of his glass to Brodie's and drank. "At least you could ask Jinny for a dance."

Caleb's eyes widened. "Jinny?"

"Aye. You know...my cousin."

Shoving Quinn lightly, he shook his head. "I know who you mean." Finishing his punch, he set the glass on the table. "Fine. I'll ask her." Taking several quick strides, he stood before her, extending his hand. "May I have this dance, Jinny?"

Jinny's eyes grew wide before a smile curved up the corners of her mouth. "Of course. I'd love a dance with you, Caleb."

He found the perfect spot next to Heather and Deke. Placing a hand on Jinny's back, they finished the dance before the band changed songs.

Jinny's eyes lit up. "Oh, a reel. Can we dance this one, Caleb?" Next to them, they could hear Heather asking Deke the same question.

"If I can remember how it's done."

Jinny took Caleb's hand. "Ach, you'll remember."

Within seconds, the floor vibrated with couples dancing a lively Scottish reel, changing partners, moving in circles. When it was over, the four of them stood next to each other, laughing.

Deke looked at Jinny. "If they play another, we should switch partners."

Caleb's face stilled. He glanced at Heather, surprised when she nodded in agreement. They didn't have to wait long. The band began another reel, keeping most everyone on the floor. Lacing his fingers through hers, Caleb led Heather back to the center of the floor. Within moments, they were laughing, ignoring the fact that when they saw each other again, they'd be at odds, the same as always.

"You were right, Emma. I did have a wonderful time." Jinny sat in the wagon on the other side of Quinn, leaning over him to talk to his wife.

"What do you think of Deke Arrington?"

Quinn straightened at Emma's question, looking over at Jinny. "Are you interested in Deke?"

"I think he's a very charming man, and no, I'm not interested in him."

"What if Sam doesn't come back? Would Deke interest you then?"

"Ach. I don't want to talk about Sam not returning...or Deke. Besides, I think he may have formed an interest in Heather."

"Heather?" Quinn choked out. "What could the lad possibly see in my sister?"

Emma shoved him from one side as Jinny did the same on the other.

Quinn frowned at his wife. "It's a fair question."

Emma glared at him. "No, it's not. Heather is a beautiful woman. Smart, funny—"

"Ach," Quinn interrupted. "The lass is opinionated, arrogant, and intolerant, seeing no value in anyone's opinion but her own. Heather is a pain in the arse."

Jinny folded her arms over her chest. "Caleb doesn't seem to think so."

"Don't be daft. Just because the lad finds her attractive doesn't mean he doesn't see her faults. And the lass has many." He looked between the two of them. "You know I'm right."

Chuckling, Emma slid an arm through his. "Heather does have her opinions. I do understand them, though."

Quinn leaned over, kissing her cheek. "Because you enjoy ranch life the same as she does. The difference is Heather angers people with her sass, acting like she'd rather be a man. You can ride, shoot, and handle chores around the ranch, the same as her, but you like being a woman. She's my sister and I love her, but I'll not be denying her faults because of it."

Jinny listened to them go back and forth, her mind on Sam. She'd wanted to ask Brodie if he'd heard from him, knowing her brother would be honest. When the opportunity arose, she'd hesitated, then lost her chance when Colin and Quinn walked up.

"You're quiet, lass." Quinn nudged her with his shoulder. "Are you thinking of Sam?"

Jinny kept her gaze on the trail ahead. "Aye. Wondering if Brodie has heard from him."

"Nae, he hasn't."

She shot a look at him. "You asked him?"

Quinn shrugged. "Colin asked him at the dance. Brodie still hopes he comes back. It's hard not knowing why the lad had to return home."

She drew in a slow breath. "Sam wanted to explain the night he told me he had to leave. I, um...didn't handle the news well. He might have explained if I'd given him a chance."

"You can't blame yourself, Jinny." Emma reached across Quinn, placing a hand on her arm and squeezing. "He didn't say he wouldn't return."

"Nae, he didn't. As each day passes without any word, I lose hope. Somehow, I always thought we'd be together." She looked at Emma, a grim smile turning up the corners of her mouth. "I hoped maybe he'd stop being an eejit, the way Quinn was with you."

"I wasn't an eejit," he protested. "There were reasons it took me so long to figure out what I wanted."

Jinny laughed. "Ach, you always wanted Emma. You were too much of a dunderhead to admit it."

"She's right, Quinn." Emma leaned into him, a sweet smile on her face.

He frowned, slapping the lines. "A lad will never win an argument with you two."

Emma rose off the seat to kiss his cheek, then sat back down. "I'm afraid you won't win with any of the MacLaren women."

Quinn shook his head. "Aye. It's the way of it."

Chapter Six

"Papa?" Robbie pushed open the door to where Sam studied documents to purchase a house a few blocks away.

Hearing his son's voice, Sam's mood improved in an instant. Standing, he moved around the desk, crouching with his arms spread. "Come in, Robbie."

Running, he jumped into his father's arms, giggling. "Read me a story." It wasn't a question. A week after moving into Sam's parents' home, they already had a routine, which included at least one chapter each night. Lifting Robbie into his arms, he settled him on one side as they left the study and walked up the stairs.

"Shall we read *Rip Van Winkle*?" Sam asked.

Robbie shook his head. "No."

"All right. How about *Swiss Family Robinson*?"

"Nooo." Robbie giggled, again shaking his head.

Sam sighed, pretending to consider the options. "Hmmm, let me see. I suppose we could read *Ivanhoe*."

"Yes." Robbie nodded his head vigorously, then laughed when Sam tossed him onto the middle of his bed.

"Let's say a prayer, then I'll read the story."

Hustling to climb under the covers, Robbie laid his head on the pillow, clasping his hands together. "God watch over Mama."

His son said the same prayer every night, and each time, Sam felt his throat tighten. Vera may have been a traitor to the Union cause, but she was still Robbie's mother, and Sam vowed he'd never say a negative word about her. Few in Baltimore were so generous.

It had been a few short months since the war ended, and anger still ran deep on both sides. Where Sam grew up, most sided with President Lincoln and the Union. Vera had done all she could to thwart the cause of keeping the country intact, choosing to spy for the South. In the end, she'd paid for it with her life. Many who'd been friends with her and her family had cut them off, bitter at her defection. As Robbie grew up, Sam feared his son would suffer the consequences of his mother's decisions.

"Story now, Papa?"

"Yes, son." Picking up the book and turning to the page where they'd left off the night before, Sam began to read, recalling how his father had read to him from the same book when he was

Robbie's age. He could almost recite the chapters by heart, which meant his mind often wandered during this quiet time each night.

He'd selected a house, securing the funds, but couldn't bring himself to sign the document declaring the property his. There were so many reasons to stay. Robbie would be near both sets of grandparents—one set who'd raised him, and the other who'd become attached within days. He'd have the advantages of a large city on the Atlantic, with an education system not yet available out west. The exposure to people from all walks of life would be invaluable as he got older, and he'd make contacts that could serve him well in whatever he chose to do. Sam had all the same advantages, and he'd still ended up in California.

Perhaps because of this, Sam still had a difficult time finding any joy in staying.

His parents made it clear they wanted them close. They never said it had to be in Baltimore. The longer Sam rolled this over in his mind, the more a plan began to develop. One that could satisfy them, and give him the life he wanted for Robbie.

Finishing the chapter, he glanced at his son, who'd fallen into a deep sleep. Setting the book aside, he leaned down to brush a strand of hair from Robbie's face before kissing his forehead.

Sam figured he had a few days to finalize the transaction on the house. If he allowed the sale to go through, he would never again leave Baltimore. He'd accept one of several job offers and build a life in the same neighborhood where he'd grown up. His stomach knotted, knowing the choice he made now would define the rest of his life...and Robbie's.

Conviction, California

"Jinny, what do you think of this fabric?" Sarah McLaren, Colin's wife, placed her hand on a blue silk taffeta at Maloney's general store. Sarah, her sister, Geneen, Jinny, and Emma had met Brodie's wife, Maggie, for lunch, then walked across the street for supplies before heading back to Circle M.

Emma nudged Jinny's arm, dropping her voice to a whisper. "Sarah asked you a question."

Blinking to clear her mind, which had wandered to Sam once again, she walked toward Sarah. "I'm sorry. What did you ask me?"

"I wondered what you thought of this fabric."

"I suppose it depends on what you'd be needing it for." Jinny drew her hand along what she knew to be expensive material.

"I'm being silly. Dreaming of what I could do with this." Sarah smiled when she spoke. No one had ever heard one word of complaint from her since Colin brought her to Circle M.

"There's nothing wrong with dreaming, Sarah. I do it all the time."

Sarah moved down the aisle, picking up a couple items on her list. "Has anyone heard from Sam?" Her gaze moved to Maggie.

"Brodie's said nothing to me, but I know how much he hopes Sam will return." Placing a hand on her stomach, she used her other to steady herself against a table filled with kitchenware.

Jinny placed her arm around Maggie's waist. "Are you all right, lass?"

"A little dizzy, and my stomach bothers me a bit. It's happened a few times in the last two weeks."

Sarah looked at Emma, then Jinny. "Have you seen either Doc Vickery or Doc Tilden?" Sarah asked, glancing at Maggie's stomach. She'd described the same symptoms Sarah had during her first months of being pregnant with Grant.

Maggie shook her head. "No. It's never seemed bad enough to bother either of them...until today."

"Let's finish with the supplies, then see if one of the doctors can see you." Sarah placed what she had on the counter, waiting until Mrs.

Maloney totaled everything up. "Can you have everything loaded into our wagon? We have one more place to go."

"Of course, dear. It will all be ready when you return."

As the women turned to leave, the front door burst open. Four men, looking like they hadn't bathed in months, walked inside, glancing around before grabbing items off the shelves and stuffing them into saddlebags swung over their shoulders.

Mrs. Maloney came around the counter, crossing her arms. "Young men, you need to bring those items to me so I can add them up."

As the men got closer, their features became more menacing. The one in the lead rested a hand on the butt of his gun, giving them a frightening smile. "The truth is, ma'am, you don't need to add up anything. Now, if you'll leave us be, we'll finish our business and get out of your way."

Mrs. Maloney took another step forward, stopping when Jinny grabbed her arm. "Let them take what they want and leave. My family will take care of it."

The older woman shrugged off Jinny's hand. "I can't let them steal from me, and I won't have the MacLarens pay for it."

The man who'd spoken moved closer to Mrs. Maloney. "You'd best do as the lady says." This time, he drew his gun, holding it at his side. "We wouldn't want to harm any of you ladies." His tone told them the men would have no reservations about hurting them if it meant getting what they wanted.

Jinny moved in front of Mrs. Maloney, blocking her from confronting the man again. "Please, Mrs. Maloney. Don't argue with him."

Sarah moved next to them. "Jinny's right. It isn't worth any of us getting hurt."

Mrs. Maloney glared at the men, then stepped around the women. "Take what you need. Just remember, there are families who also need what we have."

"Take whatever you can, boys." The leader took three long strides to stand inches away from the older woman, his gaze roaming over the others until they locked on Jinny. "You. Come with me."

Narrowing her gaze, Jinny moved away from him. "Nae. I won't be going anywhere with you."

His voice hardening, he moved quickly, grabbing her arm. "You'll do what I say."

Wrenching herself away, instinct took over. Jinny reached back, swinging her fist, missing his face by an inch as he leaned away. "Are you daft? I'll be going nowhere with you."

The women formed a circle around Jinny, Emma stepping forward. "Get what you want and leave." No one had noticed her reach into her coat, her hand gripping the six-gun she always carried.

The other three men stopped from stuffing their saddlebags, one drawing his gun. "You need help, Captain?" The other two pulled out their weapons, pointing them at the women.

"I don't need help with one feisty woman," he ground out. Storming past Emma, pushing her away before she had a chance to draw her six-shooter, he grabbed Jinny by the hair. "You're coming with us."

Ignoring the guns pointed at them, Maggie's anger peaked when the man yanked Jinny toward the back of the store. Grabbing a bucket off a shelf, she swung it at the leader, connecting with his head.

Shouting a string of curses, he released his hold on Jinny, then turned on Maggie, his gun aimed at her chest. "Make one more move and you're dead." He glanced over his shoulder at the other men. "Lock the door and keep the other women out here." Waiting until he was certain his men did as ordered, he gripped Jinny's arm in a punishing hold, causing her to shriek as he pushed her through the curtains separating the front from the storeroom in back. Shoving her forward, she stumbled, hitting her shoulder against a barrel and falling to the ground.

Sarah, Geneen, Emma, Maggie, and Mrs. Maloney huddled in a corner, glaring at the three men pointing guns at them. Flashes of her past assailed Maggie, her stomach knotting, chest tightening when she heard a groan from the back.

"What's he doing to her?" Maggie's composed features belied the rage burning within her.

"None of your business. You stay where you are, be quiet, and no one will get hurt." One of the men stepped forward, staring down at them.

Maggie held his gaze. "Just because you don't shoot us doesn't mean he's not hurting her."

A loud pounding on the front door had the men turning, drawing attention away from the women. It was all the distraction the women needed.

Emma drew her six-shooter, firing at the man closest to her, hitting him in the leg. Yelling, he lost his grip on the gun as he fell to the ground.

Maggie scrambled to retrieve it, aiming at one of the other men, ignoring the gun pointed at her. "Don't move. I'd have no problem killing you."

He snickered, but moved away. Glancing out the front window, he saw people assembling, then switched his gaze to his wounded comrade.

Geneen and Sarah grabbed cans of food from the shelves, throwing them at the men as the pounding on the door grew louder.

"Get the sheriff." Sarah's screamed request seemed to fluster the men further, prompting them to hurry toward the back, ducking when Emma fired a shot in their direction.

"Captain, we gotta get out of here. There's a crowd gathering outside."

Their leader stood over Jinny, his face hard as he glared down at her. "You'll be sorry you caused so much trouble." He looked at his men. "Where's the sergeant?"

"Shot," one answered.

"Then we leave him. Let's go." Pushing open the back door, the leader checked the back street. "Come on."

Rushing outside, they dashed between buildings, making it to the main street as the crowd burst through the door of the general store. Exchanging looks, they holstered their guns, walked to their horses, and mounted. Casting one more look at the general store, the three reined their horses around and rode out of Conviction.

Jack burst through the door of the jail. "Sheriff. There's trouble at Maloney's."

Brodie finished pouring a cup of coffee, setting the pot down, giving his deputy a bland stare. "So handle it."

"You don't understand. There was a shooting, and your family is inside."

Dropping the full cup on the wooden floor, Brodie pushed past him, running down the boardwalk, Jack right behind, to see a small crowd standing outside the general store.

"What's going on?"

"You'd best get inside, Sheriff."

Brodie couldn't remember the name of the man who stood aside, or much of anything else as his gaze landed on Maggie, bucket gripped in one hand, Sarah standing next to her. As he approached, a deep moan had him shifting his attention to the man on the ground.

"Jack, get Doc Vickery. And find Nate."

"Sure thing, Sheriff."

Turning, he went to Maggie, seeing her body tremble. "Sweetheart..." Wrapping her in his arms, he closed his eyes, letting out a deep breath.

"Sheriff, you might want to come back here." Deke stood behind the counter, his jaw tight.

Maggie pulled away, her gaze moving toward the storeroom. "Jinny's back there, Brodie." When he hesitated, she gripped his shoulders and turned him away. "Go. I'm fine."

Glancing back once, he walked past Deke to see his sister sitting on the floor, Mrs. Maloney on one side, Emma and Geneen on the other.

He knelt down in front of her, taking one of her hands in his. "What happened?"

Mrs. Maloney answered. "Four men came in, grabbing things from shelves, stuffing their saddlebags. When we objected, they pulled guns. They locked the front door, then the leader brought Jinny back here."

"Alone." Brodie's gaze didn't leave his sister's.

"Yes, alone." Mrs. Maloney stood, moving out of the way when Doc Tilden walked toward them.

Jinny squeezed Brodie's hand. "I'm fine. He threw me against the barrel. I hurt my shoulder."

"Let me take a look." Doc Tilden crouched next to them, taking Emma and Geneen's place. "Doc Vickery is looking at the man out front."

Mrs. Maloney continued. "Emma pulled a gun and shot one. When he dropped his gun,

Maggie grabbed it, pointing it at the others." She blew out a breath. "My, it all happened real fast after that."

Jinny let out a groan, grimacing as the doctor continued checking her injury, looking for any others. "You should see to Maggie."

Brodie crossed his arms, not making a move to leave. "You're the one who's hurt."

She bit her lip as a shot of pain tore through her, then looked up at Brodie. "You may need to encourage her to talk to Doc Vickery. She hasn't been feeling well."

He dropped his arms, tilting his head. "Not well?"

Jinny sighed. "Talk to her. She'll explain."

"I'll be back to help you get into the wagon." Turning, he walked to the front as three men picked up the wounded man and hauled him outside.

"Wounded in the leg. They're taking him to the clinic. I'm guessing you'll want to transport him to the jail once I patch him up." Doc Vickery stood, picking up his bag.

"Aye. I need to get his story." He moved his gaze from the doctor to Maggie, not seeing her make any attempt to talk to him. "Uh, Doc. I hear Maggie hasn't been feeling well. Can you check on her, too?"

"Brodie, I'm fine." She backed away a step.

Sarah looked at her. "He's right, Maggie. Tell Doc what's happening. I'll go to the back to see how Jinny's doing." She glanced at Brodie, a small smile tipping up the corners of her mouth.

Doc Vickery's warm gaze landed on Maggie. "All right. Tell me what's hurting."

Chapter Seven

Brodie sat at his kitchen table, staring at a cold cup of coffee, while Maggie finished making supper. Between what happened at the general store and Doc Vickery's announcement, the swing in his emotions had been extreme. He could still feel the gripping fear when Jack came into the jail, telling Brodie there were shots fired inside Maloney's. Five members of his family had been at risk, and he hadn't even known they were in danger. It made him wonder if he truly was the right person to be Conviction's sheriff.

Doc Tilden had declared Jinny safe to travel back to the ranch, but warned of using her arm for a few days. After Brodie had gone back to the front to speak with Maggie, Deke had taken his spot in front of Jinny, holding her hand, telling her she'd be fine. Brodie knew his sister still cared deeply for Sam. He also wondered if Deke might be the man to help her forget.

"Are you all right, Brodie?" Maggie's hand covered his.

He took a breath, dragging his gaze away from the tin cup to look at his wife. "Aye. I'm fine, sweetheart."

"You aren't happy about the news, are you?" She couldn't hide the fear in her voice, which made Brodie feel worse.

He pulled his hand from her grasp, cupping her face. "Maggie, darlin', besides the day we married, I've never been happier."

"Truly?"

"Aye, truly." Leaning over, he kissed her lips, taking his time, letting her know how much he wanted this. Sitting back, he grasped both her hands in his. "We've talked about starting a family, and now we'll have one."

"I know it's sooner than we planned."

"Aye, but it doesn't mean I'm not happy about having a baby."

He'd thought some about a discussion he had a few months ago with the same man who'd talked Brodie into becoming the sheriff. August Fielder had asked him to consider stepping aside to help more on the ranch. Specifically the additional land acquired in a partnership between Fielder and the MacLarens. Brodie loved being the sheriff, had wanted to be a lawman his entire life. Between the job and Maggie, his life seemed perfect.

Then there'd been an increase in random shootings as more and more dangerous men rode into Conviction. Circle M would be safer for Maggie, and their future children. There was one major problem—she'd made it clear she would never move to the ranch as long as he remained sheriff. Their little house at the end of the main street suited her fine. Being too far away from Brodie didn't appeal to her one bit.

Lately, he'd been thinking more about giving up the badge. His family did need him back at Circle M, and now he had a baby to consider.

If only Sam had stayed. With his Pinkerton background and months as a deputy, he would've made an excellent sheriff. Both Fielder and Brodie's father, prominent citizens and members of the town council, mentioned they'd support Sam.

Although he had Sam's information back east, he hadn't wanted to bother him. Perhaps it was time to send a telegram.

"Do you want to make the announcement at Sunday supper?" Maggie set a plate of roast beef and potatoes in front of him. He hadn't even realized she'd left the table.

"That would be fine, lass." Picking up his fork, he speared a piece of meat. He couldn't push away the thought of it being time for him to hand his badge to someone else. But who? Jack was eager, but not ready to become sheriff. If Nate wasn't haunted by demons he wouldn't discuss, he'd make an excellent choice.

Brodie had sent telegrams to San Francisco, Sacramento, and most of the towns in between, seeking a qualified deputy to take Sam's place. The response had been weak. When he thought of leaving, the only image that popped into his head was the man who'd left to take care of business back east.

"I need to send a telegram to Sam."

Maggie stopped chewing to stare at him. "You know how to reach him?"

"Aye. He's staying with his family in Baltimore. I want to find out if he's coming back."

"That would make Jinny very happy. She hasn't been the same since he left." As she continued eating, Brodie could almost see her mind working.

"Say nothing to her, Maggie. I don't want Jinny getting her hopes up."

"All right." She swallowed some of her coffee, then set down her fork. "Are you asking him to come back as your deputy or as the sheriff?"

"When I figure it out, lass, I'll let you know."

"You didn't have to ride all the way out to the ranch, Mr. Arrington." Jinny stood at her front door, her left arm bent and held tight to her side.

Deke fingered the brim of his hat. "I did if I wanted to see how you're doing, Miss MacLaren."

"Well then, you must come inside." Opening the door, she let him slip past her, biting her lip to stifle a grin. "My mother made lemonade. Would you like some?"

"I would. Thank you."

Jinny's lips curved into a smile. "You can either wait in here or follow me to the kitchen." She heard his footsteps as she walked through the dining room and into the kitchen. Selecting two glasses, she filled both, setting them on the table. "Is sitting in here all right?"

"Fine with me." He waited for her to sit down, then took a seat across from her. "So, how are you feeling?"

"My shoulder is healing." She wouldn't burden him with the lack of progress on her shattered heart. No word from Sam bothered her more than any injury to her arm.

"You're a lucky woman. It could've been much worse." Taking a sip of his beverage, he pursed his lips. "Did you recognize any of them?"

Shaking her head, she tightened her grip on the glass. "Nae. Brodie believes they were ex-Confederate soldiers."

"Why is that?"

"Accents, mannerisms. The lads called one a captain and another a sergeant, and one wore a cap the same as those used by the Confederate Army." Jinny's hand shook as she brought the glass to her lips.

"They left a wounded man behind. He could hang."

"Would it bother you if he did?" She thought of the man dying for threatening her and her family, the carnage he could've caused. All for a few cans of food.

"Not in the least. Those men made their choice when they walked into Maloney's and pulled guns. I'm more concerned about the rest of them staying close by, waiting for a chance to break their friend out of jail, or come after you."

Jinny worried about the same, but never voiced it out loud. "Why would they come after me? I did nothing to them."

"They probably believe you and your family are the reason one of their men is in jail. You're the reason they didn't get away with what they came for...food. And you're the woman one of them took into the back room."

Her eyes closed as she swallowed the bile in her throat. She'd never been so scared as when the man dragged her away from the others. "He didn't do anything except throw me against the barrel."

Deke leaned forward, resting his arms on the table. "Do you believe that was all he intended?"

Her eyes darkened as her gaze dropped to her lap. "I don't know," Jinny whispered the lie. She'd seen the man move his hand to his belt buckle, couldn't have missed the sick gleam in his eyes.

"Are you able to ride?"

Her head shot up. "What?"

He grinned. "Is your shoulder good enough for you to take a ride?"

"Aye, it should be."

Standing, Deke held out his hand. "Then let's saddle your horse and get you out of the house."

Jinny sat atop her horse, looking out on the vast acreage before her, all owned by her family. "Most days, I take for granted how prosperous our lives have been since moving from Pennsylvania."

Deke sat next to her, following her gaze. "Uncle Rube told me you came out as part of a wagon train. It must have been a daunting experience."

"I suppose so, especially for the adults and older cousins. For me, it was an adventure."

He looked at her, admiring her strength. "Did you already have the land?"

"Aye. My father and uncles purchased it while we still lived in York. There were times they worried about being fleeced. They had the good sense to work with an attorney in Conviction who assured them the purchase was legitimate. Have you met August Fielder?"

Deke remembered a man of average height with thinning dark hair and a goatee. "Uncle Rube introduced me to him at the dance. He makes quite an impression."

"My father and Uncle Ian created a partnership with him to purchase additional land. It doubled the size of our ranch." Relaxing into her saddle, Jinny absently rubbed her left shoulder.

Deke didn't miss the gesture. "Are you in pain?"

"No worse than normal. Doc Tilden said it could take a few weeks, but I'll not be waiting that long to get back to my chores."

Chuckling, Deke shook his head. "I'm certain you won't. Are you ready to ride back?"

"Can't we stay out a little longer?"

"As long as you want, Miss MacLaren. Lead the way."

"Are you sure, Sam? Taking us with you is a big decision." Thomas Covington didn't look up from the chore his wife, Susannah, had given him.

"Having doubts, Father?" Sam studied the elder man's face, seeing excitement, as well as concern.

"Not really, although it *is* a big decision for us. Everything else aside, your mother doesn't want to live across the country from her only grandchild." Thomas chuckled, glancing toward the kitchen where Susannah and Robbie made supper. "I believe she'd move to India if that is where you decided to live."

They stood in the dining room, under instructions to pack the family china and linens with the greatest of care. A week of intense conversations ended with his parents deciding to sell their home, agreeing to accompany Sam and Robbie to Conviction. Sam had sent a confidential telegram to August Fielder, asking if he'd be willing to locate a suitable home for all of them. The affirmative response had been immediate. He had yet to contact Brodie.

"Your mother is excited about having him in her life."

"And you, Father? What are your thoughts?"

Taking a deep breath, Thomas looked around the house they'd lived in since Sam's birth. He'd struggled more than his wife about making such a drastic change. In their sixties, both born and raised in Baltimore, they were leaving lifelong friends and a familiar routine. A deacon in his church, and a member of more than one men's club, his friends couldn't believe they would leave it all behind, following Sam to California. They didn't have the complete story.

Thomas knew Susannah had received several offers of marriage, many from men of great wealth, but she never wavered once she'd made her choice. Not after the deaths of two infants, nor when they'd struggled with money during the war. It was time to support her dream of being near her son and grandson.

"I'd do anything for your mother, Sam. If that makes me sound weak, so be it." He picked up a dish, being careful to wrap and place it in the packing crate. "The truth is, I'm excited about the journey, seeing places I've only read about."

Sam placed the last plate in the crate. "You may change your mind by the time we reach our destination."

It had been difficult to pass on purchasing a home in Baltimore. After several sleepless nights and half-eaten meals, Sam forced himself to focus on why he'd made the decision to leave—reasons that would change Robbie's life forever.

Sam wanted to return to his job as deputy, raise his son in a smaller community where people took care of one another, and build a life with Jinny. Each time he thought of her, his heart squeezed and stomach twisted. He'd made no move to contact her or any of her family, including Brodie.

A beautiful and vivacious young woman, he knew there'd be others who'd take advantage of his absence, declaring their intentions to court Jinny. Sam hoped she had turned them all away.

"Have you sent word to your lady friend about your return?"

His father's question took him by surprise, making Sam wonder if he could read his mind. "Not yet."

"Is she beautiful?"

"Very."

"A joy to be around?"

Sam sucked in a breath. "Very much so."

Thomas nodded, lowering himself into a chair. "Do you love her?"

"Yes sir, I do."

"Well, then, I feel compelled to give you some advice." Thomas leaned forward, piercing Sam with a knowing gaze. "Get word to her before we leave. You don't want to set foot in Conviction to find she's promised herself to another man."

Circle M Ranch

"Thank you, Mr. Arrington. I had a wonderful time." Jinny accepted Deke's help to the ground, then brushed her hands down her dress.

"So did I, Miss MacLaren." Grinning, he took both sets of reins. "I'll groom your horse. Go ahead inside."

"You'll have supper with us."

Glancing over his shoulder, Deke marveled at the way she didn't feel the need to request his presence. "Is that an order?"

"Aye. You may consider it one." Jinny didn't look back as she walked up the steps and into the house.

Following the sway of her hips, Deke felt a ripple of awareness, the same as he had the first day they'd met. Shaking his head, he tried to push away the rush of desire. Of all the women in Conviction, he didn't need to develop feelings for one whose heart might already be taken.

He'd heard rumors Jinny still pined for a former deputy who'd left town about the time

Deke arrived. Details were scarce, other than the man had been well-respected, and if he could believe the locals, used to work for Pinkerton. Deke still hoped to find a way to confirm it with Brodie. If anyone would have the true story, it would be her brother.

Finishing with Jinny's horse, he walked his own out of the barn as a group of riders reined their horses in a circle around him, then stopped.

"Deke?" Colin slid to the ground, extending his hand.

"Good evening, Colin."

"Did you come to visit Jinny?" Quinn walked up next, shaking Deke's hand.

"I wanted to see how she's doing." He glanced around, feeling as if he were facing a jury of his peers.

"And?" Sean, Jinny's cousin and the oldest of Ian's children, eyed him with a bit of suspicion.

Deke smiled. "She's improving. We took a short ride."

"You had the lass on a horse?" Fletcher, one of Jinny's younger brothers, came up to him, cocking his head. "Doc Tilden said for her to take it easy." His voice was the least friendly.

Caleb stepped closer, running a hand down Deke's horse. "Good to see you. She did all right, did she?"

"Jinny did fine. I think she might have been going a little crazy being in the house all day."

Quinn glanced around. "Where are the rest of the lasses?"

His younger brother, Bram, laughed, slapping him on the back. "You forgot already? You sent Emma, Geneen, Bridget, and Coral to the north range with Blaine to check on the cattle."

"Ach. That's right. I'll be seeing to my horse. Glad you came by, Deke."

Everyone said their goodbyes, except Fletcher, who hadn't budged. "Did Jinny invite you for supper?"

"She did. Is that a problem?"

Fletcher shook his head. "Nae." Turning around, he started walking toward the barn. Deke hurried to catch up.

"Fletcher?"

"Aye?" He didn't stop until he was inside, then removed his horse's saddle.

"It's not my business, but..."

Fletcher continued grooming his horse, not looking up. "You're wondering about Sam Covington."

"Yes, I am."

Standing, Fletcher straightened to his full height of close to six feet six inches, tossing the brush into a bucket. "There's not much to tell.

Jinny liked him, and from all we could tell, the lad liked her. Then business took him back home to Baltimore. From what I know, she's not heard from him since."

"How long has it been?"

"Four or five months." Finishing, Fletcher picked up his hat. "If that's all, I'm ready for supper." A slight grin curved his mouth. "You might as well follow me inside."

Deke kept pace with Fletcher, considering what little he knew about Jinny MacLaren. The last thing he wanted was to poach on another man's woman. Still, they were miles apart, and from what he'd learned, she'd heard nothing from Sam in months.

Letting out a breath, Deke followed Fletcher inside. He considered himself a good man who valued integrity, doing his best to live in an honorable way. As much as Jinny intrigued him, he wasn't ready to court a woman whose emotions were torn, or offer his own heart only to have it handed back to him if Sam returned.

A compromise formed in Deke's mind. He might not be able to court her in the way he hoped, but if she approved, he could be her friend, enjoying whatever time she allowed him.

Chapter Eight

SS Lincoln Steamship

The dense fog wrapped around the big ship, the same as it had for the last two days. They'd boarded the steamer in New York twelve days earlier, hugging the eastern seaboard before navigating through the islands of the West Indies. Until yesterday, they'd been blessed with good weather.

Over two hundred feet in length with a forty-foot beam, the *Lincoln* carried mail, cargo, and passengers to San Juan del Norte, also known as Greytown. They'd travel the short distance overland, then board the *SS Jefferson*. If all went well, they'd dock in San Francisco thirteen days later.

"Papa, where are we?" Robbie gripped Sam's neck, holding tight, as if his young life depended on it. Twisting around, his eyes blinked several times as they adjusted to the thick gray mist surrounding him.

"We're on our way to Greytown, son. The captain says we should arrive by evening."

"Is that where the horses are?"

Sam set Robbie down on the deck, grasping his hand. The steamer had room for over two hundred passengers, and this sailing was booked to capacity. He'd been fortunate to obtain four second cabin tickets, although the two hundred dollars per person put a huge hole in the money he'd set aside for the trip.

Chuckling, he ruffled his son's hair. "No, son. I'm afraid you won't be able to ride a horse until we get to our new home."

"Will I get my own horse, Papa?" Wide, hopeful eyes locked with his, once again reminding Sam of the enormous blessing he'd been given.

"Perhaps."

"I thought I'd find you two up here." Thomas Covington joined them on deck, smiling down at his grandson. "More fog, I see."

"The captain thinks we'll be moving out of it soon. Where's Mother?"

"In the cabin. I told her she needed fresh air, but she refused to budge from the warmth of the covers. Perhaps I'll be able to convince her to join us on deck after she's eaten."

"Papa says I can have a horse, Grandfather."

Stooping, Thomas lifted Robbie into his arms as a group of passengers walked past. "Is that so?"

Robbie nodded several times, a broad smile on this face. "Papa said so."

Thomas glanced over his grandson's shoulder to see Sam shrugging. "Well, if your papa says so, I'm certain you'll have a horse."

He watched Robbie's eyes widen as several children, some near his age, ran by on their way aft. Getting Sam's attention, Thomas nodded at Robbie, his brow lifting. Sam picked up the silent question.

"Would you like to see where they're going?" Sam asked his son.

He nodded, excitement obvious on his face. Setting his grandson on the deck, Thomas clasped his tiny hand as the three of them moved toward the rear of the ship, noticing a small amount of sunlight peeking through the fog. Walking next to Sam, Robbie tugging on his hand, Thomas felt a satisfaction he hadn't experienced in years. Even Susannah's occasional bouts of seasickness hadn't dampened his enjoyment of the voyage.

Reaching the spot where the other children stopped to play, a strange feeling overtook Thomas, making him glance over his shoulder. A momentary sense of panic claimed him when he saw Susannah, her face pasty white, gripping the guardrail with both hands, her gaze locked on his.

"Here, take Robbie." Transferring his grandson's hand to Sam, he hurried to his wife, slipping an arm around her waist. "What are you doing?" Although not harsh, his concerned voice had her looking up.

"I'm getting some fresh air, as you asked me to do." Removing her grip on the rail, she placed her hand in Thomas's, leaning into him. "Besides, I'm missing too much staying in the cabin. Where were you going?"

Slowly, he escorted her aft, the sound of children's laughter drifting back toward them. "Sam took Robbie to play with the other—"

The crushing sound of metal on metal and sudden pitching of the steamer slammed Susannah to the side, ripping her from Thomas's grip.

"Thomas!" Her muffled scream disappeared as the ship slammed against something hard and unforgiving.

"Susannah!" Thomas shifted from one foot to the other, reaching for anything close to regain his balance. "Susannah, where are you?"

The harsh sound of the steamer's horn startled him, as did the answering horn of another ship. Swinging around, his eyes widened in panic. They'd run into another steamer, the sound of tearing metal melting with the screams of people unable to get out of harm's way.

Blood ran down his arms and onto his hands, mixing with waves of saltwater crashing over him, making it difficult to hold on. He continued to yell his wife's name, getting nothing in response. Letting go of his tight hold, he moved toward the ship's rail, now a jagged opening—the spot where he'd last seen Susannah. A bright flash caught his attention an instant before an ear-splitting explosion pitched him forward, plummeting Thomas off the deck and into the cold water.

Sam held Robbie to his chest, his gaze darting toward the bow where he'd last seen his parents. The steamer pitched again, his shoulder crashing against the bulkhead. Searing pain ripped through him, although the tight hold on his son never faltered.

"Papa." Robbie's scared whimpers terrified Sam as much as not being able to see his parents. He had to believe they'd found safe haven somewhere out of his view. He needed to concentrate on his son, saving a life more precious than his own.

Instead of the unnerving crunching of metal and the screeching sound of wood rubbing against wood stalling Sam's actions, the sounds of certain danger triggered the opposite. His concentration sharpened as he made his way toward the bow, staying starboard, the same side of the ship where his father and mother last stood.

Children's laughter had long ago turned to terrifying screams and whimpers. Until he got Robbie to safety, he could do nothing for those already injured or in peril. Protecting his son and finding his parents controlled his thoughts as he inched his way forward, watching as the two steamers vied to control the same spot of ocean.

A burning flash caught his attention before the blast sent him flying backward and onto the deck. For an instant, Sam saw what appeared to be his father lurching to the side, then disappearing into the churning sea.

"No!" His head swiveled in search of the source of the heart-wrenching shout, only to startle, realizing he'd been the one crying out. Robbie's sobs, his arms clutching Sam's neck, forced his attention back to the critical present. No matter how much he ached to go after his father, the safety of his son came first.

Continuing toward the bow, Sam's body pitched one way, then the other as the steamer fought to stay afloat. A few steps later, the entire vessel heeled starboard, bodies flying off the deck, poorly secured cargo following into the churning sea. Sam lost his footing, sliding on the slippery surface.

Robbie's grip tightened until Sam could barely take a breath as they descended toward the breach in the side of the vessel. As suddenly as the steamer heeled starboard, it righted itself, stopping their slide toward the sea. A burst of optimism passed through Sam, only to be thwarted when another explosion rocked the vessel, sending barrels flying into the air. Still clutching Robbie to his chest, Sam's eyes widened as one barrel hit its peak, then descended. Rolling to his stomach, Sam covered Robbie with his body, praying it would be enough to shield his son from the falling debris.

Lashing out, Sam struggled toward the light beckoning just beyond his reach, an image of Robbie silhouetted against the blinding rays. Cursing, he fought against strong weights holding him back from his destination.

"Doctor, I need your help."

The urgent feminine voice lifted the haze long enough for Sam to open his eyes, his gaze fixing on a young woman. Her face flushed in determination, she used all her strength to keep his arms from thrashing.

"We have him," a male voice ground out.

She released her hold, giving way to two pairs of thick male arms.

"My son," Sam groaned. "I need to find my son."

The nurse looked at the other two, her forehead creasing in confusion. "We have no children here."

"He's hallucinating. We'll administer more laudanum, then let him sleep. When he wakes, let's hope he's more lucid."

Preparing what the doctor needed, the nurse stepped aside until Sam had been given the drug. Within minutes, his face slackened and his body stilled.

"Check the registry to see if we have a wife or child listed when they brought him in."

"Yes, Doctor." Leaving, she glanced over her shoulder, wondering if there truly was a child. If so, had the patient's son made it through alive?

Pushing through the double doors, she hurried ahead. The small hospital had been swamped with bodies and those injured after the two steamers plowed into each other off the shore of Greytown. Details were sketchy, but from what she'd heard, the *SS Lincoln* stayed on a straight course toward the docks while the other steamer drifted in the dense fog. No matter the cause, many had been lost and more injured, filling the hospital and neighboring buildings.

Reaching the desk, she checked the registry, seeing nothing to indicate the man had relatives who'd been brought in with him. She knew the records were often inaccurate, especially during an accident of this magnitude. It could be days or weeks before a full count of the survivors and those who'd perished could be made, making reuniting families a difficult task.

It had been a long night. Rubbing her eyes with the palms of her hands, she let out a deep sigh. At twenty, she'd already seen one other accident such as this. One of the vessels had sunk, the other towed back to the harbor, taking months to repair.

She had no news on the state of the two vessels that collided yesterday. By the looks of those filling the beds, she had little optimism for the fate of the steamers.

Circle M Ranch

Jinny woke with a start, her forehead damp, hands clammy. The strange dream caused her heart to race and stomach to roil with anxiety. The sickening sensation of something terrible happening held a hint of reality so strong, it made her tremble.

Tossing off the covers, she grabbed her wrapper, slipping it over her thin cotton nightgown before opening her door. The hall was still bathed in darkness, indicating it would be hours until dawn. Shaking her head, she drew in a deep breath, doing her best to calm her pounding heart. Closing the door, Jinny sat down on the edge of her bed, wondering at the sense of foreboding. She'd never had a dream so real it sent shivers coursing through her body.

Covering her face with both hands, Jinny did her best to understand the odd jumble of pictures that refused to fade away. She often dreamed, forgetting the powerful images as soon as she awoke. This was different. The faces of young and old, mouths gaping open in surprise or fear, eyes wide as waves large enough to swamp a house swept over them. Smoke and flames crowded out other images until it all ended when she jerked awake, damp hands clutching her blankets. Jinny didn't recognize anyone or understand what any of it meant.

Walking to her dresser, she picked up the pitcher, pouring a small amount of water into the bowl. Splashing her face, she studied her reflection in the mirror, noting an unnatural hollowness in her expression. A soft knock on the door had her spinning around.

"Jinny, are you awake?"

Grabbing a towel, she wiped her face, padding across the room, opening the door to find Emma on the other side. After the horrible dream, a sense of panic gripped Jinny when she saw the worried expression on Emma's face.

"Is Quinn all right?" She opened the door wide, motioning her best friend to come inside.

Walking past, worry turned to confusion as Emma studied her. "Quinn's fine. I've been lying awake and heard you moving about. I wanted to make certain you were feeling well."

"Aye, I'm fine. Except for a strange dream." Plopping down on her bed, she patted the spot next to her, encouraging Emma to sit down.

"Do you feel like talking about it?"

"I'm not certain how to describe it." Lying on her back, Jinny recounted the images, the horrified faces, the balls of fire disappearing behind thick smoke, the giant walls of water. "It makes no sense to me."

"Have you ever had a similar dream?"

"Nae. Not ever have I dreamed of something so dreadful."

"What about when your family traveled by sea from Scotland? Quinn told me how harrowing it was when storms came through."

"Aye, but I was much younger. Ma and Da made it seem like a wonderful adventure. Brodie, Colin, Quinn, and some of the others were old enough to understand the dangers, but I don't recall being scared." Jinny closed her eyes, trying to remember what she dreamed about during the journey from Scotland and the wagon train from Pennsylvania to Conviction. "Tonight's dream wasn't like any of the others."

Hearing the distress in Jinny's voice, Emma reached over to touch her arm. "It may have to do with what happened at Maloney's store. That scared all of us."

Jinny hadn't thought about the brutal men who'd threatened them. "Do *you* dream about it?"

"No, but I do think about it during the day and when I'm trying to fall asleep. I'm fortunate to have Quinn. When he wraps his arms around me, I'm asleep within minutes."

"Aye, you are a lucky woman, Emma." Jinny loved the fact her cousin fell in love with her good friend, and hoped to find a love like that for herself someday. "And I'm lucky you and Quinn stayed here tonight."

"According to Quinn, we'll be here at least one more night while the men patch the hole in the roof."

Jinny laughed. "Hopefully, I'll not have another dream and you'll not have to come in to check on me."

"I don't mind." Emma didn't move from her place on the bed as she considered what had been on her mind. "You know, I think Deke Arrington is sweet on you."

Jinny had been thinking of him, knowing if she gave Deke any encouragement, he'd ask to court her. "I like him. It's just..." Her voice trailed off as she worked to come up with a reason not to encourage him.

"He seems so nice. Did you know he used to work on a ranch before coming here to join his uncle at the saddlery?"

Jinny's eyes widened. "Nae, he never mentioned it."

"He spoke to Brodie and Quinn about it." Emma's eyes sparkled, her lips turning up at the corners. "They told him to come work for us if he ever grew tired of working for his uncle." Standing, she walked to the door, drawing it open. "I'd better get back in bed before Quinn misses me."

"Thanks, Emma. I'm glad you came to check on me."

"You're my friend. I'll always worry about you."

Watching the door close, Jinny thought of what Emma had said. Besides the fact he was handsome and smart, Deke made her laugh, and had taken the time to look in on her after what happened at Maloney's.

Since she'd met Sam, no other man had drawn her interest. Then he'd left and she'd received no word from him. Neither had Brodie. As much as it pained Jinny to forget her dream of believing a life with Sam was possible, she had to face reality. If he still held any interest in her, he'd have written or sent a telegram. It seemed to be obvious to everyone except Jinny—Sam had forgotten all about her.

Lying down, she pulled the covers under her chin, letting out a shaky breath. She'd hidden away in a make-believe world long enough. It was time to grow up and give up the daydreams of an impressionable girl—including her love for Sam.

Chapter Nine

"Good morning, Miss MacLaren." Deke set down the tool he'd been using to work on a saddle as he stood, a broad smile transforming his features from attractive to stunningly handsome. "Are you here to look at your saddle?"

It had been almost a week since the frightening dream, and each day she'd thought of the conversation with Emma, which led her to think of Deke. Not wanting to appear too forward, she'd held back from riding into town, until this morning when Quinn asked about her new saddle. It gave Jinny the excuse she needed.

"Aye. I mean, if you have the time."

"I'd be pleased to make the time for you, Miss MacLaren." His eyes crinkled at the corners as he nodded toward a corner. "It's over there."

Jinny followed, unable to pull her gaze from the wall behind the counter. She'd never noticed the broad range of leather goods hand-tooled by Rube, and now Deke. Covered with harnesses, bridles, pistol belts, holsters, cuffs, cartridge belts, and quirts, she stopped for a moment to admire the work.

"Miss MacLaren?"

"Aye?" She stepped around the counter, running her hand over a beautiful holster. "I've not seen one like this before."

"I've made three. It's a tip-up holster. The gun does not have to be drawn to shoot. The owner tips up the holster and fires."

Jinny's lips parted, her eyes widening. "Who would need such a holster?"

Chuckling, he stepped next to her. "I didn't ask, but the man who bought the first one had a reputation as a hired gun."

Her brows lifted. "And the second one you made?"

"A rancher. He'd been threatened and wanted extra protection." Deke tilted his head toward her. "From what I heard, he killed two men trying to sneak up on him at night. Of course, it could be a myth. As you may know, there are many stories told over campfires."

Jinny nodded, her eyes sparkling. "Aye, and many stories told by MacLaren lads when they've had too much of the whiskey."

Deke tilted his head back, a deep, full-throated laugh bursting from his chest. The action so surprised Jinny, she found herself laughing along with him. It felt good to let go, to forget the troubles she'd been harboring and enjoy herself. A few moments later, each calmed down, smiles on their faces.

"Well, Miss MacLaren. Are you ready to see your saddle now?"

"Aye, Mr. Arrington. I am." Walking behind him, Jinny admired his tall stature, broad shoulders, and confident stride. If she could only feel for Deke what she had the first time she'd met Sam.

The attraction had been instantaneous, catching her by surprise. The same tightness in her chest and catch in her throat happened each time she saw Sam. That was when she knew, without a doubt, she loved him.

As wonderful as their last moments together had been, he'd walked away and never looked back. Each day had been a struggle, ending when she forced herself to face the truth. Sam hadn't loved her. Not the way she loved him.

Jinny hadn't realized the depth of her mental ramblings until she smacked into Deke's back.

"Ach, I'm so sorry." She could feel her face heat when he shifted around, placing his hands on her shoulders to steady her.

Amusement shown in his eyes as he leaned down. "Are you all right?"

Catching her lower lip between her teeth, she nodded. "Aye." Clearing her throat, she glanced around him. "Is that my saddle?" Her voice came out as a breathless whisper.

Deke stood aside, allowing her to step next to it. "It is. What do you think?"

Her hand rested on the horn, then stroked the seat, moving up the cantle and over the skirt, her fingers lightly caressing the tool work of the fender. She turned to face him, moisture glistening in her eyes.

"It's magnificent. I've not seen anything so bonny, Deke."

His breath caught, hearing his name coming from her lips. Ignoring the lump in his throat, Deke nodded. "Thank you. I hoped you would like it."

She found the humble tone in his voice endearing. "I love it. Is it finished?"

"There are still a few details to complete. It will be finished by the end of the week. Would it be all right if I brought it to the ranch on Saturday? Perhaps you'd let me accompany you the first time you use it."

Jinny felt an unexpected wave of uncertainty at the offer. In her heart, she knew what Deke asked. If she agreed, it would send them on a path she wasn't ready to explore. As much as her mind told her to forget Sam and go on with her life, her heart hadn't had time to accept the message.

Once again running her hand over the leather, she sighed. Declining the offer would be unkind, and she had no desire to cause Deke discomfort. Steeling herself, her gaze locked with his.

"Aye. It would be grand to have you along the first time I use it."

A grin tipped up the corners of his mouth. "Then it's settled. I'll arrive mid-morning."

Dropping her hand from the saddle, she stepped around him. "Thank you, Mr. Arrington. I'll be looking forward to Saturday."

"Me, too, Miss MacLaren."

Greytown

Sam tossed off the covers, cursing the pain shooting through his shoulder, chest, and back. He would no longer stay another day in the bed or in the hospital, despite warnings from the doctors and nurse who'd been tending him for over a week.

"Mr. Covington. What do you think you're doing?"

His nostrils flared at the voice he'd come to love and loathe since the accident. Gentle and kind one moment, tough and unbending the next, she'd watched over him with the tenacity of a hawk after its prey.

"I'm leaving. It's been days and no one has heard news on my son or parents. I can no longer wait, hoping they're safe. It's time I learned their fate." His injuries were minor compared to the stress and worry over his family. Wincing at the pain as he slid from the bed, he held out a hand, steadying himself against it.

She dashed over to put an arm around his waist. "You're not healed enough to leave. The doctor says it will be several more days."

He looked down at her for an instant, getting caught in the glow of her soft gray eyes. If another woman didn't own his heart, he might find the young nurse attractive. Instead, he saw her as an impediment, a person who stood in the way of finding Robbie and his parents. Straightening as best as he could, Sam glared at her.

"You and the doctor have done all you can for me. Please, I'd be grateful if you would bring me my clothes."

"Your clothes?" She sucked in a breath, her gaze darting around the room. "They were ruined. I'm afraid they were tossed out days ago."

Closing his eyes, a muscle in his jaw ticked. "My personal things. Did you save them?"

"I believe so. They should be locked in a room near the front. What will you do for clothes?"

"If I have to walk outside stark naked, I will. I'll not wait one more hour to search for my son."

Resigned, the nurse nodded. "In that case, we may have some extra clothes in the same room. If you'll sit down, I'll take a quick look." She didn't stop to check on any other patients as she hurried to the front.

Doing as she asked, Sam rested his hip against the bed, unwilling to do more. If she didn't return within five minutes, he'd do what he threatened and leave. He knew the hospital staff had done what they could to learn about survivors, but so far, their efforts had turned up nothing.

"Here you are." Rushing up to him, she set the clothes on the bed. "I don't know how well they'll fit, but they should be close, at least until you can buy new ones." She set a leather pouch next to the clothes. "There's money and a few other personal items in there. If you need a place to stay..." Her voice trailed off.

"Don't worry any further about me. I'll find a place to stay, even if it's under the docks." Pushing up, he grabbed the pants, allowing her to assist him with them, the shirt, and coat. She was right. They didn't fit properly, but he preferred them being too big rather than too small.

"The boots may be a little awkward." She held them up, stifling a giggle at the large size.

"It won't matter. I'll stuff rocks in them if I have to." He shoved a foot into one boot.

"Wait here a moment."

He almost laughed. Where would he go with one boot on and the other held tight in her hand? Moving to a row of cabinets, she pulled out a stack of clean cloths.

"Here we are." Taking the boot in her hand, she stuffed a couple rags inside, then handed it to him. "Do those help?"

Slipping it on, he nodded. "Yes, thank you." After doing the same with the other boot, he stood, stuffing the pouch into a pocket. "I don't know how to thank you."

She shook her head. "There's no need. This is my job. I'm glad you're one of the ones who can walk out. Well, best of luck to you, Mr. Covington."

Glancing around, he tilted his head. "Who runs this hospital? Everyone speaks perfect English."

She smiled. "It's because we're all from America. The hospital is owned by a consortium of shipping companies. I'll be here another year, then plan to return home."

"And where is that?"

"Baltimore, Mr. Covington."

"I'm sorry, sir. What did you say your name was?" The older woman, obviously overworked and harried, brushed graying hair away from her face, her gaze darting to him, then behind her to those crowded into the school. It had been converted into temporary living quarters where survivors of the wreck could stay until learning the fate of loved ones.

He repeated the story for the second time. "Samuel Covington. I've been in the hospital, recovering from my injuries. I lost contact with my son, father, and mother during the steamship collision."

She glanced down at the list in front of her. "Their names?"

Repeating them, he tried to peer around her and into the room housing close to a hundred people. "Robbie is only four." Sam didn't know why he felt the need to emphasize the fact, other than to underscore his worry.

Shaking her head, she looked up. "I'm sorry, but they're not on my list." Her face clouded, shoulders slumping. "There's a temporary morgue at the end of town."

Sam's heart squeezed. He refused to let himself accept the possibility they hadn't survived.

"I wish there was more I could do, Mr. Covington. It was a terrible tragedy..." Her voice faded as he turned away.

He couldn't respond, couldn't draw a full breath. His hands fisting at his sides, he took a few tentative steps away.

"Mr. Covington?" The woman came up beside him, placing a hand on his arm. "I should've thought of this sooner. A church next to the hospital is housing a few children who were separated from family members. Perhaps your son is there."

A sliver of hope took hold as he hurried to the door. Grabbing the knob, he looked back. "Thank you."

The wind gusted, kicking up clouds of dust as he hurried toward the hospital. When he walked outside an hour ago, he hadn't noticed a church, determined to get to the school where he heard survivors were housed. Approaching the one-story hospital, he stopped, turning in a circle, letting out a frustrated breath when he didn't see a church. Continuing, he stopped again, hearing the sound of children's laughter. Tiring, he stumbled toward a crumbling building and leaned against an old wooden post. Sucking in a breath, he placed a hand against his aching shoulder. He knew if he walked back into the hospital, the nurse would give him laudanum.

Until Sam found his family, he needed his mind clear. The drug would take that, along with the ability to walk, away. Whiskey, however, could help dull the pain. Unfortunately, there would be no time for liquor until he learned the fate of his loved ones.

Again, the sound of young laughter poured onto the street. The children were close, which meant the church had to be nearby.

Pushing away from the post, he staggered into the street, looking around. His gaze locked on a small structure. Moving closer, he could just make out a cross carved into the front door. Ignoring the pain in his shoulder, he walked up and knocked. It took several attempts before the door opened, an elderly man, stooped with gnarled hands, raising his glassy eyes to meet Sam's.

"I'm looking for my son. He was a passenger on the *SS Lincoln*. I heard..." The sound of laughter drew his gaze toward the back.

"Come." The old man motioned behind him.

Sam's breath came in ragged gulps as he walked through the darkened room. Benches took up most of the space. An alter at one end held what appeared to be a hand-carved cross similar to the one he saw in the door. On both sides, candles burned, providing a warm glow.

Following a stream of sunlight coming from the back, he stepped into a primitive kitchen, nodding at an older woman standing over a wood fire. He pointed to the back yard, receiving a nod before she turned her attention back to her chores.

The sun shining, children ran about, unmindful of Sam's presence. His gaze darted around, searching, praying Robbie would be among them.

"Yes?"

He didn't even see the woman walk up. Taller than some of the locals he'd seen, she had long dark hair clasped at the nape of her neck, a wary expression on her face.

"My name is Samuel Covington. I'm looking for my son, Robbie. He's four, and..."

His voice broke, his balance faltering. Before he could take a step, the woman put an arm around his waist, guiding him to a bench several feet away. When she started to walk away, he grabbed her arm.

"Wait."

Shaking her head, she pulled free, taking several purposeful steps to the corner of the church, then disappearing. Disappointment and a sense of deep failure shook him. He glanced around once more, his heart sinking when he saw no sign of Robbie. Bracing his hands on the bench, he pushed up, falling back at the sound of a startled shout.

"Papa!" Rushing from around the building, Robbie ran to him, his arms outstretched, tears streaking down his face. "Papa..." His deep sobs were muffled in Sam's chest as Robbie's small hands tightened on his father's shirt.

"I'm here, son." Stroking Robbie's head, Sam didn't try to stop his own tears. "You're safe now, Robbie. I have you." Settling Robbie on his lap, Sam wrapped his arms around him, rocking back and forth, thanking God for this miracle.

They sat there a long time before Sam loosened his hold, scrubbing a hand down his face.

"Where were you, Papa?"

Sam's body shuddered as he took a deep breath, wanting to say the right words, not knowing what they were. "I was hurt. They put me in the hospital, but I'm better now."

"Is that why it took so long?"

Rubbing Robbie's back, Sam nodded.

Turning his head one way, then the other, Robbie looked at his father. "Where are Grandfather and Grandmother?"

"I don't know, son."

His eyes wide, Robbie pursed his lips, a serious expression on his face. "We should find them."

Sam would've chuckled if he wasn't in so much pain—physically, mentally, and emotionally.

"Yes, son. We should."

Taking Robbie's hand, he spoke briefly to the woman who'd given them privacy. Reaching into his pocket, he removed the pouch. Pulling out money, he handed it to her, not backing down when she shook her head.

"Please. There's no other way I can repay you. Use it to feed the children." He pressed it into her hand before he led Robbie through the church and out the door.

Chapter Ten

Circle M Ranch

"I love it." Jinny had said the words more than once since Deke arrived, carrying her new saddle into the barn. "And the stamp on the back of the cantle. I've not seen it before."

Shrugging, Deke ran his fingers over the updated maker's mark—*Ferguson & Arrington Saddlery.* "Uncle Rube insisted I be included. He said the shop will be mine one day, so I might as well start getting some recognition."

"And he would be right." Placing her left foot in the stirrup, she swung up into the saddle.

"Does it feel all right?" Deke had unharnessed the horse from the wagon he drove out, then saddled it. He mounted in one smooth motion.

"Aye. She's perfect."

"She?" He followed her lead, reining his horse toward the north.

"Aye. As bonny as the saddle is, I've no doubt it's a she." Sending him a devious smile, she dug her heels into Dancer, sending the mare into a canter.

Deke stayed back a moment, enjoying the view. She rode as if she and Dancer were one, with fluid movements and beautiful form. He considered himself a good rider. Jinny rode with an accomplished expertise he envied. Following behind for a good distance, he caught up to ride alongside for a couple miles, unable to miss the joy on her face.

Taking an overgrown trail toward the eastern mountains, she led him through thick groupings of cypress, manzanita, and stands of tall pine toward the bubbling sound of a nearby creek. Entering a small clearing, Jinny reined Dancer to a stop.

"How did you ever find this place?" Sliding off his horse, Deke lifted his arms to help Jinny down. He didn't linger, removing his hold on her waist the instant her feet touched the ground.

"Brodie, Quinn, Colin, and Blaine found it not long after we reached California. Whenever possible, they explored as much as they could, going north some days, east or south other days. If they found an interesting spot, such as this one, they'd bring several of us back."

He led the horses to the creek, allowing them to drink. "They didn't explore west of the ranch?"

"Nae. They already knew Conviction and several ranches were to the west. The lads looked for unsettled spots. My opinion is my da and his brothers wanted them to search out people living on our land and *encourage* them to move."

"Encourage, huh?"

"Aye. You'll not want to be asking Brodie or Quinn about it, though. They'll not be saying anything." Walking a few feet away, she sat on a flat-topped rock, motioning for Deke to sit next to her. "Now tell me, Mr. Arrington. Why did you leave home?"

Instead of sitting beside her, he took a spot on the ground, crossing his legs. Watching the creek, he pulled small blades of grass out of the dirt, tossing them into the water. Every time someone asked this question, he tried to come up with a good answer—simple and final, as he found that was what most people wanted. Something told him Jinny wanted neither.

"My parents are good people. Hardworking, kind, tolerant." He glanced up at her. "I couldn't have asked for a better family."

She tilted her head, watching as he continued to pull grass and toss it into the stream. "Then why would you leave?"

"It seemed time. As one of the middle children in a brood of seven, I was never lonely. My brothers and sisters all got along as well as you'd expect in a large family. I'm certain you know what I mean." Studying his hands, he didn't look up to see the knowing look in her eyes.

"Aye. Family can be your closest friends, or your fiercest enemies."

"I find it hard to imagine any of the MacLarens having strong conflicts. Not the kind that tear some families apart."

"Nae, we don't. It doesn't mean we don't fight. We're all too pigheaded, as Da and Ma remind us all the time. Still, I can't imagine living across the country from any of them."

A quick pain flashed through him, thinking of his mother the day he left. Strong and opinionated, she'd made it clear she didn't want him to go. It had taken months for her to soften, accepting his decision within days of him leaving.

"It wasn't easy. Ma took it hard. I write her every week, but I know it's not enough. The one good aspect about coming to Conviction is Uncle Rube. He's my mother's older brother." A wistful smile crossed his face. "As soon as I save enough, I'll send her money for a visit."

"What about your da. Won't he come?"

"You know how it is, Jinny. Even with six children old enough to work the place, Pa won't leave it. Going to town for supplies and church on Sunday is as far away as he cares to travel. She might bring one of the younger children, if Pa allows it."

"Is it a big ranch?"

His smile broadened. "Not nearly as large as Circle M. And it's as much a farm as a ranch. We have enough cows to provide milk for many in the closest town. Same with vegetables and meat. The cattle were my responsibility, along with one older brother. We have up to thirty head. Not a lot, but enough for our family's needs and to sell to restaurants and boardinghouses. It's a good life..."

"But?"

"I wish I knew. Before Uncle Rube left, he taught me his trade, believing I might need the skills if I stayed on the family ranch. From the first moment, working with leather felt right, the same as sitting a horse and rounding up cattle. In my mind, they all went together. I had to have a good understanding of what it took to control a horse in order to create the right saddle." He let out a breath, shaking his head. "Pa didn't agree. He thought my time should've been spent only on the cattle, not on some trade providing leather goods others already offered. Somehow, in my heart, I knew working with leather was something I had to do. The telegram from Uncle Rube, inviting me to Conviction, finalized a decision that had been brewing a long time. He wired the money for the trip, and here I am."

"No regrets?"

"Not a one."

"Did you leave a sweetheart behind, Mr. Arrington?" Jinny's face scrunched into a frown the instant the words were out. Thank goodness he chuckled, easing her embarrassment.

"No sweetheart waiting for me to return. Now, how about you, Miss MacLaren?"

"Me? I would think it obvious I'm here with my family."

Leaning back on his elbows, he looked up at her. "There's no sweetheart you're pining after?"

She shook her head, clasping her hands in her lap. "Nae. No sweetheart."

"That's not what I asked."

Biting her bottom lip, color crept up her neck and onto her cheeks.

"Tell me about him." Deke didn't admit to knowing more about Sam than he should. He wanted to hear it from Jinny.

Shifting on the hard rock, smoothing her hands down her dress, she struggled with what to say. "His name is Samuel Covington, and he is the most remarkable man I've ever met."

When she didn't continue, he prodded her. "Explain remarkable."

"He's done so much. When he came to Conviction, he was under the employ of Allan Pinkerton. He gathered, um...information for the Union Army for part of the war, then worked other assignments for the agency. After he finished a job in Conviction, he left Pinkerton. Brodie offered him a job as deputy, which he accepted." A grin lifted the corners of her mouth. "The truth is, he got in a wee bit of trouble and Brodie needed a deputy. They made a bargain, which kept Sam here for six months. Then they agreed he could stay on as deputy as long as he wanted."

"A fast courtship then."

Her eyes widened. "It...we..." She shook her head. "Ach. We never courted, Mr. Arrington. I think Sam and I just knew the instant we met that we were meant to be together." Looking away, some of the enthusiasm left her voice. "At least, *I* knew. We saw each other on Sundays when he'd ride out with Brodie for supper. I rode into town at least once a week, making certain we saw each other. A few times, Brodie asked me to join them for lunch. And, of course, we saw each other at church."

Deke lifted a brow. "I still don't understand why he didn't court you, let you and your family know of his interest."

She'd asked herself the same many times, wishing she had a good answer. "I believe Sam had concerns about my brother being his boss." Blowing out a breath, she brushed strands of hair off her forehead. Jinny hated stating the second reason, thinking it would become real if she said it out loud. "Either that, or...maybe he didn't care as much as I thought."

Deke reached over, placing his hand over hers. "I'm sorry his leaving has been so hard on you." He waited a moment, noticing she didn't pull her hand away. "Why did he leave?"

Her shoulders slumped as she shook her head. "I don't know. He mentioned his family back east and business he needed to take care of." Pulling her hand from Deke's, she shifted a little away, staring at the bubbling creek.

"Does he plan to return?" He couldn't imagine a man leaving without asking a woman who so obviously cared about him to either wait or forget about him.

"Sam didn't know if he'd be able to return to Conviction."

The news stunned Deke. "He didn't ask you to wait?"

"Nae, Mr. Arrington, he didn't." She bit the words out an instant before standing. Staring into the water, she didn't turn as she spoke. "I know what I'm saying must seem daft...being in love with a man who doesn't feel the same."

Walking up behind her, Deke let his arms hang loose at his sides. "No, it doesn't sound daft at all. You love a man who left, but your heart hasn't forgotten him."

Shifting around, Jinny looked up at him. "Aye. I've been unable to push my feelings aside. I keep hoping he'll return."

Deke's concerned face softened as he placed his hands on her shoulders. "It's only been a few months. Perhaps you will still hear from him. In the meantime, I would be honored if you'd allow me to be your friend."

She enjoyed Deke's company, even if he didn't garner her interest in the same way as Sam. "Aye, Mr. Arrington. I would value your friendship."

Smiling, he turned them toward their horses, tucking her hand through his arm. "Then I would request you call me Deke."

A resigned smile crossed her face. "Then you must call me Jinny."

"It would be my pleasure, Jinny."

Greytown

Sam hesitated taking Robbie with him to the makeshift morgue, yet his options were few. As they walked down the center of the small town, a village really when one took it all in, he realized he had no options at all. He didn't have a place to stay or anyone to watch his son while he continued searching for his parents.

Getting close to the other end of town, the location the woman had directed him, he passed several groups of people hovering together. Sam shuddered at their ragged, despondent features, the look of total disillusionment on their faces. Approaching a small cluster of men, he waited to speak until they turned toward him.

"By chance, were you on the *SS Lincoln*?"

Robbie clutched Sam's hand tighter, his eyes wide as he looked up at the hard faces. Leaning down, Sam whispered something in his ear, getting a nod in response.

One of the men, older, haggard-looking, with thinning gray hair and a week's stubble, stepped closer. "Yes." He raised an arm, sweeping it toward the others milling about, looking as if they'd lost everything. And they probably had. "These are the survivors. At least the ones we know about. Half of those in steerage and in cabins were lost."

Sam's gaze moved over the crowd, finding no trace of his parents. "Could there be others?"

Red-rimmed eyes met Sam's. "It's been a week. I doubt there are others." He glanced down at Robbie, clearing his throat. "There's a morgue a little farther down. It's where I found my family." The man's voice broke on the last.

Sam's gut twisted at the hopelessness on the man's face. "I am so sorry."

Using an arm, he swiped at the wetness in his eyes. "It was my wife's wish to move west, see

San Francisco. When we were rammed by the other ship, my daughter and son-in-law were with her on our bunks in steerage. My daughter was pregnant." He glanced away for a moment, then back at Sam. "They had no chance." As the man turned away, Sam couldn't miss the way his body shuddered.

"Papa?" Robbie's tiny voice reached ears already reeling from hearing the depth of loss for those around them. Bending down, Sam picked him up.

"What is it, son?"

Wrapping his arms around his father's neck, he rested his head on Sam's shoulder. "I don't like it here."

"I know, Robbie. Neither do I, but we have to look for your grandfather and grandmother. Then we have to find a place to sleep tonight."

A big yawn stretched Robbie's mouth wide as he nodded. "All right."

Walking in the direction the man indicated, Sam came to the end of the street, seeing no sign of a makeshift morgue. Then his nose picked up a scent Sam had hoped to never encounter again. The smell of death, as thick as on the battlefields, assaulted him, making him gag.

Putting one foot in front of the other, he followed the stench straight toward a steamer docked nearby. Stepping onto the deck, he continued forward, stopping the first person he saw.

"I, um…" Sam glanced at Robbie, who'd thankfully fallen asleep.

The man didn't wait for more. "The morgue is on the next deck down."

"Thank you." Balancing Robbie in his arms, he moved toward the steps, dreading what he might find, knowing he had no choice.

An hour later, exhausted and nauseous, Sam emerged, sucking in a lungful of fresh air. He had checked every body, finding no sign of his parents among them. He should've been overjoyed. Instead, for one of the few times in his life, Sam felt uncertain of what to do next.

Staggering toward the dock, he leaned against the rail, taking a moment to clear his head. The sun hung low in the sky. Finding a place to stay the night and food for Robbie became his priorities. He'd have to resume his search tomorrow.

Pushing away, his thoughts jumbled, he stepped onto dry land, taking a cursory look around. His gaze swept past a thin figure braced against the side of a crumbling stone building, then returned. Something about the man seemed familiar. Getting closer, his heart began to beat in a wild rhythm.

"Father." It came out as a choked whisper, impossible for anyone to hear. Hurrying his pace, Sam tightened his hold on Robbie and broke into a run, not slowing until he knelt beside a man he barely recognized. "Father?"

Deep sunken eyes met his, a mere hint of recognition passing through them before Thomas turned his head away. Placing a hand on his father's shoulder, he leaned closer.

"Father, it's Sam and Robbie. We've been looking everywhere for you."

Shifting, Thomas's hollow, red-rimmed eyes searched Sam's face. Lowering his head, he began to sob, tears falling onto his torn and filthy clothing.

Sam's eyes moistened, his heart breaking as he watched the man who'd been stoic and controlled his entire life break in front of him. Not a single obstacle had ever changed his resolve—until now. And Sam felt responsible.

"Is it Mother?"

Scrubbing a trembling hand down his face, Thomas looked up, the life gone from his eyes. "She's gone, Samuel. Lost in the water."

"Papa?" Robbie tugged on his father's collar. "Why is Grandfather crying?"

His throat thick with emotion, he held his son close, doing his best to control his own sorrow.

"Papa?"

Unable to voice what he couldn't accept, Sam stood, setting Robbie on the ground. Reaching out his hand, his voice sounded hollow. "Come with us, Father. We'll find a place to stay and clean up. Then we'll continue the search for Mother."

Chapter Eleven

Circle M Ranch

Captain Howard Eplett lay flat on his belly, adjusting his field glasses to get a better view of the two riders. He wanted to be certain of the target before he sent his men out.

"Is that her, Captain?"

Eplett glanced at the man lying beside him, Sergeant Claude Parry, his second-in-command. The officer and his ex-Confederate soldiers had refused to accept the South had lost, carrying their anger and vengeance across an entire country until they'd landed in Conviction. A town he wished they'd never ventured into. The option had been taken from him when their visit went wrong, ending with the sheriff taking one of his men into custody. Eplett refused to leave him behind.

"It is." His low voice spat the words out, disgust coursing through him.

"That's three times now he's ridden out to meet the girl. Three Saturdays without a miss." Parry inched away from the crest of the hill before standing. "Do you want me to talk to the men?"

Eplett knew what Parry asked. The men were beyond angry at being held back from breaking into the jail and taking their companion. More than once, he'd ordered them to put down their arms and wait until the time was right. They couldn't afford to have anything go wrong, nor did he want to lose any of his men in a gunfight. His plan was simple and without the danger of trying to break a man out of jail.

"Tell them to be ready next Saturday, nothing more. I don't want anyone anticipating what's expected. I'll give them the orders Friday night." Eplett inched back, the same as Parry, and pushed himself up. "Have them pack everything. We won't be returning to camp." He walked to his horse, then glanced over his shoulder. "And no drinking the night before. I need everyone sober."

Conviction

"Doc Tilden says he's healed enough for the trial. Do you want me to send word to San Francisco?" Deputy Nate Hollis leaned against the wall separating the front of the jail from the cells, his eyes as clear as Brodie could remember.

"Aye, Nate. I'd appreciate it. The last word was to expect the judge in another week." Brodie leaned back in his chair, stretching his arms above his head, letting out a groan.

"It's late. Why don't you go home to Maggie and a hot supper? I'll keep watch on the prisoner."

Brodie had worked long days for weeks, taking Sundays off for the MacLaren family supper. The way Nate had been acting the last few months, Brodie hadn't been comfortable leaving unless Jack was available. Tonight, Jack had plans for supper with Reverend Andrews. With Sam gone, it would be the first time Nate would be the sole deputy on duty.

He thought of Maggie, a smile tugging at the corners of his mouth. She'd be thrilled to have him home for supper instead of bringing his food, as had become the custom, keeping him company until he'd finished every bite. Pulling out his pocket watch, he figured she wouldn't have left the house yet. After a couple hours, he'd come back and check on the prisoner—and Nate. Standing, he reached for his hat.

"I'll be taking you up on the offer, lad. Jack should be by after supper with the reverend."

Nate rubbed the back of his neck with his right hand, then walked to one of the chairs and sat down, adjusting himself to accommodate the gun at his side. With a partial left arm, he seldom took the gunbelt off during the day, refusing anyone's help when offered. Brodie knew pain still plagued him, blaming the loss of his arm for Nate's erratic behavior.

No amount of concern breached the deputy's control on whatever problems he concealed. Nate refused to discuss any of his reasons for coming in late or never leaving his bed at all. If he had been any other man, Brodie would have lost patience months ago. The man's skill at handling a gun with just one arm, along with his determination and sense of justice, made it hard to give up on him. Besides, he'd become a friend, and a sheriff could never have too many of those.

"Take your time. I've eaten, and the town has been quiet. I know where to find you if something comes up."

Brodie studied Nate's face, noting the weary features, even if the eyes had lost most of their glassy redness. "You don't want me bringing any of Maggie's cooking back then?"

Nate grinned, the first Brodie had seen in a long time. "I'll never refuse any of Maggie's cooking."

"Aye. I'll remember that." Grasping the doorknob, he paused. An unnerving tremor surged up his back, a sense of dread washing over him. Looking at Nate, he shook his head, pushing aside his unease. "Send word if you need me."

Closing the door behind him, Brodie looked up and down the original road through Conviction. The street where it all started. It had been over three decades since the town had begun with little fanfare and a great deal of hope. Over time, it had swelled to a thriving riverfront community surrounded by successful ranches and farms, the largest being Circle M, the vast MacLaren spread.

Turning toward his house at the end of town, Brodie thought of the men who'd terrorized his family at Maloney's, how all but one had escaped through the back door of the general store. Brodie expected an attempt to free the prisoner. After several weeks, and no indication they'd stayed in the area, he'd begun to breathe a little easier.

A cheerful shout caught his attention. He looked up to see Maggie hurrying toward him, a basket over one arm. Unmindful of onlookers, she set the basket down, laughing as she wrapped her arms around his neck.

"Ah, lass. You're going to have everyone talking." His smile and warm kiss belied the warning.

She dropped her arms, a brow lifting as the corners of her mouth tilted up. "As if you care."

"Aye, I do care. But I care more about getting you home and feasting on the fine meal you've brought me." Bending, he picked up the basket, wrapping his arm around her waist. Guiding her back down the street, he leaned over to press a kiss on her head, his worries about the prisoner and his companions forgotten in the happiness he found with Maggie.

Greytown

Holding Robbie's hand, Sam settled an arm around his father's trembling shoulders, watching the retreating coastline as the *SS Jefferson* steamship traveled out of San Juan del Sur harbor and into the Northern Pacific. It carried far fewer passengers than the captain or crew had anticipated just weeks before.

Bodies of less than half the drowning victims had been recovered. Susannah Covington hadn't been among them. A single memorial service took place for those who'd lost loved ones, including those whose final resting place was the turbulent Caribbean Sea.

They'd almost missed the final journey of survivors overland to San Juan del Sur, where the *SS Jefferson* had been docked. Rumors had abounded about the ship pulling up anchor, unable to wait any longer for the passengers. It had taken every bit of persuasive skill Sam owned to convince

Thomas his wife had been lost in the tragic event.

In front of his father and son, Sam remained strong, making sure they had food and a place to stay until the trek to the Pacific. At night, he lay in bed, pain slicing through him at the death of his mother. At those times, he thought of Jinny. All he wanted was to wrap his arms around her, letting her warmth flow through him, and never let go.

"Papa?"

Sam looked down into wide, questioning eyes, then lowered himself into a crouch. "Yes, Robbie?"

"Why is Grandfather crying?"

Brushing hair off Robbie's forehead, he swallowed the knot in his throat, wanting to appear strong for his son. "He misses your grandmother."

Wrapping his arms around Sam's neck, Robbie rested his head on his father's shoulder. "I miss her, too."

Tightening his grip, Sam fought tears welling in his eyes as guilt washed over him. If he'd been satisfied raising Robbie in Baltimore, his mother would never have been on board the steamer. She would still be alive, and his father would spend his final days on earth with the woman he loved by his side. If only Sam had known the consequences of his decision. Loosening his hold, he pulled back.

"Grandmother wouldn't like you being sad for her, son. She loved you very much and wanted you to enjoy your new life." Sam winced at the deep throbbing in his chest. The loss was too new, much too fresh to deal with in a rational way, yet he had his son and father to consider. They needed him to be tough and steadfast. "We'll be at our new home in no time. There'll be other children to play with—"

Robbie's eyes lit up. "And a horse. Right, Papa?"

Despite the pain he couldn't shake, Sam chuckled. "Yes, son. As soon as we're settled in our new home, we'll find you a horse. And I know just who to visit." His mind skipped to Jinny, renewed hope and a sense of purpose taking hold. By the time they arrived, Brodie would've received the letter he'd asked a friend to send from Baltimore, telling him of his return and requesting his job back. He had no doubt Brodie had held the deputy position for him.

Standing, grasping Robbie's hand, Sam found himself wondering if Jinny still felt the same, saving her heart only for him.

Circle M Ranch

"Ma, are you here?" Heather MacLaren hurried through the downstairs, then bounded up the steps to the second floor. Calling again, she checked the rooms, then let out a frustrated breath.

"Heather, lass. Are you upstairs?" Audrey stood at the bottom of the stairs, her arms crossed.

"Aye, Ma." Meeting her at the bottom, Heather gave her mother a hug.

Audrey stepped back, narrowing her gaze to study her oldest daughter's face. "Is there something wrong? I didn't expect you until Sunday supper."

"Nae. All is good. I've come with news. Is Quinn around?"

"He and Colin rode north this morning. I expect them back later today." She slipped an arm through her daughter's. "I'll make tea for us, then you'll tell me what is so important you rode over in the middle of the morning."

Heather didn't protest as Audrey pointed to a chair and made tea, setting a cup in front of her and sitting down.

"Tell me what has you on fire this morning."

Heather chuckled at the phrase her mother had used often when they were younger. "Mrs. Evanston has decided to sell."

Audrey's eyes widened at the news. Over a year before, the widow had hired Heather to help at her ranch, creating tension within the MacLaren family when all of them were needed at Circle M. Looking at her daughter, she had to admit living at the next ranch south had been an excellent change for Heather.

Before the offer to work for the widow, Heather had struggled with her place in the family. An accomplished rider, excellent shot, and hard worker, she challenged her brothers and male cousins on everything, arguing to the point they'd been forced to tolerate her rather than welcome her help.

The situation changed somewhat when Caleb Stewart joined them at the ranch. Sparks flew from the instant they met, Heather insisting she couldn't stand his arrogant attitude. Audrey never accepted the excuse. She believed the reason for their sparring had little to do with his behavior and more to do with emotions Heather kept buried and feelings Caleb chose not to voice.

When Heather accepted the offer to work at the Evanston ranch, the rancorous behavior vanished. Sparks now flew only when Caleb joined them for Sunday supper.

"She wants to sell, does she?" Audrey sipped her tea, considering the news. "Does she have a buyer?"

Heather shook her head. "Nae, not that she's mentioned. I know Uncle Ewan and Uncle Ian are always eager to add more land. I thought they'd want to speak with her."

Audrey, like the other aunts, Kyla, Lorna, and Gail, knew much more about the business of running a ranch than most women who'd crossed the frontier. Although they worked alongside their husbands, few women held an interest in the revenue and costs. Fewer had more than a passing interest in bankers, lawyers, and cattle buyers.

"When we purchased the Estrada property with August Fielder, we used a great deal of our cash. We'll not be wanting to increase our debt."

"Perhaps there are other ways to buy her ranch." Heather gripped her cup with both hands, staring at the contents, not meeting her mother's gaze.

Audrey watched her, a slow grin spreading across her face. "There are ways to get what you want, lass. If the family wants the Evanston ranch, I've no doubt we'll have it." Taking the last sip of tea, she set her cup aside. "Would you want to stay there or come back home?"

Heather glanced up, the question coming as a surprise. She'd always railed against orders, even those from her deceased father. When he died, she'd taken the anger of the loss out on her brothers and cousins. Mildred Evanston had helped her learn to control the devil within her, although Heather knew she still had a long way to go.

"I'll do whatever the family wants."

Standing, Audrey placed a hand on her daughter's shoulder, looking down at her. "That is a good answer, lass. We'll see if you truly mean it."

Howie Eplett and his men sat huddled around a campfire, doing their best to stay out of the pounding Saturday morning rain. They'd discovered a spot on the Circle M ranch where they could hide. Near a creek, the indent in the hillside provided a small amount of shelter, allowing them to remain undetected by the MacLarens.

They'd planned to follow the woman and her beau on their regular Saturday ride, taking her hostage, holding her in exchange for Private Terrence Card. The weather forced them to stay put, pushing out the abduction another week. The men didn't hesitate to voice their objections. Most wanted to ride into Conviction, break the private out of jail, and leave. Eplett refused. There might not be many deputies, but from what he'd seen and learned from his secret trips to town, the men were good shots and vigilant. He knew they'd never get out of town without losing at least one man—a risk he wasn't prepared to take.

"We can't continue to let the men sit around with nothing to do, Captain. They're talking of leaving, breaking off to head out on their own." Sergeant Claude Parry sat next to Howie, his arms resting on his legs, his voice low. "They're talking of going north to Ophir City. It's about a day's ride."

"I know where it is, Claude," Howie hissed. "It's where we planned to go after Conviction." He tossed the cheroot he'd been smoking on the ground, mumbling a curse. "We can't leave Card behind."

"No one wants to leave him behind. They want to hit the bank, then ride back here. It's a week before the MacLaren woman and her gentleman friend ride out again." Leaning back, Claude crossed his arms. "Might be a good idea,

Captain. Give the men something to do while we wait to get Card back."

Even though the men tried to keep their thoughts amongst themselves, Eplett had heard the rumblings. They had plenty of cash from robbing banks along their route from east to west. He'd marveled at how easy it had been. So easy, they'd tried their luck with stagecoaches. Those hadn't been as lucrative, and to his way of thinking, were riskier than banks. They'd been cooped up for weeks, waiting for the chance to get Card, and Howie still berated himself for the failed attempt to rob the general store. They had the money for supplies and should've purchased what they needed, then robbed the bank. It had turned into a fiasco, one Eplett didn't care to repeat.

A trip to Ophir City would alleviate the tension and get the men focused on the reason they'd stayed so long near Conviction. Pulling another cheroot from his pocket, he lit it, taking a deep drag before blowing the smoke out in a thin stream.

"Tell the men we ride out tomorrow. Afterward, we come back here. No matter the weather next week, we grab the girl and get Card out of jail."

Chapter Twelve

Conviction

Brodie walked toward the jail, the letter from Sam tucked in his pocket. He'd hoped to hear from him for weeks, and now that he had, he anticipated good news.

Pushing open the door, his gaze landed on Jack. The youngest deputy had been doing more than his share of night shifts and early mornings, allowing Brodie and Nate to make most of the rounds. This morning, Nate had been assigned the early shift. Poking his head around the corner toward the cells, he let out a sigh.

"Where's Nate?"

Standing, Jack picked up his hat, anticipating Brodie's request. "Don't know, Sheriff. I got here right after sunup and didn't see him. You want me to check the hotel?"

"Aye. Come back and let me know if you find him." He hoped Nate had already started his rounds without stopping by the jail first. His gut told him that wasn't the case.

"Sure thing, Sheriff." Nodding, Jack hurried outside, turning in the direction of the Gold Dust.

Settling into his chair, Brodie pulled the letter from his pocket. Ripping it open, he read quickly, hoping Sam had made the decision to return to Conviction and his job. And possibly Jinny.

His initial smile froze on his face as he continued reading. Sam had indeed decided to return, but he wouldn't be alone. He'd be bringing his family. *Family?* Sam had never mentioned a family, other than his parents. Brodie wondered if he had a wife and children, people he loved and never mentioned. If Sam had led Jinny on, there'd be hell to pay.

Anger began to swell as he reread the letter, then placed it on his desk. Sam had shown a strong interest in Brodie's sister, leading her to believe he had feelings for her. He knew Sam had tried to keep his interest in Jinny a secret, but Brodie had figured it out, confirming it with Maggie, who'd spoken with his sister. Going through their wives was often the only way the MacLaren men learned what was going on in the minds of the women.

Glancing down, he noticed the date, then read further until his gaze focused on Sam's expected arrival. The letter must've taken much longer to reach Conviction than anticipated as they were already almost two weeks late. Sam also mentioned August Fielder finding a house with at least three bedrooms. A bachelor wouldn't need such a large place.

Running his hands through his hair, he struggled with what to do with the news. Although she'd do her best to hide it, Jinny would be heartsick to learn Sam hadn't been truthful. The letter caused a dilemma. How could he trust a deputy who hadn't been honest? He was already dealing with Nate, who refused to discuss his change in behavior. So far, he hadn't done anything illegal or unbefitting a deputy, forcing Brodie to take away his badge.

Sam had created perhaps a bigger injustice—to Jinny.

Pinching the bridge of his nose, Brodie considered what to do. Again, he stared at the letter, August Fielder's name drawing his attention. He needed to talk with him. Before he spoke with Jinny or anyone else, Brodie wanted to learn as much as he could about Sam's return, and the family he'd kept hidden.

Off the Coast of California

"How much longer, Papa?" Robbie swiped at the saltwater splashing his face as the steamer made its way through the swells toward San Francisco.

"Not much longer, son. The captain says we should reach the harbor this afternoon." Sam, his father, and Robbie had been watching the journey from amidships on the starboard side.

Sam gripped the rail with both hands, enjoying the first sunshine they'd had in days. He hadn't confined himself or Robbie below deck, but the cold chill kept them bundled up, even in the middle of summer. Once they reached shore and traveled to Conviction, their bulky clothes could be packed away, hopefully for months.

Glancing to his side, he watched his father stare straight ahead, one hand wrapped around Robbie's much smaller one. To Sam's relief, he'd improved a little each day as the threads of acceptance took hold. Thomas had mentioned he was glad he didn't have to return to Baltimore alone, walking into an empty house with so many memories. For Sam, it affirmed continuing to Conviction might be what they needed.

Out of the corner of his eye, Sam noticed three men approaching, stopping several feet away. The same three he'd seen for several days. They never got too close, didn't speak to him, but watched his movements. Their intense scrutiny unsettled him. He guessed they traveled in steerage with the other passengers who, for various reasons, were unable to book a cabin. They had the look of men accustomed to working the docks, yet he knew they weren't part of the crew. And they hadn't been passengers on the *SS Lincoln*, which sank outside Greytown.

"Is something wrong, Samuel?" His father stared at him with eyes less haunted than the day before.

Keeping the men in sight, Sam shook his head. "Nothing's wrong, Father. Do you have all your possessions together for when we dock?"

A bitter laugh escaped Thomas's lips. "There isn't much to pack. As with everyone else, most of my belongings were lost or ruined." He reached into his breast pocket, pulling out the watch Susannah had given him on their twenty-fifth wedding anniversary. "I'm thankful to still have this." He held it up, moisture filling his eyes. It had been tucked securely in his pocket the morning of the wreck. It no longer worked, but Sam hoped the watchmaker in Conviction could work his magic and fix it.

"You also have what you shipped overland, Father." Sam shifted, leaning an arm on the railing, noting the men still watched. "Would you mind taking Robbie below deck for a bit? He's looking a little tired."

"I'm not tired, Papa. I want to stay with you."

Thomas looked over Robbie's head at Sam. "Why don't I take Robbie for a walk around the ship? By the time we're done, I'm certain we'll both be ready for a rest."

Sam nodded, returning his gaze to the men, who made no attempt to disguise their interest in him and his family.

Looking down at Robbie, Thomas smiled. "All right, young man. Come along with me."

Waiting until they were out of earshot, Sam straightened, turning his full attention to the three men. They made no move to walk away, almost taunting him to come to them. He had no intention of disappointing them.

Making eye contact with each, he walked forward, stopping a couple feet away. "Gentlemen. It is a nice day, don't you think?"

One of the three drew himself up to his full height, which Sam guessed to be close to six feet. At six-three, the gesture didn't intimidate him.

"Me and the boys was just commenting on the weather, wasn't we?" He looked at the others, who nodded.

They stared at each other for long moments, no one speaking as the ship rolled over the swells.

The tallest crossed his arms. "You got something to say?"

"I noticed you've been keeping watch on me and my family. Any particular reason?"

Glancing at the others, the man smirked. "Lovely family you got. We heard you already lost one in the accident. Be a shame to lose more."

Taking a step forward, Sam clenched his fists at his sides, his face becoming a steely mask. "I don't appreciate threats. You touch my family, make one move to harm them, and I will see each of you hang."

Ignoring the threat, or the potential danger in angering Sam, the man continued. "We hear San Francisco's a rough town. Me and the boys could provide protection. You know, keep the riffraff away."

Sam studied each of the three, memorizing their faces and build. He'd been approached by men like them before, offering *protection* when extortion was the more appropriate word.

"I appreciate the offer, gentlemen." Moving his coat aside, he watched the men's eyes widen at the sight of his gun. In Greytown, he'd been fortunate to find a retired ship's captain with a six-shooter he'd been willing to part with. Sam also added a knife strapped to his ankle, as well as one on his belt. He'd learned the hard way what happened when you weren't prepared. Traveling with his son and father had him more cautious than ever.

"You might think about it, gent. Bad things can happen in such a big city."

Sam stiffened at the knowing sneer on the man's face. If it were just him, he would think little of the threat. Having his son and father under his protection made him more vigilant, and more suspicious.

"Again, I appreciate the offer." Sam touched the brim of his hat. "Enjoy the rest of the cruise, *gentlemen.*"

Turning, he took his time strolling to the front of the ship where his father and Robbie stood looking toward the open sea. The moment they docked, he'd hustle them to shore, find a hotel, and book passage to Conviction. Lingering in San Francisco, seeing some of the boisterous city, no longer held any appeal.

Conviction

"I wish I had more to tell you, Brodie, but Sam mentioned bringing his family and the need for a house with three bedrooms. It wasn't easy, but I found one north of town." August Fielder pushed the letter across the desk. "You can read it if you'd like. I would have mentioned it sooner, but assumed he'd contacted you about getting his job back."

Reading the letter, Brodie felt a rush of disappointment. He didn't mention a wife and children. Jumping to conclusions didn't sit well with him, but nothing else made sense. Sliding it back across the desk, he pulled the letter he'd received out of his pocket and held it out.

"This is what came in the mail today." As August read it, Brodie looked around the large room where the attorney worked when home, remembering their discussion a few months earlier. He'd yet to give the man an answer. With Sam returning, it might be time to consider leaving his sheriff's position and returning to work on the Circle M. His chest tightened as he thought of giving up the profession he'd wanted since a child.

"Sam says pretty much the same as in my letter." Handing it back to Brodie, August leaned back in his chair, crossing his arms. "I'm assuming you plan to give him his job back."

He didn't want to see Jinny hurt, yet withholding the job from Sam seemed pointless. He'd proven himself many times since arriving in Conviction, doing more than what Brodie expected. Once settled in their new home, he planned to have a hard discussion, insisting Sam stay away from Jinny. She deserved more than a man who couldn't be honest.

"Aye. I see no reason not to give him back his badge."

Standing, August walked around his desk, crossing his arms and leaning his hip against the edge. "Have you thought any more about transferring the sheriff job to Sam and returning to the ranch?"

Expelling a deep breath, Brodie shook his head. "Not since he left. Even with him returning, we need at least one more deputy, maybe two. The town is growing so fast, Nate, Jack, and I can't keep up with it. Sam being back will help." Standing, he walked to the window, staring out at the lush yard.

"I won't push you, Brodie. As I mentioned before, it's your decision. No one is going to push you out of the job."

Brodie pursed his lips, nodding. "Thank you." He didn't know what else to say. Whatever he decided, it would be painful and not without some regrets.

"There is, however, something else to consider. Widow Evanston has decided to sell her ranch. She approached me confidentially yesterday to see if I'd be interested. I need to discuss the matter with your father and Ian, but it's a good spread we should consider buying."

August and the MacLarens had partnered to purchase a large part of the Estrada ranch. The original land grant had been divided so the Estrada family still had a good number of acres.

Quinn had ridden into town the day before, saying the family expected him at Sunday supper. They had business to discuss and wanted him there. Brodie hadn't pushed for the reason, but it made sense now. Heather must have learned of the widow's desire to sell and told the family. After the success of the Estrada purchase, he had no doubt his father and uncle would be interested in the same arrangement for the Evanston ranch.

"I'll send telegrams to the sheriffs in Sacramento and San Francisco, letting them know we're in need of deputies. Once Sam returns, and we're certain he'll stay, I'll make my decision."

"That's fair. I know it will be a tough decision, given your success as the sheriff."

Walking to the door, Brodie paused. "Is there anything I can do to help get Sam's house ready?"

"It's been ready for two weeks. I can't deny I'm curious about the delay and hope nothing has gone wrong. Unfortunately, Sam didn't provide any other contacts, so all we can do is wait."

"Aye. Good day to you, Mr. Fielder. I'll let you know when I hear from him."

Letting himself out, Brodie swung up on Hunter, reining the horse toward the docks. He'd spread the word about needing deputies, then do the same at the Gold Dust Hotel, keeping his usual watch for the men who'd terrorized the women at Maloney's. It had been weeks since they'd arrested Terrence Card, and no attempt had been made to break him out. Still, Brodie's instincts told him they hadn't heard the last of the ex-Confederate gang.

Ophir City

"We rob the bank as soon as they open. We'll be in and out before the law or anyone else knows what happened." Captain Eplett squatted, pointing to a crude layout in the dirt. It showed the main street, bank, jail, and other businesses Claude Parry had noted on a trip the day before to a town half the size of Conviction. He didn't anticipate a big haul. What he did expect was all his men to get away alive and unwounded.

The men had been up, their horses saddled and gear packed, long before the sun rose. Now they waited. The camp was less than a mile from town, right off the trail from Conviction. Eplett planned a different route back, identifying a meeting spot should they get separated.

"We can't afford casualties. No one takes chances, and no killing. Two go inside, the rest wait with the horses."

"What if they draw on us, Captain?"

"Defend yourselves, but don't shoot to kill, Private." Satisfied, Eplett stood, glancing around. "Everyone ready?"

"Yes, sir," they replied in unison.

"Then let's ride."

The robbery went as planned, two men entering the bank and filling saddlebags with money. After one last admonishment to the clerks and the lone customer not to follow, they holstered their guns, leaving less than ten minutes after they'd entered. Swinging into their saddles, they kicked their horses as they raced out of town.

Eplett thought they'd gotten safely away when a shot rang out. Sergeant Parry cursed, leaning down to grasp his leg. Reining his horse around, Eplett pointed his six-shooter at a boy, no more than twelve, who still shouldered his rifle. In a split-second decision, the captain aimed at the boy's feet and fired. Dropping the rifle, the boy fled inside. Satisfied, he reined back toward his men, kicking his horse into a run as he leaned low over the saddle. The entire episode took no more than a few seconds.

Keeping to the trail, he caught up to his men in minutes, moving his horse alongside Parry's, the man struggling to stay in the saddle. Leaning down, he pulled the reins out of the sergeant's weak grasp.

"Hang on, Sergeant. We'll get you out of here." Signaling his men to keep going, Eplett held tight to Parry's reins. Waiting too long to treat the wound could prove deadly, yet they had to get far enough away from town to be safe.

Glancing over his shoulder, he saw Parry slump forward, swaying in the saddle. Eplett had to get him to safety, and fast.

Signaling the others to ride ahead, he reined the horses right, into a section of large boulders and thick shrubs about a hundred yards off the trail. A good tracker could find them. If a posse was on their trail, he hoped they'd follow the others, knowing the route he'd laid out for his men would get them to safety.

Reining to a stop, he slid off his horse, catching Parry in his arms as the man slipped from the saddle.

Conscious and in great pain, Parry gripped Eplett's arm. "Leave me here, Captain."

Settling him on the ground, Eplett ripped open his pants, checking the wound on his thigh, letting out a relieved breath when he saw the bullet had gone straight through. Dashing to his horse, he pulled a shirt from his saddlebags, along with an almost empty bottle of whiskey.

"I'm not leaving you, Claude. I just need to clean it up and put a bandage around it, then we'll be back on the trail." Opening the whiskey, he held the bottle over the wound. "This will hurt."

When Parry nodded, gritting his teeth, Eplett doused the wound, then covered it with the shirt. Applying pressure, he held it steady for several minutes until the sound of horses had him looking in the direction of the trail. He placed a hand over Parry's mouth.

"Stay quiet."

The sound of pounding hooves grew louder, men shouting at each other, unaware of the two men a few yards away as they rode past. Lifting his hand, Eplett focused on the wound. Tearing the shirt, he wrapped a strip around Parry's thigh.

He couldn't count the number of men he'd tended to during the war. He couldn't abide men or children suffering. Women, however, were a different matter. He'd never held the same respect for them, had never met a woman who earned it. Not his deceitful mother, who'd run off when he was six, and certainly not his cheating fiancée.

"That will have to do until we reach camp."

Pushing up on his elbows, Parry's pained gaze locked on Eplett's. "Leave me. Come back when you know it's safe."

Ignoring the plea, Eplett hoisted him into his arms and onto the saddle. "Can you hold on?"

"Yes, sir," Parry ground out, gripping the saddle horn with both hands.

Holding the reins of both horses, he swung onto his horse. "We're heading away from the others."

"Do whatever you have to, Captain. I trust you."

With that affirmation, Eplett kicked his horse, riding west and away from the posse.

Chapter Thirteen

San Francisco

"Come quickly, Robbie. We need to reach the stagecoach before it leaves." Holding his son's hand, his father a few feet behind, Sam followed the porter who'd agreed to carry their luggage from the hotel. According to the front desk clerk, the stage boarded a short three blocks away.

Fog hung thick in the early morning, the same as when the steamship docked the day before. They'd arrived in port and disembarked without incident. Sam assumed the men he confronted understood his message, moving on to others who might be more agreeable to their *help*.

Glancing over his shoulder, he noted his father falling farther behind, his normal brisk pace slowed by age and a heavy heart. In Sam's mind, they couldn't get to Conviction soon enough. They needed a fresh start in a town with good people where new memories could be made.

"Are you all right, Father?"

"I'm fine, Samuel. Perhaps a little winded is all."

Accepting the reply, Sam continued to follow the porter around a corner, spotting the stagecoach a block away. In a short while, they'd be loaded and on their way. It wasn't until a few minutes later, when they stopped in front of the stage, that Sam noticed his father wasn't with them.

"Would you like me to take care of your passage, sir?" The porter stood next to him, oblivious to the concern on Sam's face.

"Yes, please." Digging into his pocket, he pulled out the fare. "Here. Apparently, we've lost my father. Make sure they wait until I return." Looking into the stage, he spotted an older couple. Glancing behind him, still not seeing his father, Sam made a quick decision. "Excuse me. My father seems to have been delayed. He should only be a block behind us. Would you mind watching my son for a few minutes while I find him?"

"Well, I don't think—" the man began, only to be interrupted by his wife.

"Of course, young man. You go find your father. This young gentleman will be safe with us." The woman leaned forward, offering her hand to Robbie. "I'm Mrs. Jaeger and this is my husband, Mr. Jaeger. What is your name?"

Robbie looked at the woman, then up at his father, his face scrunching together.

"His name is Robbie Covington, and I'm Samuel Covington." His worry grew the longer his father failed to appear. Lifting his son, he set him inside the stage. "Robbie, I need to find your grandfather. You need to stay here with Mr. and Mrs. Jaeger. Do you understand?" A reluctant nod was all Sam needed before he ran back toward the hotel.

Scanning every store and alley, he called his father's name, getting no response. He'd been right behind them until the last corner. Afterward, Sam had lost track of him.

"Thomas Covington?" He called the name over and over before noticing an opening between two buildings. Not wide enough for an alley, Sam assumed the merchants used it to travel between stores.

His desperation grew, his voice hard and loud. "Tom Covington!"

"Help!"

Sam swore as he jogged down the opening, turning at the end to find his father on the ground, the three men from the ship bending over him, rifling through his clothes. Drawing his gun, he aimed at the tallest.

"Back away from him or, by God, I'll shoot you where you stand." Taking a breath, Sam leveled the six-shooter, no doubt in his mind he could hit all three before they got to him. He had no desire to kill them, but he would if they gave him no choice.

The tallest held up his hands. "No need for shooting. We were just helping the old man after some men roughed him up."

"That's a lie," Thomas replied, doing his best to sit up as the men began to back away. "They jumped me, Sam."

"Quiet, old man." The tallest looked at the other two, giving a slight nod toward Sam. The three rushed at him.

With no time to change his mind, he fired at the tallest, hitting him in the leg. The second took a bullet to the shoulder, the third in his arm. Shouts from the street, the men moaning on the ground, his father's worried voice all mingled together as Sam holstered his gun and helped Thomas up. Without sparing a glance at the men he'd shot, he brushed his father off, straightening his clothes and checking for injuries.

"Did they hurt you?"

"No. Roughed me up a bit, though."

"What's going on here?" Two men with badges rushed up, staring at the three injured men, then at Sam and Thomas, who pointed at his attackers.

"Those men jumped me." Straightening, Thomas glared down at them.

"That's not true," the tallest ground out, gripping his leg. "They attacked us."

The officers knelt beside the men, checking their wounds as the medical wagon came to a stop on the street. One of the officers stood, looking at Sam.

"Who shot them?"

"I did. They were attacking my father, then rushed at me." Sam looked at the three, smirking. "As you can see, I didn't aim to kill."

"That may be, but we'll need all of you to come to the police station. Looks like these men will need a trip to the hospital."

Sam thought of Robbie and the Jaegers. "How long will this take?"

"Can't say. You have somewhere you have to be?"

Sam didn't appreciate the officer's tone, but ignored it.

Rubbing a hand behind his neck, he glanced at his father. "We've passage on the stage to Conviction. An older couple is watching my son. I left Robbie with them when my father disappeared."

The officers turned away, talking in quiet tones as the medical personnel loaded the injured men into the wagon. The older of the two officers looked at Sam.

"The stage office is a block away. Let's go there and talk so you can be with your son."

Sam knew what to expect, knowing it would take a miracle to make it on today's stage. "Thank you. I appreciate it."

Walking with the younger officer, Sam could hear his father behind them, talking to the older one.

"My son, Samuel, is a deputy in Conviction. He was with Allan Pinkerton's agency before that, working with the Union Army."

"That explains how he got all three of them. Most men wouldn't even attempt it."

Sam stifled a chuckle as the conversation continued. As far as he knew, his father had never met anyone who didn't become a friend. He hoped it would work in their favor today. As they approached the stage, Robbie jumped down, running to his father.

"You took so long, Papa."

"I know, son. But we're here now." He looked at the Jaegers. "I apologize for the inconvenience and am most grateful for you watching Robbie."

Mrs. Jaeger stepped down from the stage. "It was no bother at all, young man. Now, you must tell us what happened."

After hearing the condensed story, Mr. and Mrs. Jaeger refused to leave without them. She fussed over Thomas and clucked her approval of Robbie. Somehow, between the Jaegers' determination not to leave, his father's cooperation, and Sam's position as a deputy in Conviction, the officers took their stories and told them they were free to leave.

"It's doubtful, but we may need you to come back for the trial. Unless you don't want to press charges."

Thomas crossed his arms, indignation in his voice. "I'm pressing charges, officer. Those men should not get away with what they did. They'll only do it to someone else. I'll be happy to return for their trial."

Sam agreed. He planned to ask August Fielder if he'd take their statements, hoping the court would accept them in lieu of returning to San Francisco.

Through all of this, the stage driver let his displeasure be known, stalking about and interrupting every few minutes. By rights, Sam knew he could drive off, leave them all behind— and lose the passage of five people. He'd waited, pocketing the extra money Sam slid to him in private.

Shaking the officers' hands, they boarded the stage, exhausted and ready to leave. As the stage rolled out of the city, Robbie resting in Sam's lap, he closed his eyes. So much had happened in such a short time. He'd gained a son, lost his mother, then almost his father. They'd made it this far and now headed toward their new life.

Sam could only hope Jinny would be waiting for him.

Outskirts of Circle M Ranch

"The sergeant isn't going anywhere soon, Captain." Private Krahl packed away his few medical supplies, slinging the saddlebag over his shoulder. "At least two weeks."

"Forget it, Krahl. I'm not lying on my ass anywhere close to that." Claude Parry looked over at Eplett. "I'm not holding up the plans, Captain. Give me a few days and I'll be good as new."

Howie looked down at him, believing the private was right, knowing they still had to be concerned about infection. They'd all evaded the posse, meeting at the camp hidden within MacLaren land. Rough, rocky, and thick with shrubs, they hadn't seen a single person come this way since they'd claimed it. Now they'd be stuck another week, maybe two, while Parry healed.

"Get some rest, Sergeant. When you're better, we'll go after the woman and get Card out of jail."

Parry tried to sit up, groaning when his body didn't cooperate, and dropped back down.

Eplett kneeled on one knee, checking the bandage. "Take it easy. You'll ruin the private's good work."

Mumbling a curse, Parry stared at the captain. "We both know it can't wait any longer. The news we heard was the judge would be in town this week. Card and the rest of us need to be far away from Conviction by then."

At first, Eplett had thought the same, cursing their luck, wishing for the hundredth time they'd never entered the town. He knew the way justice worked. Even if the judge found Card guilty of a crime, he wouldn't be sentenced to hang. The judge would send him to San Quentin, at least two days' ride in a wagon, which would stop in towns along the way to pick up other sentenced prisoners. If they missed their chance to take the MacLaren woman, bartering her for Card's release, they'd have other chances before he reached prison.

Eplett had no intention of waiting. He wanted the woman for more than her value as a hostage. From the moment he'd seen her in the general store, he'd wanted more than what he knew she'd willingly offer. Watching her the last few weeks, his interest had increased until it was a fever in his blood. It made no sense, but he wasn't a man who spent much time evaluating his feelings for women. He'd satisfy his need, then make the exchange, leaving the area without a backward glance.

Nothing in his character warned him his thinking was wrong, and he wouldn't care if it did. He'd long ago pushed aside guilt and honor for what mattered most—his men, money, and vengeance against those who supported the North. From what he'd learned, the MacLaren family, and the majority of those in Conviction, supported Lincoln, which made them his enemies. In his mind, he and his men were the instruments of justice, and he meant to see justice served.

Conviction

Brodie's patience had come to an end. For several days in a row, Nate hadn't arrived for his morning shift at the jail. Jack hadn't found him in his room at the Gold Dust, nor on his rounds. He'd walk through the door mid-morning, his appearance haggard, eyes pinched in pain, offering no explanation while evading questions. Today, Brodie vowed to learn what had turned a good man and a responsible deputy into a man he didn't recognize. It may mean losing Nate, but Brodie's responsibility was to the people of

Conviction, not to a man who refused to accept help.

"Good morning."

Brodie looked up from his desk, a grin lifting the corners of his mouth when he saw Maggie walk in with Colin's wife, Sarah, and her sister, Geneen. Grant, Sarah and Colin's son, squirmed in Maggie's arms, a broad smile on his wife's face as she spoke to the boy in a quiet voice. His eyes softened as he gave Maggie a knowing look. Soon, they'd be making their own announcement.

"What a nice surprise. What brings you lasses to town this lovely day?" Walking around his desk, he placed a kiss on Maggie's cheek. "Did the lads come with you?"

"Not today. Colin, Quinn, and Caleb are searching for strays. We decided to make the trip ourselves." Geneen took a casual stroll around the room, poking her head around the wall toward the cells to see the prisoner. She stepped back, a shiver running down her spine when she remembered the day at Maloney's. "When will the judge arrive for his trial?"

Brodie placed his hands on his hips, shaking his head. "He should be here now. I got word he's delayed...again. I'm hoping he'll be here by the end of the week."

"Maybe it's time we had our own judge." Sarah settled into a chair as Maggie continued to coo over Grant.

"Aye, it is. I've talked with August Fielder about it. He's preparing a request for a permanent judge in Conviction. Unfortunately, it could be months before he gets an answer." Brodie took Grant from Maggie, rocking him in his arms as he spoke. "In the meantime, I'm in need of more deputies."

Geneen's brows lifted. "Are Nate and Jack not enough?"

Her question reminded Brodie she had a sweet spot for Nate, knowing she hoped the deputy would ask permission to court her one day. Although she tried to hide it, her attraction to Nate was no secret to any of the MacLarens. And from what Brodie could tell, Nate felt the same, although his interest hadn't been as obvious as the feelings Sam showed for Jinny.

This left him with an additional dilemma. He already struggled with what to say to Jinny about Sam. Now he had to consider Geneen when he made a decision about Nate.

"Nae, lass. I needed more men *before* Sam left." His face clouded. "If I'd had more deputies when the ex-Confederate raiders rode in, I might've been able to stop what happened."

Maggie moved next to him, placing a hand on his arm. "It wasn't your fault, love." She took Grant from Brodie when he offered him to her.

"Perhaps, but I'll not be putting more people in danger if there's a way to stop it. Adding more deputies will be a good start."

Geneen leaned against a wall, her gaze moving to the door. "It's quiet in here today. Do you expect Nate to come by soon?"

Brodie noticed Maggie and Sarah glance at Geneen, neither commenting. They both knew her interest wasn't casual curiosity.

"He'll be by sometime today, lass, although I'm not sure when. What plans do you three have today?"

Maggie handed Grant back to Sarah. She stood up, cradling her son to her chest, then looked at Brodie. "We're going to Maloney's to place an order, then we need to speak with Stein Tharaldson. Sean and Fletcher have requested some specific items they want him to order for the horses."

Brodie chuckled, thinking of his younger brother, Fletcher, and his cousin, Sean. They were in charge of the horse breeding program and, along with Emma, were making significant progress. Sean had an enormous appetite for anything related to animals, and hoped to attend the Highland Society's Veterinary School in

Edinburgh, Scotland. It would mean leaving the ranch for years.

"The lads are always wanting to try whatever Sean has read about in the latest journals." His eyes shifted to the door, seeing Nate walk in. The deputy nodded at Brodie before his attention turned to Geneen.

"Ladies. You're all looking well today." Removing his hat, he stepped closer to Geneen, his gaze softening as he leaned down, lowering his voice. "You're looking especially beautiful, Miss Geneen."

Brodie could see the blush creep up her cheeks at whatever Nate had said. He sucked in a slow breath, then let it out, realizing he had to talk to him soon, discover his deputy's hidden secret. Protecting the town was his job. Safeguarding his family meant a great deal more. Geneen might not be a MacLaren like her sister, Sarah, but in the eyes and hearts of the family, she was one of them.

Geneen cleared her throat. "We were about to go to Maloney's, then to see Stein Tharaldson. Would you care to come along?"

Nate shifted, his gaze landing on Brodie, seeing the wariness in his boss's features. "I'd like to, but it's my turn to watch the prisoner. The sheriff can't be expected to stay inside all day."

Brodie didn't have to look at Geneen to know she hoped he'd say something. "Jack is due back any time now, Nate. Why don't you go with the lasses? Find me when they're ready to ride back to the ranch. I need to speak with you."

"Sure, Brodie." Offering his arm to Geneen, he smiled at her. "Are you ready?"

Brodie saw Maggie and Sarah hide their grins at the way Nate focused on Geneen. They believed she deserved the attention, and both liked the deputy, thinking the two were a perfect match. He wished he could feel the same.

Maggie kissed him on the cheek before joining the others at the door. "I'll see you at home tonight, Brodie."

"Aye, lass. I'm looking forward to supper with you."

He couldn't help the tinge of worry crawling up his spine as the door closed. Nate had problems, secrets he'd chosen not to share, and Brodie had sent him along with his family. He let out a breath, hoping he hadn't made a mistake.

Chapter Fourteen

Nate had seen the look in Brodie's eyes, knowing his boss wouldn't put up with excuses any longer. The time had come to either be honest or quit his job and leave Conviction.

Strolling along the boardwalk with Geneen on his arm, he couldn't imagine leaving the town, a job he loved, or the woman who mattered to him. Similar to Sam's feelings for Jinny, he and Geneen had been drawn to each other from the first moment they'd met. He'd attended as many MacLaren Sunday suppers as he could, always sitting next to her at the table, making small talk afterward before the men congregated in the den for whiskey.

Over the last few months, he'd been forced to deal with another, more urgent problem. As much as he regretted not seeing Geneen, he'd been unable to attend many Sunday suppers.

"We've missed you on Sundays, Nate." Geneen kept her gaze focused ahead, her voice soft with no trace of censure.

Glancing at her, he couldn't help the pang of regret when he noticed the pretty day dress she'd worn to town. Like Heather and Emily, she often preferred men's trousers and shirts while working on the ranch. They'd been able to ride once when supper ended early on a beautiful summer afternoon. She'd noticed his surprise at her expertise in handling a horse, setting him straight right away by besting him in a race across an expansive meadow. He guessed she might be able to shoot better than him, too, but wasn't about to test his theory.

"My apologies. I've had...business that's kept me in town."

Looking up at him, her brows furrowed. "On a Sunday?"

Clearing his throat, he nodded, his jaw tightening. "I'm afraid so." He wouldn't say more. The reason for his absence was a burden for him, and he had no intention of sharing it with anyone else. Which brought him back to the dilemma of what to tell Brodie. A decision had to be made before the women left town, yet he had no idea what to do. Perhaps turning in his badge and riding out of town was the best for everyone— especially Geneen.

Nate gently removed her arm from his as they stepped to the door of Maloney's. "I'll stay outside while you ladies do your shopping."

"It's a shame you must stay with us. It must be such a bother." Sarah shifted Grant in her arms, looking at Nate.

"I assure you, it isn't a bother. Until we're certain the ex-Confederate raiders are well away from Conviction, you'll have to suffer with one of us or your family escorting you. It simply isn't safe."

Geneen leaned toward him, keeping her voice low as Sarah and Maggie entered the general store. "There's no suffering involved when I'm with you, Nate." She could feel her face heat at the shameless statement, forgetting her embarrassment when he began to laugh.

"Ah, Miss Geneen, you are the most delightful woman I've ever met." He reached up, stroking the back of his hand down her cheek. When she closed her eyes, her tongue darting out to moisten her lips, he couldn't control his body's response. Dropping his hand, he stepped away. "No matter what happens, don't ever change."

Before she could respond, the door opened, Maggie poking her head out, her eyes gleaming in excitement. "You must come inside and see all the new items."

"I'll be right there." Geneen let out a breath. "I suppose I should join them. You'll stay while we shop?"

"As long as you want." Making a slight bow, he moved to the edge of the boardwalk, feigning interest in the activity up and down the busy street. Touching her had been a mistake. They'd made contact numerous times in the past, Geneen even kissing his cheek on more than one occasion. He'd sworn she'd be his wife someday, but that was before the uncertainty he now faced—a setback he had no defense against. Only a slow decline to his inevitable fate.

"How much longer, Papa?" Robbie's voice shook as the coach jerked along the rutted road.

Looking out the open window, Sam felt a sense of familiarity as he recognized the hills they passed. "The driver says we'll be there by late today."

He glanced at the Jaegers sitting across from them, both watching as Robbie got on his knees to gaze at the passing landscape. "Look, Papa. More cows." Enthusiasm overtook him as he pointed out the window.

Sam leaned forward to see the small herd. "Those are called cattle. Cows are used for milk."

Turning, Robbie's brows drew together. "What are the cattle for?"

"Meat." Sam chuckled when his son's eyes widened.

"We *eat* them?" A flash of horror crossed his face as he began to understand his father's meaning.

"Cattle are where we get steaks and roasts."

Looking back out the window, Robbie pursed his lips. "Do we get ham from them, too?"

Mr. Jaeger grinned. "Ham comes from pigs, young man...and so does bacon."

Robbie's face screwed up, as if he couldn't quite imagine his morning bacon coming from a pig. Sitting back down next to Sam, he pulled on his father's jacket. "Do we get bacon from pigs?"

Sam's eyes glinted with amusement. "Yes, son. We do."

"Will we have cattle and pigs, Papa?"

"Someday perhaps. For now, will you settle for a horse?"

Clapping his hands together, Robbie's face lit up. "Yes, a horse."

Mrs. Jaeger leaned forward, patting Robbie on the knee. "I think you'll make a fine rider, Robbie."

"Will you have a horse, too?"

She smiled at that, then settled back against her seat. "Well now, I don't know. Mr. Jaeger and I used to ride quite a bit. We sold the horses when we decided to come west. Maybe someday we'll get new ones."

Not long into the journey, Sam had been surprised to learn the Jaegers were moving to Conviction at the encouragement of an old friend—August Fielder. They'd be living with him until they found a place of their own. When Sam had told them Fielder had been the one to find a home for his family, a lively discussion had ensued, the couple recounting stories of the three of them before August got the urge to explore the rest of the country.

Mr. Jaeger crossed his arms, taking a quick glance outside, then looked at Sam. "Have you had word from August since leaving Baltimore?"

"Just one. He left a brief message at the hotel in San Francisco saying he'd found a house for us. We don't have much, so moving in should take very little time." His mother's china and a few other personal items should've arrived by the overland route. She'd been hesitant to put it all on the steamer, saying she didn't trust them to get her precious belongings safely to California. His chest squeezed at the memory. It turned out she'd been right.

"As soon as you're settled, you'll have to come over for supper."

Mr. Jaeger shot a look at his wife. "Mama, August may not want us inviting people over to his house."

"Nonsense. He's always enjoyed my cooking, and I don't intend to sit around and do nothing while you men are off having fun. Besides, his letter said we should treat his house as our own."

Sam's lips turned up at the corners, picturing the August Fielder he knew having fun. He didn't believe he'd ever heard the older man tell a joke, and never knew him to imbibe in more than two drinks.

"We'd be honored to join you for supper when it's convenient, Mrs. Jaeger."

Sam glanced at his father, who snored softly next to him. He didn't know how the elder Covington could sleep during such a rough trip, but he'd been dozing for much of the time since leaving San Francisco.

"And your young lady. You must also bring her along."

Clearing his throat, Sam began to regret sharing the fact he had feelings for a woman in Conviction. Somehow, he'd even confessed his hope she wouldn't mind him having a son. Thankfully, he hadn't mentioned her name or the association between Fielder and the MacLarens.

"We'll see, Mrs. Jaeger. I've been gone a while and have a lot of work ahead of me." Sam assumed Brodie had received his letter. Once his father and son were settled, he looked forward to returning to his job as a deputy, knowing the sheriff would welcome him back.

"A family?" Colin choked on his beer, spewing part of it onto the table he occupied with Quinn and Brodie at Buckie's Castle. There were no empty chairs at the saloon tonight. He and Quinn had ridden in to speak with August Fielder about the decision to purchase Widow Evanston's ranch, then stopped by the jail, convincing Brodie he needed a drink before heading home to Maggie.

"Aye. That's what the letter said. Fielder has found them a house with three bedrooms." Brodie brought the beer to his lips and drank.

Quinn narrowed his gaze, staring into what remained of his drink. "I'll be having strong words with the lad if he's been trifling with Jinny."

"You? She's *my* sister, and he wants to return as a deputy. If he lied to us, I'll be taking the lad on myself, deputy or not." Brodie drained the last of his beer, slamming the glass down on the table before signaling the bartender for another.

"You'll not be doing it alone."

At the sound of the stage approaching, Colin's chair scraped across the scarred wood floor as he pushed back from the table, moving to the front window. Pulling out his pocket watch, he glanced outside as the stage came to a stop a few doors away. "It's running late today."

"When did you say Sam is supposed to be coming back?" Quinn also stood, walking to the window to peer out.

"Any day now."

Joining them, Brodie's gaze hardened as a small boy jumped to the ground, followed by an older couple. A moment later, a tall, slender man with gray hair and alert eyes stepped down, taking a look around before glancing up as the last passenger left the stage.

"Sam." Colin's one word had them heading outside.

Brodie's gaze focused on the small boy, who appeared to be a miniature version of Sam. Jumping up and down, he pointed to a group of cowboys riding up the street, their guns in clear view.

"Papa, look."

Sam followed the path of the riders until he caught sight of three men moving his way. A smile broke across his face, recognizing the MacLaren men. Holding out his hand to Brodie, his smile faltered when his ex-boss, and friend, glared at him.

"I know I'm a little late arriving—"

"You have a family?" Quinn interrupted before Brodie had a chance to respond. "Do you not think you should've mentioned them to us, and to Jinny?"

Dropping his hand, Sam took a step back, clasping Robbie's shoulder. "Now isn't the time."

"Now's a fine time, lad." Brodie kept his voice level as he looked at the wide-eyed boy. "Is this your wee lad?"

Clearing his throat, Sam leveled stern eyes on him. "Yes. This is my son, Robbie Covington, and my father, Thomas." Although the elder Covington had no idea what to make of the conversation, he held out his hand.

"And Mrs. Covington?" Colin asked, shaking Thomas's hand.

The older man's face clouded in pain. "My wife died when our steamship sank outside Greytown."

"I'm sorry to hear that, sir." Colin turned back to Sam. "And the *other* Mrs. Covington?"

Seeing anger replace confusion on Sam's face, Brodie stepped forward. "Sam's right. We've no business talking about this on the street." Glancing around, he noticed the older couple standing to the side, concern on their faces. Walking toward them, he held out his hand. "I'm Brodie MacLaren, sheriff of Conviction. These are my cousins, Colin and Quinn."

Shaking the outstretched hand, Mr. Jaeger narrowed his gaze. "We've heard many fine things about you and your family from Sam. We hope he was right in his assessment."

Brodie felt his face heat at the rebuke, knowing he'd crossed a line in front of strangers. "I apologize for our behavior." He turned to glance at Sam. "We've many questions, but here isn't the place to ask them." Shifting, he focused his attention on the older couple. "May I direct you somewhere?"

"My wife and I are visiting August Fielder. We'd be grateful for your help in finding his home."

Brodie winced at the familiar name, feeling another wave of embarrassment at how he and the others had behaved. Counting three trunks on the boardwalk, he turned to Quinn. "Would you ride to Stein's and ask for the use of his wagon?"

Tipping his hat, his own face a light shed of red, Quinn nodded. "Aye. I'll be right back."

Holding Robbie in his arms, Sam walked up to the Jaegers, ignoring Brodie and Colin. "Would you care to join us for supper at the Gold Rush?"

Mrs. Jaeger raised a hand, stroking Robbie's hair. "We appreciate the invitation, but it's been a long journey and we're quite tired. Plus, I think it's time you were alone with your family and friends."

"Another time then." Sam's jaw hardened, his face a mask as he did his best to control the anger coursing through him.

"Come by August's house once you've settled into your new home. I was quite serious about having you over for supper."

"We'll be sure to do that, Mrs. Jaeger. Now, I believe it's time to feed my father and son, then find them rooms. It was a pleasure traveling with you."

"Same here, young man. You be sure to let us know if you need anything, such as someone to watch Robbie."

"I just may do that." Sam appreciated the offer, especially after being on the receiving end of the MacLarens' rage. He had an inkling what triggered their displeasure, but wasn't yet ready to set aside his irritation at their method of confronting him. Then a flash of concern hit him, wondering if Brodie had said something to Jinny about him returning to Conviction with his family. For the first time, Sam began to understand how his poorly worded letter may have caused the men to approach him with such hostility.

Brodie walked up. "Why don't you take them to the Gold Dust? Colin and I will wait here for Quinn, then make certain they get to Fielder's."

"Thanks, Brodie. Once they're settled, I'll meet you at the jail. It seems we have much to discuss."

"Aye. It seems we do."

Several hours later, the three MacLarens and Sam sat around Brodie's desk at the jail, an untouched bottle of whiskey and four glasses before them. His normally impeccable attire—brown brocade vest, white shirt, black jacket, and black string tie—showed the effects of days on a stage.

"I've mishandled this from the start." Sam pushed a hand through his hair, then rubbed his eyes with the palms of his hands.

"Aye, the letter could've been more clear. The rest though..." Brodie leaned forward, resting his arms on the desk.

"What more could you have done, Sam?" Quinn picked up the bottle, pouring them each a shot and passing the glasses around. "You knew nothing of your son until you received the telegram asking you to return to Baltimore."

"I should've mentioned the reason for leaving." Sam let out a slow breath, closing his eyes. He was dead tired, but needed to take care of any misunderstandings tonight. "If I'd known for certain Robbie was my son...but I didn't. I chose to keep my reasons confidential until I knew without doubt Robbie belonged to me." Standing, he paced to the window, looking out onto an almost empty, dark street. "Vera never contacted me. What kind of woman keeps that information from the father?"

"A scared one." Colin held the glass in his hand, then took a sip, his voice contemplative. "Maybe she didn't know how to reach you. Or she died before she had a chance to deliver a message."

Turning, Sam leaned back against the window, his eyes glassy. "After Robbie was born, she told her parents she'd quit passing on information to the South. Like much of what she said, it was a lie. Her body was found one day at dawn, a few miles from their home, a bullet in her chest. A Union captain delivered the news—a man she'd known in school. Robbie was less than a year old." Pushing away, he stalked to the desk, picked up a glass, and downed the contents in one swallow. "I'd already moved away, taking on a different assignment with General McClellan. Time passed, and my final assignment brought me out here. The Fosters found me by contacting Allan Pinkerton. They'd still be searching if he hadn't given them my whereabouts."

"You did what was right, Sam. No one can fault you for that." Brodie rolled the shot glass in his hand, then set it down, his expression serious. "Jinny, though...the lass is a mystery. She's done nothing to hide her feelings for you, so don't be asking to court her unless you intend to marry my sister."

Sam opened his mouth to speak, then closed it when Quinn spoke. "What of the Arrington lad?"

Sam's brows furrowed. "Arrington lad? Who's he?"

An uneasy look passed between the MacLarens before Brodie spoke. "Deke Arrington is Rube Ferguson's nephew. He works at the saddlery."

Sam waited for Brodie to continue, cocking his head when he offered nothing more. "And?"

Brodie sighed. "And the lad spends a great deal of time with Jinny. They ride every Saturday."

"On the saddle Deke made for her," Quinn added.

Sam didn't attempt to stifle his cursing. Shredding both hands through his hair, he sat down, his shoulders slumping. "How long?"

Quinn glanced at Colin and Brodie. "Only a few weeks. It's clear they like each other well enough, but it's not the same as when you were here."

His defeated gaze sought out Brodie. "Has he asked to court her?"

"Nae. At least not officially, although he did ask Da if he could call on her."

Another oath slipped through Sam's lips. "It's the same thing, Brodie."

"If you'd be asking my thoughts, I think they're just friends." Brodie gripped his glass, finishing the contents.

Sam snorted. "Most in town would've said the same about Jinny and me."

Colin gave him a sympathetic smile, filling Sam's glass a second time. "Aye, but the lass doesn't look at Deke the way she used to look at you."

"*Used to*, Colin. It's been months since we've seen each other. I should've sent a telegram, told her how I felt. If I'd only known for certain I'd be returning...but I didn't."

Brodie sat up, stretching his hands above his head. "Perhaps we're worried for nothing. Why don't you ask Jinny? You could ride to the ranch tomorrow and speak with her."

Quinn winced. "Uh, tomorrow is Saturday, Brodie."

"So?"

"Saturday is when Deke and Jinny ride, then he stays for supper."

Quinn's words sliced through Sam. The more they spoke, the more it became apparent Deke was indeed courting Jinny. He'd lost her because he couldn't tell her the truth.

Sam loved Jinny, wanted her for his wife, and knew she felt the same. At least she had before he left, telling her he didn't know when, or if, he'd be returning. He wanted to slam his fist into a wall, shout at his own stupidity. Instead, he downed another glass of whiskey, then a third one.

Brodie felt terrible for the man he considered a good friend. "No sense drinking yourself blind, lad. Come to supper on Sunday. I'll let Jinny know so she'll be prepared to see you. It's the only way to learn the truth."

Sam swallowed the hard knot in his throat. "Don't tell her about Robbie. I need to do that myself."

"I'll not say a word, except that you've returned and are coming to supper."

Seeing the surprise on the others' faces, Sam drank one more shot of whiskey, then set the glass down before standing and walking to the door. "Sunday it is. The day I learn my fate."

Chapter Fifteen

Outskirts of Circle M Ranch

"I'm not staying behind, Captain." Sergeant Parry pushed to a sitting position, then fell back when his injured leg couldn't support his attempt to stand.

Eplett studied him with his arms crossed, shaking his head. "I've already made my decision. You're not able to stand or ride, but you can guard our camp while we're gone. I'm leaving one man here with you."

Disgust filled Parry's voice. "I don't need anyone else with me. Give me a gun and lots of ammunition and I'll keep any intruders away."

Eplett figured the sergeant would feel this way. There wasn't much anyone would want in their meager camp, except the stash of cash from the bank robberies. Only he and Parry knew the money's location, and he trusted the man with his life. Still, he hesitated leaving him alone.

"Don't think so hard on this, Captain. You need all the men with you today, the same as you'll need all of us when the sheriff agrees to the exchange. Go on and grab the girl. I'll be fine here by myself." Parry adjusted his position, leaning back against a tree.

"All right, but be careful." Eplett placed a rifle across Parry's lap, setting extra ammunition beside him. "This shouldn't take long. How much trouble can one girl and her companion be?" He chuckled, looking forward to the look on Miss MacLaren's face when she recognized him and his men. Opening a pouch, he tossed Parry some hardtack and jerky. "You've got plenty of water."

"By the time we're ready to ride out of here, I'll be strong enough to get on my horse." Parry grumbled a few more words, then looked up at Eplett. "You're certain you want to do it this way, Captain? Seems easier to ride into town and take Card from the jail."

Eplett battled his frustration. They'd had this discussion several times and he was through talking about it. "I'm certain."

Without another word, he walked toward his horse and mounted, signaling the men to follow him. Within a few hours, they'd have their hostage and exchange her for Card. If something happened between those two events, so be it. He wouldn't second-guess himself or the motivation behind it. In the end, no one would get hurt and they'd be on their way south, toward the Mexican border.

"Are you ready?" Jinny glanced over her shoulder at Deke, who finished checking his saddle cinches before mounting.

"I am. Are we still riding to the old Estrada hacienda?" They moved at a slow walk, leaving behind the barns, corrals, and houses forming the MacLaren compound.

"If you have the time. It will take us most of the day." Jinny leaned back, patting her saddlebags. "Ma packed us enough food for a week."

Deke chuckled at the way Lorna MacLaren fussed over them. He didn't know how much Jinny had told her mother about them, but it seemed she had the impression they were courting, moving toward a serious relationship rather than just being friends. At one point, he'd hoped for more. It had taken time with Jinny to realize he didn't feel the spark of passion he'd anticipated. He wanted a woman who could be his friend, as well as set his blood on fire. Jinny fit well into the first, and he was content with that.

"Who takes care of the land around the hacienda?"

"Quinn, Caleb, Bram, and Blaine take turns staying there and overseeing the men. Before

Quinn married Emma, he and Caleb stayed there most often. Caleb makes most decisions regarding the men who work the northern property. Pa says that may change now that the family and Mr. Fielder have decided to buy the Evanston ranch."

"I heard your father talking to Quinn about it this morning while you were getting ready. He mentioned Caleb."

Jinny reined her horse to an abrupt stop. "Did he say Caleb would be made foreman of the Evanston property?"

Taking off his hat, Deke scratched his head, then swiped an arm across his forehead. "No. He said he wanted Caleb involved. Why? I didn't think the MacLarens made anyone a foreman."

Jinny thought of Heather and how easily she became upset at any possible slight. If her da and Uncle Ian put Caleb in charge, Jinny felt certain Heather would return to the main ranch rather than take orders from him.

"They didn't used to, but times are changing. The four elder MacLarens ran the ranch with Angus, who was the oldest, having final say. When he and Uncle Gillis were murdered, Da and Uncle Ian took over. As the ranch expands, they're not able to manage all the men themselves, so they identify who is in charge each day."

Deke settled the hat back on his head, nudging his horse as Jinny picked up the pace. "Seems it could be confusing, changing who's in charge each day in each section of the ranch."

Nodding, Jinny glanced toward him. "It is. With the family owning half the Estrada spread and buying the Evanston ranch, it will get worse. Colin, Quinn, and the others have talked about it with Da and Uncle Ian. They'd much prefer having one foreman named for the Estrada land, another for the main ranchland, and one for the Evanston ranch. So far, they've made no final decisions."

She worried her lower lip. Emma, Sarah, and Jinny had talked a couple times about who they thought would make the best foremen. If there were three, Colin, Quinn, and Blaine seemed to make the most sense. Fletcher and Sean were needed at the main ranch for the horse breeding. Neither Bram nor Camden had an interest in being a foreman, at least not yet, and the others still had much to learn. Although not a MacLaren, Caleb would make a strong foreman. When he spoke, everyone listened. She knew he'd be put in a position of authority someday.

Then there were the MacLaren women. Heather and Emma were the most accomplished and understood how to run a ranch. After her marriage to Quinn, Emma had started working with Fletcher, Bram, and Sean.

Heather could be a problem. She saw herself as a foreman, believed her skills were as good as any man's, and would fight to make her wishes known. Somehow, Jinny didn't see her getting her wish anytime soon.

That left Geneen and Coral. They were good ranch hands, but had no interest in being in charge.

Of course, if Brodie quit his job as sheriff, it would change everything. He, Colin, and Quinn would be the three chosen as foremen. She snorted, knowing he'd never give up the job he'd dreamed of his entire life.

"What's so funny?"

Shaking her head, Jinny smiled. "Nothing. Sometimes it's a bit of a challenge being part of a large family. Race you to the ridge." Without further warning, she kicked Dancer into a run, leaving Deke behind.

"There they are, Captain. Looks like they're in a race." The private handed over the field glasses.

Eplett watched Jinny laugh as her horse pulled farther ahead of her companion. He wondered if she knew the man held back on the reins just a little, allowing her to cross an imaginary finish line ahead of him. Probably not. Women like her thought they were owed everything, even victory in a meaningless race.

"Excellent. We'll follow, staying far enough behind to keep them close without spotting us. They'll stop at some point. That's when we'll close in." Handing the glasses back, Eplett turned to the others. "Let's go."

They didn't have long to wait for the two to find a spot under some trees and dismount. Eplett slid his own field glasses from their pouch in his saddlebag, holding them so he had a clear view of their actions. Untying a blanket, the man spread it out as the woman unwrapped their food. Eplett smirked at the perfect timing.

Stowing the glasses, he turned to his men. "It's time to move into position."

The group of men split off. Half skirted behind the couple, and the others moved forward. Their experience in battle, as well as their lawless journey across the country, trained them to move silently, even when mounted on temperamental horses. It took little time to surround the man and woman who were so engrossed in their own conversation that they didn't notice the group of men ride up until it was too late.

Eplett leaned forward, resting his arms on the saddle horn. "So, we meet again."

Jinny gasped, her stomach clenching when she recognized the man who'd terrorized her at Maloney's.

Jumping to his feet, Deke reached for the six-gun strapped around his hips.

"I wouldn't if I were you." Eplett nodded behind them, causing Deke to spin around toward the second group of men, all with guns aimed at him. Letting his arms hang loose at his sides, he took a step toward Eplett.

"Who are you and what do you want?"

"I'd think it obvious." Eplett swung his leg over the saddle to dismount. "We want the woman. She and I have unfinished business...don't we." It was less a question than a statement. His feral gaze settled on Jinny, his mouth twisting into a confident sneer. "She'll be leaving with us."

Deke rushed forward, stopping when a series of bullets hit the ground at his feet. Before he could move again, two men came up behind him, removed his gun from its holster, then bound his wrists and stuffed a handkerchief into his mouth.

"We've no reason to harm you. It's the girl we want."

Her throat thick with fear, Jinny steeled her courage, crossing her arms. "I'll not go anywhere with hoodlums such as yourselves. You'll be releasing Deke now, or my family will come for you. And trust me, you'll not be liking the consequences."

A burst of laughter surrounded her, doing nothing to dampen her anger.

"I don't believe you're in a position to dictate what my men and I will do, Miss MacLaren. And *Deke* will not be harmed if you come with us without a struggle. However, if you put up a fight, it will be my distinct pleasure to put a bullet in him and leave him for the varmints to discover."

Her eyes widened in shock. "You wouldn't."

Crossing his arms, his voice hardened. "I would. He means nothing to me. You, however, are worth a great deal."

She glanced at Deke. To her surprise, no fear showed in his eyes, only anger and disgust at the men, or the situation, or perhaps both. His helpless struggle to loosen the ties reminded her of the danger.

"If I leave with you, do you swear Deke will be safe?" She ignored Deke's growl as he shook his head.

Eplett took a step closer. "I swear he won't die from one of our bullets."

Swallowing the fear gnawing in her gut, Jinny nodded. "Fine. I'll go, but know this. If anything happens to either of us, my family won't rest until they track you down and watch every last one of you hang."

Yanking her toward him, he tied her hands together. "It's doubtful, but I do admire your spirit and belief that your family can save you. Few people would put that much trust in someone else." She yelped when Eplett yanked the rope tighter. "Sorry, but I don't want you to think you'll be able to get away."

Turning her around, he shoved her toward his horse, signaling to one of his men. "Untether their horses and run them off."

Jinny stopped, shifting to face him. "No. You promised he'd be safe. He'll have no way to get back if you run off the horses."

"I promised we wouldn't *shoot* him, Miss MacLaren, not that he'd be safe." Before she could reply, he mounted, then waited while another of his men lifted her onto the horse. "I know you're an excellent rider, so I'll expect you to still be sitting behind me when we reach our destination."

Jinny glanced back at Deke, mouthing an apology, then looked forward again. "And what is our destination?"

"Someplace your family will never find you."

"What do you mean they're not back?" Quinn paced away from the front porch, staring north into the darkening sky. "Did they take the usual trail?" Hands fisted on his hips, he turned to glare at Emma.

"They planned to ride to the old Estrada hacienda, then come back. Maybe they decided to stay the night." Emma covered her mouth as soon as the words were out. Too late, she saw the flaring of her husband's nostrils at the insinuation. She walked down the steps to join him. "Not that they would ever, well...you know."

He moved toward her. "Not what? Behave like you and I did?" Removing his hat, he shoved a hand through his hair. "This isn't at all like Jinny. We have to start searching for them. I'll let Colin and Blaine know." His features stilled. "Does Uncle Ewan know she's not come home?"

"You're the first."

"I'd best be the one to tell him. You head up to Colin and..." His voice trailed off at the sound of horses. Spinning around, his chest tightened at the sight of Dancer and Deke's horse running into the compound and toward the barn.

"My God, Quinn. It's their horses." Emma took off at a run, Quinn right behind her, following the horses into the barn. "Something terrible must have happened. I'll take care of them while you get Uncle Ewan and the others."

He turned to leave, then stopped, sending an anxious look at Emma. "Find Bram. Tell him to ride into town and get Brodie."

"Where are you taking me?" Jinny gripped the horse with her legs, doing her best to grasp the cantle, swaying as they moved over the rocky terrain. No matter how experienced the rider, having your hands tied together and riding behind someone, made it difficult to stay on top. The fact her heart raced from worry didn't help.

Eplett ignored her question, the same as he had the others she'd shouted at him. He had to admire her courage, even as she tested his patience. With weapons pointed at her friend, she held her head high, chin jutting out. Jinny MacLaren wasn't a woman who'd grovel.

The raiders needed to get back to camp, make certain his friend and fellow soldier hadn't been surprised by any unknown visitors. For several nights, they'd heard the unmistakable roar of a mountain lion. The animal hadn't been spotted. Still, a wounded man was powerful bait for a large and dangerous cat.

They wound through the low hills, across two streams, and through thick brush before coming upon their camp. Eplett knew something had happened. The air had changed, the feel of death surrounding the area.

Staring at the spot where he'd left the sergeant, Eplett reined his horse to a stop, swinging his leg over the horse's neck to dismount. He glanced over his shoulder at one of the men.

"Get her down while I find Parry."

His gut twisted as he followed the unmistakable tracks of someone dragging themselves to a bush a few yards away. Once there, his stomach lurched. Parry's body lay in a heap, blood soaking the ground around him, his dead eyes wide with fear. Turning and bending at the waist, Eplett retched, his face and neck breaking out into a cold sweat.

"Captain..." The words died as the private stared at the sight before him, then turned to mimic Eplett's reaction. Straightening, he swiped an arm across his mouth. "My God. It must've been the cat we've been hearing."

Gulping down deep breaths, Eplett turned to face the carnage. "Parry didn't stand a chance." Regret twisted its way through him, making him wish he'd allowed the sergeant to ride along to get the MacLaren woman.

Scrubbing a hand down his face, he let out a bone-chilling cry, cursing the cat, their circumstances, and the people of Conviction.

"Get some men and dig a grave. We'll bury the sergeant, then send word to the sheriff about our hostage."

"Yes, sir." Reeling from what he'd seen, the man's shaky feet propelled him to the others, who hadn't dared approach when they'd heard their captain's anguished cry.

Eplett watched as they dragged Parry's lifeless form away, a cold knot burning its way from his throat to his gut. He'd lost a close friend, an ally, and a darn fine soldier. None of the other men compared to him, which meant Eplett was as alone as he'd ever been.

His need for the young woman no longer held any appeal. Of all the remaining men, Private Terrence Card had been with him the longest. A sudden need to make the exchange and ride hard and fast from Conviction claimed him. He wanted to leave this place and all the bad memories behind.

Chapter Sixteen

Jinny sagged against a boulder, her back, arms, and legs aching. They hadn't untied her hands or allowed her to take a much needed relief in the bushes. Instead, their attention had been focused on something behind a group of thick bushes.

Shifting to get more comfortable, her gaze snapped up as the men dragged a blanket-covered body across camp, one carrying a shovel. Pulling him past a low shrub, the blanket snagged, revealing the ravaged body. A scream tore from her throat as her stomach convulsed.

"Shut your mouth." Eplett loomed over her, his features twisted.

"But..." Jinny couldn't finish, her stomach roiling again.

"Look the other way if it's too much for you," he hissed, bending to check the rope around her hands, tugging one end until she whimpered in pain.

"His throat. It was...it was—"

"Gone. He was attacked by a mountain lion while we went after you." Leaning closer, his hot, foul-smelling breath nauseated her. "All you need to do is stay quiet and wait until the sheriff gets word about my demands."

"My brother?"

Eplett's eyes widened before narrowing. "Your brother is the sheriff?"

"Aye, if you're speaking of Brodie MacLaren."

He'd known the sheriff was one of the many MacLarens. Eplett had no idea the woman he'd captured was his sister. A feral smile crossed his face as he realized the prize sitting at his feet. MacLaren would do whatever it took to get his sister back, including releasing Terrence Card.

"Is your brother a reasonable man, Miss MacLaren?"

A thin, blonde brow lifted as she cocked her head to the side. "Aye. He can be. My brother can also be fiercely stubborn when it comes to family."

Rearing his head back, he laughed, the deranged sound making Jinny cringe. "I'm counting on him being stubborn about his family. The decision he makes will determine whether you live and are returned to your young man, or if you'll face the same fate as the man being buried."

Gasping at the threat, Jinny stared past Eplett to where the men dug a shallow grave, fighting the fear slicing through her. His meaning left no doubt as to her fate should Brodie not do as the madman asked. They'd abandon her, letting her destiny rest with the mountain lion who'd already killed one of the men.

Jinny dragged her gaze to where Eplett had been standing a moment before, seeing him move quickly across the camp to speak with one of his men. Less than a minute later, the man saluted, mounting his horse and reining it south toward Conviction. She didn't have to be told where the messenger rode.

Sucking in a shaky breath, she thought of Deke, praying he'd been able to loosen his ties and find one of their horses. Bram had trained Dancer well. Her horse could be attacked by a snake, but her flight of fear would take her no more than a couple hundred yards away. Worst case, her mare would run home, alerting the family something was wrong.

For so many months, her thoughts had centered on Sam, wishing he'd return or at least send word of his intentions. Being taken captive, held against her will, forced Jinny to think of the present and the reality of her life. Sam had no intention of returning. No matter how much he might have cared, he left her behind without a backward glance.

The thought of never seeing him again left a cold ache in her chest—a dull throb she'd lived with day and night since he'd walked away.

Even if he returned to Conviction, resumed his role as a deputy, it would be with Jinny knowing he'd never taken the time to pen even one letter or a brief telegram. She refused to see him as a man without character. Instead, she forced herself to accept whatever duty called Sam home meant more to him than a future with her. Returning to Conviction wouldn't change the fact he'd forgotten all about her within moments of riding out of town.

Resting her head against the tree trunk, she closed her eyes, pushing away her current predicament to dream of what her life might be like if the right man came along. She wanted someone who loved and valued her above all others. A man who appreciated the open land and accepted her large, unruly family. Someone who had the same sense of dedication to the ranch while craving a home and children. A man who could laugh at himself, respect others, and worked hard.

For an instant, Sam's face crossed her mind before being replaced by an image of Deke. Her heart didn't race the way it did when she thought of Sam. Thinking of her brief time around Deke, she experienced a sense of comfort, similar to the feeling she got each time she walked into her bedroom. It was a familiar space with no surprises, comfortable, like a well-worn dress.

She yawned, her thoughts drifting to Brodie and Maggie, Quinn and Emma, Colin and Sarah. Jinny knew each couple possessed a passion so strong a stranger could sense it. Love and devotion flowed between them, creating a bond strong enough to withstand all obstacles. Jinny wanted what they had, and wondered, if given enough time, she might find it with Deke.

"Get up."

The gruff voice jolted her, reminding Jinny of the danger and uncertain outcome she faced. Bracing her back against the tree, she pushed up with her legs. She felt herself sway, about to topple to the side, when a rough hand gripped her arm, jerking her forward.

"The captain says you're to, well...do what women have to do." He shoved her toward a group of bushes.

She thought of a haughty response. Instead, she decided to focus her energy on formulating a plan of escape rather than angering the man guarding her.

Stopping, she turned to face him. "You'll have to untie my hands."

"The captain said nothing about removing the rope."

"I'll not be doing my business with my hands tied. Untie them or take me back." Jinny saw the man rub his chin, then look behind him before leaning down to untie her hands.

"You better not try anything. Captain Eplett don't want you hurt before he hears from the sheriff."

The knowledge Eplett had sent word to Brodie should've given her a sense of relief. Instead, a shot of fear claimed her, reminding Jinny that Eplett and his men couldn't be trusted.

Stepping behind the bushes, she scanned the area, trying to see any landmarks identifying where they held her. She knew they were still on Circle M land. They would've had to ride a great deal farther west to get off MacLaren property. Then something familiar caught her attention. A specific rock formation she hadn't noticed when they rode in. *The Boulders.* She and a few of the MacLaren women had named the place during one of their rides. If only she had a way to get them a message, they'd know exactly where to find her.

"Hurry up."

"Didn't your mother teach you it isn't polite to rush a lady?" She hurried with her business, wanting more time to check the area before deciding what to do next.

"I didn't have a mother and don't recall knowing any ladies. Just finish up and get back over here."

Odd, but she didn't feel a shred of remorse for the man growing up without a mother. Any other time, the story would've cut to her heart, begging her to reach out and say something soothing. Right now, all she wanted was to find a path to freedom. If she could just get a horse...

The sound of bushes rustling had her fiddling with her dress, giving the impression she'd just finished. "I'm not ready yet."

"It don't matter. The captain wants you back where you were." The man pushed through the bushes, grabbed her arm, and pulled her back into the clearing. "Hold out your hands."

To her relief, he secured her hands in front of her. If she could get to a horse, it would be a simple matter to mount and ride away. Jinny had watched them ride, knowing she had a good chance of getting away if she had a couple minute head start.

"Sit back down where you were." He turned to leave.

"What about water, or some food?"

"You don't ask for much, do you...*lady*?" The taunt didn't bother Jinny.

Her gaze focused on his gun, reminding her she needed a weapon. Glancing at the horses, she saw three rifles still in scabbards, guessing the ammunition would be in the saddlebags. If not, they'd be fools not to keep them loaded, ready for any threat.

Even if Eplett posted a guard tonight, she reasoned the rest would fall asleep at some point. They were only human. Their bodies required sleep. It would be the perfect time to grab a horse and get away. She refused to think of the consequences if they caught her. All her focus had to be on escape.

Rolling to his side, Deke grimaced at the pounding in his head, trying to remember what happened. Sitting up, he lifted his hands, still bound together in front of him, and felt the sticky substance on his forehead. Someone had hit him with the butt of a rifle as they rode away, Jinny on the back of the leader's horse.

Shouting a curse, Deke forced himself to stand and look around. He remembered one of the men scattering their horses. His gaze lit on what was left of the food Lorna had prepared. The knife. She'd put a knife in one of the bundles. Rushing to the blanket, he knelt down, pushing aside one bundle after another before he found it.

After one false start, then another, he found a way to stabilize the knife, using it to cut through the binding. Ripping it from his wrists, he stood, lifted his fingers to his mouth, and blew. The whistle echoed through the air. Moving away from the trees, he whistled again, getting no response. Whistling once more, pounding hooves had him shifting, his gaze landing on a group of riders moving toward him.

"Thank you, God," he mumbled, watching as several MacLaren men reined their horses to a stop.

"Where's Jinny?" Quinn jumped down, taking a quick look around at the blanket and scattered wrappings his Aunt Lorna used to pack food.

"I don't know."

Colin joined them, his features stoic. "What do you mean you don't know?"

Looking past Colin, Deke recognized Blaine, Sean, and Camden. "The ex-Confederates who terrorized the women at Maloney's found us. They bound me and took Jinny."

Quinn grabbed his shoulders. "Which way did they ride?"

"West." Deke pointed toward a group of low hills as another group of riders approached. Brodie, Fletcher, Bram, and Caleb stopped beside the others. Brodie slid from his horse. Before he could ask, Colin nodded in the direction Deke had pointed.

"The ex-Confederate raiders grabbed her and rode off. They left Deke tied up, and by the looks of it, roughed him up a wee bit."

Quinn examined Deke's wound. "Aye. Looks like the butt of a gun landed on the lad's head."

"A rifle," Deke corrected, then looked around. Spotting his gun in the dirt several yards away, he brushed it off, then holstered it. "I see you brought my horse."

"And Jinny's," Quinn added.

Grabbing the reins, Deke swung up on his gelding, noting the rifle still in its scabbard. Glancing up, he saw the sun sitting above the western hills, indicating it would be dark within an hour.

"We have to get moving before we lose our light." Kicking the horse, Deke led the way, heading in the direction where he'd last seen Jinny.

Conviction

"I'm Nate Hollis, a deputy and friend of Sam's. Is he here?" Out of breath, his body trembling, Nate rushed past the older man, looking around.

"He took Robbie to the river, but should return soon. I'm his father, Thomas Covington. Can I help you?"

Nate sucked in a breath, his face flushed, and thrust out his hand, waiting until Thomas shook it. "It's a pleasure to meet you. I'm sorry to intrude, but a message came for Brodie, telling him he had to get to Circle M right away. Jinny is missing."

Thomas rubbed the back of his neck, trying to remember the significance of the name. "I'm sorry. I don't recall the name."

"Jinny is the sheriff's sister. She and Sam, well...they were close before he left town."

"Ah, that's right. My son has mentioned Miss MacLaren several times. I believe she's the reason he came back. You say she's missing?" Thomas moved into the parlor, nodding for Nate to follow him and sit down.

"I'd prefer to stand...if you don't mind." Shoving his right hand into his pocket, doing his best to hold what was left of his left arm at his side, he worked to control his shaking.

Thomas walked to a table, took a glass, and poured a measure of whiskey. "Take this, young man. It may help."

"Thank you." Accepting the glass, Nate downed the whiskey in one swallow, turning at the sound of a door opening.

"Grandfather, we're back." Robbie raced into the room, coming to a halt when he spotted the stranger.

225

"Nate Hollis. It's good to see you." Sam strolled in, clasping Nate's hand, his eyes narrowing as he studied his friend's face. "Are you all right?"

"He's come with bad news, son. Robbie, come with me while your father and Mr. Hollis talk."

When the door closed, Sam took a step toward Nate. "What happened?"

"Brodie told me where to find you. Quinn sent word he needed to get to the ranch right away."

Sam's stomach clenched as he thought of Jinny. "Was someone hurt?"

"Jinny is missing. Brodie thought you'd want to know."

Sam's hands fisted at his sides as he murmured an oath. Tossing his black hat aside, he shredded his fingers through his hair and paced away. "Did he have any other details?"

"Quinn sent Bram to town to fetch Brodie. He said Jinny's and Deke Arrington's horses came back to the barn alone. Bram also said something about the two riding to the original Estrada hacienda today, so that's the direction they were headed."

Sam knew the location of the Estrada ranch house. He and Jinny had ridden there a couple times before returning to the main house for

Sunday supper. Today, she rode with Deke Arrington, the man Brodie had mentioned. From what Sam understood, the man courting Jinny.

"I'll meet you outside." Grabbing his hat, he dashed out of the room to find his father and son. Sam didn't even consider Nate not riding with him. Slowing his pace, he turned to see him walk from the parlor toward the door, his face pale.

"Are you all right, Nate?"

He waved him off. "I'm fine."

Sam didn't have time to question him further. Finding Jinny, making certain she was unharmed, was all that mattered. Everything else could be dealt with once he knew she was back at Circle M.

Belford Ranch

Mrs. Belford stood on her porch, staring out at the evening sky. She needed to get busy if supper was to be ready by the time the men rode in from checking stock. Her two sons and the three cowboys she'd rescued from hanging were all she had for help. At almost fifteen and thirteen, her boys did the best they could to balance their work at the ranch and school, which she insisted they attend. And, so far, the young men who served their sentences working her ranch had more than met her expectations.

She'd taken a huge risk bringing them to the ranch after their drunken actions had caused the death of her husband. Allowing them to hang, knowing her husband's cancer left him with little time and in a great deal of pain, wasn't something the widow wanted on her conscience. With no intention of selling the family ranch, she needed men. The decision to take them on seemed to be working out for everyone.

A chorus of whoops and hollers caught her attention, a slight smile curving the corners of her mouth at the sight of five riders approaching the barn. At first, her sons resented having the three cowboys guilty of killing their father living on the ranch. It had taken time, and learning their father would've died anyway, to get them to work beside the new ranch hands. After several months, they behaved like five brothers.

"Ma!" Martin, her oldest, waved as he slid to the ground, then disappeared inside the barn. The youngest, Brandon, did the same, a broad smile covering his dirt-smudged face. The others, Theo, Walt, and Cy nodded, their expressions grim. Curious, she ignored the need to finish supper and made her way across the open space to the barn. After years working around different men, she'd learned to recognize when something wasn't quite right.

"Theo, I'd like to speak with you."

He glanced at the others, handing his reins to Walt. "Yes, ma'am."

"Did anything unusual happen today?"

Settling his hands on his hips, he looked at the ground. "Not sure it's anything to worry about."

"You let me decide that. Tell me what's bothering you."

Looking over his shoulder, he paced away, knowing she'd follow. He stopped when they reached the corral at the side of the barn.

"Some men are camping at the edge of Circle M where it butts up to your place. It may be nothing, but it seems strange. They didn't look like men who'd work for the MacLarens."

"What do you mean?"

Shaking his head, he blew out a breath. "We didn't stay to get a real good look, but they were shabby, not what I'd expect from Circle M ranch hands. I only know the sheriff and his cousins, Quinn and Colin, and that's from being in jail." Rubbing the back of his neck, he glanced up. "I'm probably wrong, but Cy and Walt felt the same. Could be they're friends of the MacLarens."

Crossing her arms, she studied Theo's face. He'd always been honest with her, even about the killing of her husband. She had no reason to doubt his instincts.

"How far away are they?"

"About an hour ride northeast of here. Their camp is near the junction where your land, Circle M, and the old Pearce ranch intersect."

"Well, it's too late to ride out there tonight. We'll plan to leave early in the morning and pay them a visit."

"Ma'am, I don't think you need to ride with us. Fact is, I'd rather you stay here, in case the men aren't working for Circle M."

Laying a hand on his arm, she squeezed. "I appreciate your concern, but I want to ride out with you. I've been cooped up around this place too long."

Theo had learned not to argue with her once she made up her mind. "Yes, ma'am."

"I'd appreciate it if you'd saddle my horse for me in the morning. We'll leave right after breakfast." She didn't miss his hesitant expression before he nodded.

"Yes, ma'am. What about Martin and Brandon?"

"I'll talk to them at supper and let them know I need them to stay close to the ranch tomorrow." She headed toward the house, Theo keeping pace beside her. "As I recall, they have some schoolwork to finish. They can ride out with you, Walt, and Cy once we return."

Mrs. Belford refused to voice her concern about her ranch hands going alone. With their past, and the fact many still considered them killers, it would be too easy to blame them if something went wrong. With her along, the chance of that happening decreased. Even with the many chores she had around the ranch, she wasn't willing to take the chance of having them ride out alone.

Chapter Seventeen

"It's too dark to follow their tracks. We'll have to wait until morning." Colin hated being the voice of reason when fear drove them forward, everyone's tempers running high. He'd pulled his horse next to Brodie to see the determined scowl on his cousin's face.

"Morning might be too late."

Quinn joined them. "Nae, Brodie. They don't plan to kill Jinny. Not before they get what they want."

"And what would that be?" Brodie couldn't keep the sarcasm from his voice.

Quinn glanced at Colin, who nodded. "Your prisoner."

Brodie's brows drew together. "Terrence Card? They'd risk their lives, and Jinny's, for him?"

"It's a guess, lad, but it makes sense." Colin slid to the ground, signaling the others to do the same. "They'll not do anything until they hear from you."

"You think they sent word to me at the jail?"

Colin nodded. "Aye. Since you're not there, they'll need to decide what to do next. Jinny will be safe for tonight."

"Shouldn't we ride on?" Deke walked up, his eyes blazing, his face twisted in misery. "The moon is bright. We need to keep looking."

Quinn shook his head. "Nae, lad. It's too dark to go farther. We'll start again at first light."

"You can choose to stay here and sit around, but I'm going on." Deke turned, halting when Quinn grabbed his arm.

"You'll not be going anywhere alone."

Deke wrenched his arm away. "But Jinny's out there with those men. There's no telling what they'll do to her."

Brodie stood a few feet away, his jaw taut, chest squeezing at the thought of his sister being abused. Sweet Jinny. A woman who didn't have an evil bone in her body and who everybody loved. It seemed Deke was one of those people.

The rest of the family crowded around, some siding with Deke, most understanding the need for caution. It would do no good if others were hurt by rushing on.

Fletcher stepped next to Deke. "The land we must cross is rocky, with huge boulders surrounded by thick shrubs and trees. It's the home of mountain lions and an occasional bear. Rattlesnakes are thick in the area. We've lost more than a few head of cattle to the terrain on this part of the ranch." He shook his head. "Colin and Quinn are right. We need to camp here tonight."

Pushing past Fletcher, Deke walked toward Brodie. "She's your sister. What do you say?"

Brodie ignored the bile burning in his throat, doing his best to think as a lawman and hunter rather than a worried brother. By now, Sam would have learned about Jinny. No doubt he and Nate were already searching. Brodie just wished he knew where they were.

Fletcher was right. The roughest terrains on Circle M were at opposite ends of the ranch. The west and east borders formed rugged boundaries, discouraging some from entering their vast holdings, providing excellent cover for those seeking shelter—or those who wanted to disappear. People unfamiliar with the land could get lost, risking injury to themselves and others.

"There's nothing more we can do tonight, lad. It's best to make camp."

Deke walked a few feet away, hands fisted at his sides. Leaving without the MacLarens would be foolish. He didn't know the land, and even if he found her, he'd be no match against half a dozen treacherous men.

Staring up at the darkening sky, he thought of Jinny, praying she'd be safe one more night. He blamed himself for her capture. Until today, he'd thought his feelings for her were clear. Now, he wasn't so sure.

"The sheriff and two of his deputies had left town by the time I got there, Captain. I gave your message to the deputy at the jail."

Eplett stifled his anger at having to wait to make the exchange. "Did the deputy say when he expected the sheriff back?"

"Nope, and I didn't ask. Delivered the message and rode out. I didn't want to take a chance of him locking me up, too."

One of the men listening stepped forward. "If all but one deputy is gone, maybe we should ride in and take Card. Why go through with the exchange when there's no one to protect him?"

Eplett nodded, then looked at the man who'd ridden into town. "Is the deputy you saw the only one left?"

"Funny, but when I gave him the message, he looked uneasy. Made it a point to let me know there were several other deputies who weren't at the jail. He could've been lying. I don't know if it's worth taking the chance and riding in to find them waiting for us."

Eplett wondered if MacLaren had left because he'd already heard about his sister being

235

taken. He pushed the idea aside, figuring there hadn't been enough time for them to suspect anything. Not unless...

He turned to one of the men. "Those horses you spooked. Where did they go?"

"North, Captain. Away from the Circle M ranch house."

"Good." Eplett believed it would take the horses hours to find their way home, then more time for the family to alert the sheriff.

"What do you want to do, Captain?"

"Wait. When the sheriff gets the message, he'll do everything possible to save his sister. Until then, we bide our time."

The man who'd ridden to town looked at Eplett. "Do you plan to return her once we get Card?"

Eplett crossed his arms, his eyes gleaming. "Well now, I don't know. Could be we'll use her to get away, then abandon her somewhere along the trail. I don't care what happens to her once we get Card back and get away."

No one spoke after Eplett turned his back and walked toward Jinny. Kneeling down, he lifted her chin with his hand. "Seems you may be with us a while." He noticed the tin plate still full of beans and hardtack. "You don't like our food?"

Jinny pinned him with an angry glare. "I don't like anything about you and your men,

Captain Eplett. You're nothing but vulgar thugs. Dunderheads without honor."

He barked out a laugh. "Such language from such a fine lady. What would your young man think of it?"

Her mind flashed to Sam, then realized he meant Deke. "If he's been hurt, you and your men will pay for it."

"Such fire from a woman who's at my mercy. I'd think you'd be a little more careful with your tongue, Miss MacLaren."

Lifting her chin, she spat the next words out. "Mark my words, Captain. If anything happens to me or Deke, you'll not have a single day of rest. My family will hunt you until they've put you and your men in the ground."

Something about the way she spoke the words made his jaw clench. Standing, he stared down at her. "We'll see who goes into the ground first. You, me, or that sheriff brother of yours. Trust me. Killing any of your family will mean nothing to me."

"Everyone ready?" Brodie looked at the men, seeing them nod, their resolute expressions telling him how determined they were to find Jinny and bring her home. "Let's go."

It had been an uneasy night. No one wanted to make camp, believing every minute the raiders held Jinny was a minute too long. The grim reality of the terrain ahead had been all that held them back. They'd used the time to come up with a plan to divide the group to cover more ground. Brodie would take one, Colin the other. At any one time, they would be no more than a mile apart, close enough to signal each other with rifle fire.

Brodie thought of the MacLarens back at Circle M, wondering if they were safe. His father, Ewan, had insisted on going with them on the search. Colin and Quinn urged him and Uncle Ian to stay behind. No one knew if there'd been an accident or if Jinny and Deke had been taken. In case they were abducted, someone had to be ready if a message arrived, or guard the family if they were threatened. Since no word had been sent, the group had to assume no one at the ranch had been contacted.

Colin rode up beside Brodie. "We go as planned?"

Looking toward the two paths they'd take, Brodie nodded. "Aye. Blaine, Cam, Caleb, and Sean go with you. Quinn, Bram, Fletcher, and Deke with me." He pulled out his pocket watch. "If no one finds her, we meet at the designated spot at ten and regroup."

Colin reined his horse close, clasping Brodie on the shoulder. "We'll find her, lad. They'll not be taking Jinny away from us."

Mrs. Belford walked to her horse and mounted, then looked at Theo, Walt, and Cy. "Martin and Brandon know why we're leaving and where we're headed. You lead the way, Theo."

"Yes, ma'am."

They'd had an early breakfast, eager to get going to assess if the men camped north of them were friend or foe. She suspected foe, which meant they'd be looking to steal cattle from one of the ranches. As boundaries went, her house was much closer to the camp than the other two spreads.

They planned to approach from the south, on the same trail Theo and the others had spotted the men the day before. He figured it would take no more than an hour to reach their destination. If all went well, they'd be back at the Belford ranch and eating dinner before noon.

Sam slid off Pirate, glad he hadn't sent word to Stein to sell the horse he'd left in Conviction. Bram had trained him well, selling the gelding to Sam at a fair price.

Kneeling beside a set of tracks, he pinched the bridge of his nose and shook his head. He and Nate had ridden well into the night before making camp on the western edge of MacLaren land. They could've covered more ground, but he didn't want to miss anything that would give him a clue as to Jinny's whereabouts. From previous rides, he knew they were about two hours from their ultimate destination—the original Estrada hacienda.

Nate watched him from his saddle. "If we keep going, we'll pass through the old Pearce place, then some of Mrs. Belford's land before returning to Circle M. If she and Deke rode from the ranch to the hacienda, do you think they would've been this far west?"

"No. Just being cautious." Mounting, Sam knew they had no more time to waste. They had to make their way in the direction Jinny would've taken, find tracks, then go from there. They'd gained nothing by moving slow. "We'll head to The Boulders, then veer north." Reining his horse around, they started up the trail.

"The Boulders?"

Sam smiled. "It's what Jinny calls the big outcropping of large rocks, shrubs, and trees up ahead. It spans a large area and is hard to ride through. If someone took them, it would be a perfect place to hide."

"We don't know if they were abducted, Sam. All we know is they're missing."

"True." He pursed his lips. Both Jinny and Deke having an accident seemed too coincidental, and he'd never been one to believe in coincidences. "Did anything happen in Conviction while I was gone? Something that would encourage someone to go after Jinny?"

Nate rubbed the upper part of his left arm, feeling the phantom pain of his missing left hand. Yesterday had been brutal. Today threatened to be worse.

"Nothing except the incident at Maloney's."

Sam shifted in his saddle to look at Nate. "What incident?"

"That's right. You were back east when it happened." Nate explained how the ex-Confederate raiders had threatened the women at the general store, showing a special interest in Jinny. With each word, he could see the anger on Sam's face build.

Trying to control the rage at the knowledge someone had threatened the woman he loved,

Sam's mind raced with questions. "Were they seen again?"

"One is still in jail, awaiting trial. Nobody has seen the others since they rode out of town. We kept expecting them to try to break the prisoner out of jail, but so far, nothing. Brodie figures they took off and left him behind."

Sam's instincts had always been sharp, saving him from serious injury or death many times. What Nate told him had his entire body on alert.

"They didn't leave."

Nate stared at him. "What do you mean?"

"The raiders never left. They have Jinny." And he thought he knew just where they'd be hiding her. "We have to find them." Without waiting for Nate to respond, he kicked Pirate, reining him in the direction of The Boulders.

"There they are, Mrs. Belford." Theo held the field glasses, pointing toward the camp, his eyes widening when he saw a woman. Walt and Cy had stayed a good distance away with the horses, not wanting to alert the men until Mrs. Belford saw them. "I didn't see her before, but there's a woman with them."

242

"A woman? Let me see the glasses." Taking them from Theo's hand, she focused on the camp. "Oh no. It can't be." She looked again, watching the woman stare into space, her hair in disarray, clothing dirty. Mrs. Belford's hand shook as she lowered the glasses.

"Do you know her?"

"It's Jinny MacLaren, the sheriff's sister." She handed the glasses back to Theo, who took another look.

"They have her tied up. What do you want to do?"

She thought of the distance between here and Circle M, wondering if the MacLarens knew Jinny was missing. If they did, there'd already be a search party looking for her. "We have to let the MacLarens know she's here. The four of us aren't enough to go up against those men. And truthfully, I'm not that good a shot."

Theo cocked a brow. "Pardon me, Mrs. Belford, but we wouldn't let you go down there anyway." Pushing away from their perch between two boulders, he stood, helping her to her feet. "I'll send Cy to the Circle M. I think you should head back to the ranch."

"Absolutely not. I may not be the right person to confront those no good varmints, but I'm not leaving. We'll keep watch on Jinny, make certain they don't do her any harm before the

MacLarens arrive." Anger and unease settled in Mrs. Belford's stomach. All the MacLaren women were good people. Jinny, though, was special. Sweet, kind, smart, and stubborn when it came to those she cared about. Well, a lot of people cared about her, too, and it wouldn't be long before Jinny knew it.

Finding nothing, the two groups of men met as planned. Each showed a different emotion on his face, but no one had lost the sense of urgency to find Jinny.

"There's one place out here for them to hide her."

Brodie stared at him. "And where would that be, Quinn?"

"The Boulders."

Brodie blew out a frustrated breath. "That's where we've been looking for three hours."

"Emma told me there's a particular area where the women like to ride to, uh...get away from us." A sad smile curved the corners of his mouth. "It's still a big area, but from what Emma said, it's right in the middle of the rock formation."

Colin raised a brow. "That's due west of where we are now."

"Aye." Quinn drank from his canteen, swiping the excess away with the sleeve of his shirt. "If it's true they're holding her in exchange for the prisoner, it's the perfect place to hide without anyone finding them. We've searched the north and south ends. We need to search the middle."

Brodie remembered Jinny mentioning the specific area a few times during Sunday supper. Now he wished he'd paid more attention, learned of landmarks or anything else that could help them find her.

Quinn handed the canteen to Brodie, who thought about their next move. Taking a deep swallow, he narrowed his gaze on the area directly ahead of them. "We'll need to ride in slow. Sound carries, bouncing off the boulders."

Colin nodded. "Aye. If we find them, we may need to leave the horses behind and go in on foot. Less chance of them hearing us."

"Agreed." Brodie rubbed the back of his neck, wishing he knew where Sam and Nate were. If they found the raiders, they'd need every man to make sure Jinny got away.

Colin turned to the others, who stood in a circle around them. "Did you all hear?"

They nodded, Fletcher speaking for all of them. "We search The Boulders. Slow and easy so as not to spook them or bring harm to Jinny. We'll follow your lead, Brodie."

Brodie clasped his younger brother on the shoulder. "We'll find her, Fletch, and bring her home."

"Aye. I've no doubt we will."

Chapter Eighteen

Jinny leaned back against the tree, or as she'd come to think of it, her home away from home. Her body hurt from spending so much time in the same position. They had loosened the rope around her wrists, allowing her to take care of her needs whenever she asked.

With each passing hour, Jinny worried more about Deke. Besides being at the mercy of wild animals, he had no one to provide food or water. She had to believe he'd loosened his ties, found his horse, and ridden back to Circle M. If so, she had no doubt he'd be part of any search party her family organized.

She'd slept little the night before. Eplett had forced her to lay down next to him, tying a rope around her waist and his so she couldn't sneak away. Worse, the continuous roars of the mountain lion kept everyone on edge. After the death of one of his men, Eplett had posted two guards and kept the fire burning. The glowing flames comforted Jinny and gave her hope someone would see them and ride into the camp. That hadn't happened.

"Here."

Jinny lifted her gaze, seeing the dented tin cup full of water Eplett held out to her, a knowing sneer on his face. She wondered what he had planned for her if no one came to her rescue. If she weren't so thirsty, she'd shove it away, spilling the contents on the ground. Impulse gave way to the practical need to sate her dry mouth. Lifting her bound wrists, she took the cup and drank, looking over Eplett's shoulder, seeing a glint of light in the rock formation behind him.

Her heart sped up. Nothing natural could reflect the light in such a way. The flash had to be created by something manmade.

"What's wrong?" Eplett glanced over his shoulder.

Finishing the water, she held up the empty cup, refusing to return her gaze to where she'd seen the light.

"Nothing's wrong. Thank you."

Turning back to her, Eplett narrowed his gaze. Jinny's body tensed under his penetrating scrutiny. He grabbed the cup and stalked away, his head once again lifting to the rocks where she'd been looking. As the air rushed from her lungs, she chastised herself for being so careless. She could think of one reason for the flash she'd seen—someone watched the camp.

"Did you hear something?" Sam raised his hand, indicating for Nate to rein up, then listened again. A moment later, the sound of voices could be heard in the distance.

"Men shouting." Nate closed his eyes, focusing on the sound.

"There it is again. They're up ahead." Excitement coursed through Sam's veins, believing they may have found the men they sought. "We'll ride a little farther, then continue on foot. I don't want to alert them to our presence until we know if they are friend or foe."

Riding on, it seemed like forever until they heard the voices again, much closer this time. Approaching from the west, they dismounted, ground tying the horses behind shrubs. Their cautious steps took them through a series of boulders until they stood on high ground, looking down on the camp below.

Sweeping his gaze from one man to another, he spotted a small figure on the ground. Holding up his field glasses, he looked again, rage sweeping through him. Lowering them, he turned to Nate, his features twisted.

"Is it Jinny?"

He nodded. "Yes. They have her hands bound. She's dirty and looks like she hasn't slept in days."

"But she's alive, Sam. We need to figure a way to get to her." Nate drew his six-shooter from its holster, then checked the cylinder. "I'll get our rifles."

"Wait. There's no good path from here. They'll spot us before we're halfway down."

Holding the glasses up to his face again, Sam scanned the area. He counted six men, all armed, but no one on alert. Shifting his gaze upward, he scanned the area surrounding the camp, stopping when a flash of light caught his attention. Concentrating on the spot, he waited, seeing the flash again, mumbling a curse when he couldn't get a clear view.

Nate crouched beside him. "What is it?"

"Someone with a rifle or gun is hiding in the rocks south of us."

"Friend or foe?"

"I wish I knew. I can't get a good look at them." Moving to the horses, Sam shoved the glasses back into his saddlebag. "We can't go after Jinny until we know who's watching from those rocks."

Mounting, they rode south, careful not to alert anyone to their location. Sam estimated it wouldn't take long to move behind the person watching the camp. A few minutes later, they spotted horses grazing. Sliding to the ground, slipping rifles from their scabbards, Sam and

Nate moved cautiously toward the rocks. Two men and a woman stood with their backs to them, their attention focused on the camp below. Lifting their rifles, Sam and Nate aimed at the trio.

Sam took a step forward. "Drop your guns, then raise your hands and turn around."

The three froze, doing as he asked.

The woman pierced him with an exasperated expression. "Why, Sam Covington. You lower that rifle right now."

Shock registered on his face when he recognized the widow. "Mrs. Belford? What are you doing out here?"

"The same as you and Nate. Trying to figure a way to get Jinny away from those thugs. We sent Cy to the Circle M, letting them know we found her. I expect it won't take long for them to get here."

Sam recognized Walt and Theo, two of the men who'd killed Bob Belford. He knew they could shoot, and from what he could see, were loyal to Mrs. Belford.

Sam leaned toward Nate, lowering his voice. "Can we trust those two?"

"I don't know them well enough. If Mrs. Belford trusts them, I guess we can, too."

Sam breathed a little easier. This location provided a better path to the camp. With four men, they could ride their horses down, surprising them before the raiders had a chance to respond. First, they had to find a way to keep Jinny safe.

"Excuse me, Deputies." Sam and Nate looked at Theo, who motioned them over. "I think there are riders up above, coming from the northeast." He motioned up high, toward the other side of the camp.

Theo handed Sam his field glasses. He put them to his face, staring across the distance, seeing movement. He spotted the horses first, then moved his gaze up, expelling a deep breath. "It's the MacLarens. Brodie is in front."

"Thank God." Mrs. Belford took a step away, a hand going to her chest as she rested against a boulder. "I knew those boys would come."

Nate accepted the field glasses Sam held out, watching the riders for several minutes. "I don't think they've seen the camp. They seem to still be searching." Handing the glasses back, he took another look at the men in the camp. "There aren't any guards posted. The raiders seem oblivious to the activity around them."

Sam looked at Theo. "You need to let the MacLarens know we're here without alerting the camp. Can you do that?"

"Yes, sir."

Sam looked through the glasses, then held up his hand. "Wait, Theo. Brodie's signaling the others to rein up. He's dismounting and looking over the edge of the trail to the camp below." He lowered the glasses to his side. "They've found them. We need to be prepared to move when they do. My guess is Brodie and the others will plan to go in at nightfall when it will be harder to spot them."

Mrs. Belford placed a hand on his arm. "Who'll protect Jinny from getting shot?"

Sam's mouth went dry, his throat tightening at the thought of her getting hurt. He had to believe Brodie wouldn't do anything to endanger his sister. The sheriff always thought everything through as he formulated a plan.

Sam pushed aside his own concerns, facing the widow. "Don't worry, Mrs. Belford. The MacLarens won't make a move until they're certain Jinny is safe." He turned toward Theo. "It's time for you to let the MacLarens know we're here. Tell Brodie we'll be waiting to move when they do. The more confusion we can cause in camp, the better the chances of rescuing Jinny."

As much as he hated waiting, they needed to move when the others did, and not before. He and Nate walked with Theo to his horse, waiting for him to mount. Sam grabbed the reins before Theo could ride off.

"Don't worry about coming back here. Go in with them. I don't want to take a chance of the raiders seeing you."

"Yes, sir."

Sam let out a frustrated breath, dropping the reins so he could ride away. All they could do was wait for the MacLarens to act, and pray nothing happened to Jinny.

Switching his gaze between the camp below and the rim across from them, Sam saw the instant the MacLarens became aware of a rider approaching. Most drew their guns, aiming at Theo, before Brodie recognized him and stepped forward.

It had taken him longer than Sam anticipated to reach the MacLarens. He continued to watch through the glasses as Theo's animated gestures had the others turning to look in the direction he pointed. A moment later, several pulled out their own glasses, searching the rim until they spotted Sam, Nate, and Walt. Even from this distance, Sam could see the relief on their faces.

"Here. Eat this." Mrs. Belford had left a few minutes before, returning with a couple wrapped packages containing hardtack and jerky. "I don't have a lot, but you'll need it all before nightfall." When her hands were empty, she looked at Sam, lines of worry creasing her eyes and the corners of her mouth. "Did Theo make it?"

"Yes, ma'am. The MacLarens know we're here."

Her features relaxed at the news. "Then I'll get ready."

"Ready?" Sam asked.

"To ride when you do. I hope you didn't think I'd stay up here by myself while you young men went for Jinny." As she started to turn, Sam grabbed her arm.

"Listen to me, Mrs. Belford. You have two boys at home who need you. Think about what will happen to them if you get hurt or killed. From what I can see, there are six men in camp and fourteen of us. With those odds, it would be real foolish of me to let you go down there."

Her brows knit together as she crossed her arms. "*Let* me go down?"

If it weren't for the dire situation they found themselves in, Sam would've laughed. "I mean no disrespect, ma'am. I just want you to think of Martin and Brandon. You've already done your part by riding out in search of Jinny. You and your men found her. Now let the rest of us go down and get her."

He could see her rolling his words around in her head before she nodded. "All right. But when you've got those varmints cornered, I'm joining you. Jinny will need another woman with her once everything settles down."

The sun finally began its descent behind the western hills. For Brodie, it couldn't come soon enough. He and his family had discussed their options several times before agreeing on a plan. Brodie, Fletcher, and Deke had ridden in a wide arc to the east, then a little south, coming up behind the camp. On the northeast rim, the others waited for his signal—a bird call he and his cousins had perfected when they were boys. Once Colin responded, it would be his signal to ride in. He hoped Sam and Nate were ready when the MacLarens made their move.

His job was simple. He'd move up behind Jinny and pull her out of the line of fire, clearing the path for the others to surround the camp. It all made sense, but Brodie pinched the bridge of his nose, knowing nothing ever worked out quite as planned. He prayed the chaos would pull the raiders attention from Jinny long enough to get her to safety.

"How much longer, Brodie?" Fletcher knelt beside him, his hand steady as it rested against the butt of his gun.

"A few more minutes. Then it will still be light enough for the lads to see, but dark enough to help conceal their path. Make sure you and Deke are ready to cover me." Brodie looked at Jinny once more, who hadn't moved. "I'll be moving a wee bit closer to see if I can get Jinny's attention."

Fletcher's stern gaze locked on his brother. "Aye, Brodie. We'll be ready for your signal."

Leaving his rifle between Deke and Fletcher, he started forward, keeping low to the ground. He didn't want to scare her or alert the men in camp while he found a spot to hide until the sun dropped behind the hills. Getting to within five feet of Jinny, he crouched, drawing his gun from its holder.

"Jinny," he whispered, his voice a low rasp. Getting no response, he tried again, this time a little louder. "Jinny."

Her head snapped up, back straightening.

He edged a little closer. "I'm behind you, lass."

"Brodie." She breathed out his name, almost too low for him to hear. He could see her chest rise and fall as she bent her legs, turning her head a couple inches toward him.

"Aye, lass. Are the men close?"

"Nae. They're on the other side of the camp. Are you alone?"

"Nae. The others are hidden in the rocks, waiting for my signal. Once the sun sets a little more, I'll alert them we're ready. As soon as Colin replies, you'll be needing to scramble toward me as fast as you can. Can you do that, lass?"

Her relief was so great, she could barely think. It wouldn't be long before she'd be free of the rope around her wrists and the men who held her.

"Lass?"

She nodded enough so Brodie could see. "Aye. On your signal, I'll move to you."

He wanted to ask if she was hurt, but couldn't afford to chance being noticed when they were so close to reclaiming her. Instead, he leaned back, his heart in his throat as dusk approached. It wouldn't be long now.

His gaze wandered past Jinny, seeing the men milling about, unaware of the wrath about to rain down on them. They seemed relaxed. One group played cards while a couple other men drank coffee. Their inattention made Brodie wonder if he'd missed something. Was there a seventh man posted in the rocks, guarding the camp in stoic silence? It was what Brodie would do, especially holding a prize as rare as Jinny.

These men seemed to have no worries, not a single concern about being discovered. Sucking in a breath, Brodie counted down as the sun disappeared, throwing the camp into twilight.

"Ready, lass?"

She nodded once, pulling her legs closer to her chest, prepared to run at his signal.

"Be sure to wait until Colin replies and the lads start to ride. There will be a few others coming from your left. Don't be worried. They're with us." He didn't mention Sam, concerned his presence might distract her at a time she had to focus on getting away.

Glancing behind him, he sent a grim smile to Fletcher and Deke. Both stared back, their faces set. Taking in a slow breath, then letting it out, he brought both hands up, cupping them together. Bringing them to his lips, he blew, shifting his hands to create the bird call his family would recognize.

Jinny swallowed her fear, knowing a wrong move on her part could result in someone she loved getting shot. Her body began to tremble as she waited for Colin's answering call. A moment later, the reply came, followed by the sound of horses. She sprang into motion, scrambling to reach Brodie's outstretched arms as gunfire ripped through the still evening air.

Stumbling into his embrace, she closed her eyes, burying her face in his chest.

"I've got you, lass." His grip tightened as her hands dug into his shirt. He barely registered Fletcher and Deke moving in front of him, guns firing, covering the men who rode into a camp mired in confusion.

Jinny's body shook with such force, she could barely take a breath. The sound of gunfire, men shouting, and the subsequent moans of those hit sliced through her. She wanted to move out of Brodie's embrace, unable to find the strength.

"I must help the lads, Jinny. Will you be all right?"

She nodded vigorously. "Aye. Go. Help the others."

Gripping his gun, he pinned her with a stern look. "Do not come out until one of us comes for you. Do you understand, lass?"

She nodded, her eyes wide with fear. Not so much for herself as for the family who'd come to rescue her. She gripped his arm. "Be safe, Brodie. Please..."

He didn't respond before turning away, finding a target, and firing. Brodie could see Fletcher and Deke on his left and right, hidden behind rocks as they fired. A yell drew his attention. One of the raiders scrambled for cover as shots hit the ground around him. Lifting his gun, the man screamed as Brodie's bullet blasted through his shoulder, spinning him around and to the ground.

Jinny watched from her hidden position, wishing she had a gun, wanting to be part of doling out justice to those who'd taken her. Most of her family remained hidden behind rocks and shrubs, mere ghosts, turning lawlessness into righteousness.

To her right, she spotted Deke, relief rolling through her. He'd survived, joining in the search with her family. Covering her ears, she took a deep breath, opening them again when she heard the MacLaren war cry. *Creag an Tuirc*, the Boar's Rock, fought to be heard over the blasts of gunfire, shouts of the raiders, and screams of those injured. Jinny prayed none of her family had been shot. She'd never forgive herself if any of them gave his life to rescue her. Brodie's loud voice broke over the noise, silencing the sounds of gunfire.

"Drop your weapons and hold up your hands."

Jinny leaned out from her hiding place, her breath catching at the sight of Eplett and one of his men standing at the edge of camp, their guns aimed in the direction where Brodie stood with Fletcher, Deke, Caleb, and Quinn. More of her family circled the two men, ready to shoot if they didn't comply with Brodie's order.

Brodie tried again. "There's no chance you'll make it out of here alive. Give yourselves up, stand trial, and perhaps you'll live."

She could see Eplett waver, the ex-Confederate beside him glancing at Brodie, then the captain, his gun arm shaking.

"Four of your men are dead. You'll never make it out of here alive unless you give up."

Jinny saw the instant Eplett made his decision. She'd thought he'd fire, refuse to be taken prisoner. Instead, he threw back his head and laughed, lowering his gun, then dropping it into the dirt. A moment later, the man beside him did the same.

"You win, Sheriff." Eplett held his hands in front of him, an unapologetic sneer on his face. "Let's see if you can keep me locked up."

Sam's heart beat wildly at the scene before him. Four were dead, and from his vantage point, not one of the MacLarens or their cohorts had been shot. A miracle, considering the chaos that ensued when Brodie gave the signal.

Holstering his gun, Sam moved his horse out of the shelter of the trees. He had a mission to get to Jinny. She hadn't seen him, had no idea he'd been part of the group who searched for her. Brodie had planned for her to learn of his return at Sunday supper—a meal that hadn't happened. Instead, she'd learn now. The thought didn't bother him at all, until Jinny dashed from her hiding spot, running toward a man Sam didn't recognize, throwing herself into his arms.

Sam's gut clenched, his heart squeezing in pain as he watched the way they looked at each other. Great affection passed between them, the kind he and Jinny had once shown for each other. The man he believed to be Deke Arrington tightened his hold around her, then pulled back. He placed a kiss on her forehead and her cheek, then tucked her head against his chest.

Pain tore through Sam as he continued to stare, unable to pull his gaze away. As he began to rein his horse around, he heard a gasp. A piercing ache sliced through him when Jinny pulled away from the man, an agonized look of disbelief on her face when she recognized him.

Chapter Nineteen

Less than a week had passed since Jinny's rescue, and Sam hadn't seen or heard from her. Not that he expected to. He stayed busy, trying not to dwell on what he'd witnessed at the camp or the look on her face when she'd seen him.

He settled his family into their home, accepted his badge from Brodie, and returned to the same routine before his abrupt departure. To those who didn't know him, his life fell right back into place. To Sam, all his hopes and dreams for the future died at the sight of Jinny in Deke's arms.

He'd left the camp soon after the shooting stopped, satisfied Jinny was all right. At the time, he hadn't returned to his official capacity as a deputy, and knew Brodie didn't need him to help transport the two prisoners to Conviction. From what he'd heard, half the MacLarens took Jinny back to Circle M while the other half accompanied Brodie, Nate, and the prisoners to jail. They'd be facing trial within days.

"It's good to have you back, Sam." Jack set his hat on a hook before filling a cup with coffee.

Sam looked at the revolver he'd been cleaning, mulling over how to respond. Nothing about the last few days had been anything like the first time he'd come to Conviction when he worked for Pinkerton.

"I'm glad to be back." It wasn't a complete lie. He'd always liked the town and the people, feeling a sense of belonging he'd never achieved in Baltimore.

"Brodie says your father came back with you."

"And my son."

Jack choked on his coffee, wiping moisture from his chin. "Your son? I didn't know you were married."

"I'm not. I found out about Robbie when I went back east." Sam had already told the story to August Fielder, Brodie, and Nate. He had no desire to repeat it again, except to Jinny, and he doubted if she'd care.

Scratching the stubble on his jaw, Jack lowered himself into a chair. "Well, I'll be. How old is he?"

Sam grinned, thinking about Robbie this morning when his grandfather told him he'd take him for a ride around town. "Almost five. I told him he could have a horse."

"Guess you'll be riding out to Circle M. From what the sheriff says, Fletcher and Sean are the best at breeding horses."

"That's what I understand." After the rescue, he'd put off riding to the MacLaren ranch. He didn't know when he'd be ready to see her again. Accepting she'd moved on didn't come easily.

"Lads." Brodie walked in, his gaze landing on Jack. "Are the prisoners causing any trouble?"

"No sir, Sheriff. Quiet as lambs."

Sam smirked at Jack's comment. They all knew the three men wouldn't remain quiet for long. They'd raised an uproar several times each day, demanding to be released, later insisting they needed an attorney. Brodie had ignored the first request, introducing them to a lawyer to meet the second. The man wasn't bad at his chosen profession, except for the days he buried himself in a bottle of whiskey—which he did with regularity.

Brodie shook his head. "Well, they've a lawyer, so that should satisfy them until their trial on Friday."

"Do you think the judge will make it this time?" Sam had heard how many times Terrence Card's trial had been postponed.

"Aye. He'll be here. If not, I'll be riding the trail to find the man."

Sam stared at the wall separating the front of the jail from the cells, knowing the prisoners could hear them. "And I'll go with you, Brodie. The men who took Jinny need to meet their fate."

Jumping up from the chair, Jack hurried to grab his hat. "I'm off, Sheriff. Need to make my rounds so I can be at the docks before the next steamboat arrives. I don't know why some of those gamblers have to cause so much trouble on every trip."

Watching Jack close the door behind him, Brodie's mouth twitched. "He's a fine lad."

"Very exuberant," Sam added, his lips twisting into a reluctant grin.

"Aye. And dedicated. I could use a couple more like him."

Sam laughed. "I believe he's one of a kind, Brodie."

Brodie leaned forward, resting his elbows on the desk, steepling his fingers below his chin. After a moment, his shoulders relaxed, as did his features. "Jinny is one of a kind, too."

The comment jolted Sam. "No one knows that better than me."

"Aye, but you've made no time to visit her. I thought you cared about her more than it appears."

Pushing from the chair, Sam paced toward the wood stove, then back to the other wall, shoving his hands through his hair. "She's not mine to care about any longer, Brodie. You saw her with Arrington at the camp. It's him she wants. Not me."

"You're so sure of this you'd be willing to lose her?"

Sam stopped pacing, glaring at his friend. "Can you deny her feelings for the man?"

"The lass has said nothing to me about Deke, other than they are friends. Unlike the many times you've been to Sunday supper, he's been once. It may be that I'm wrong, but are you willing to take the chance?"

Letting out a breath, Sam forced his racing heart to calm, lowering himself into a chair. "I don't know what to do." He glanced at Brodie, his features lined with the stress he'd been under. "Does she know about Robbie?"

"No one at the ranch knows. It's your story to tell, and Jinny deserves to hear it from you."

"She's young, with big dreams. She may not want to take on another man's child."

"Ach. Do you think so little of her?"

Sam's brows lifted. "You know that isn't true."

"Then you need to give the lass a chance. Join us for supper on Sunday. Bring your father and Robbie. Jinny has waited for months to hear from you. She deserves the whole story."

Sam rubbed his eyes with the palms of his hands. He'd wrestled with thoughts of Jinny for months, knowing he loved her, not knowing how to proceed. So caught up in the changes in his own life, he'd put off contacting her. After such a long time without hearing from him, she'd met someone else and forged a friendship. Maybe more, if appearances were accurate.

"If you think it's wise, then yes, I'll be there Sunday."

"With your family?" Brodie studied Sam's face. After going through what he had with his wife, Maggie, he knew how hard it was to love a woman and believe you've lost her forever.

Sam forced a wry grin. "Yes, Sheriff. I'll bring my family."

Brodie chuckled. "All right then. It's time you got to work, Deputy."

Standing, Sam grabbed his hat from the hook. "What would you have me do first?"

"Send telegrams to Sacramento and San Francisco, maybe even to Pinkerton. We need at least two more deputies. Afterward, you'll be patrolling Chinatown and keeping watch for Nate."

Sam's hand stilled on the doorknob. "Nate? Is something going on I should know about?"

Rubbing his chin, Brodie's features tensed. "Aye. Something is going on. I want you to discover what."

Jinny sat in the old rocking chair on the porch, tucking the quilt tight around her shoulders. Since returning to the ranch, she'd claimed this spot, spending hours watching blue skies or star-filled nights. The weather had been glorious. Her mood had not.

She couldn't get the look of Sam's face out of her head. He'd helped rescue her, yet hadn't stayed around to talk, explain about his return. Brodie had given her few details, other than he'd arrived the day before she and Deke went missing, not hesitating to join the search.

"Would you like some company?"

Jinny glanced into the yard to see Emma and Sarah approach. They'd stopped by each day asking vague questions, hoping to learn if she'd heard from Sam. She thought the whole thing daft. If Sam came to visit, they would know. Nothing stayed secret around the MacLaren ranch for long.

"Aye. Company would be grand."

Pulling two chairs close, Sarah and Emma sat down, following Jinny's gaze. No one spoke for several moments, content to enjoy the evening air. After a while, Emma shifted in her chair, looking at Jinny.

"Sarah and I are going to town tomorrow. Would you like to come along?"

Not lowering her gaze from the brilliant sky, Jinny shook her head. The last thing she wanted was to see Sam before she was ready. "Nae. I have to be in town on Friday for the trial."

Sarah sat up straighter. "How could I forget about the trial? Then we'll wait until Friday and go with you. In fact, I'm certain most of the family will be there."

"Brodie will be there. I don't think having the whole family at the trial will make it any easier for me."

Emma and Sarah exchanged glances. Vibrant, funny, and often outspoken, they'd seen Jinny this sullen just one other time—when Sam had left Conviction. Now he'd returned, and so had Jinny's brooding mood. They understood her reasons for drawing within herself, keeping her emotions close. This time, though, there seemed to be hope, yet Jinny refused to see it.

"Maybe so, but I'm going anyway," Emma said.

Sarah nodded, resting her head against the back of the chair. "Me, too. I suppose you'll have to live with us being there, Jinny."

She knew they meant well, and if they were going through the same ordeal, she'd be there for them. It's what the MacLarens did.

"You'll have to speak with him sometime." Emma shot a look at her, a soft smile on her face.

Jinny didn't consider pretending she didn't know who Emma meant. "Why hasn't he come to see me? It's been almost a week without word from him." Letting out a deep sigh, she shook her head. "I no longer hold his heart."

"You know that isn't true." Emma reached over, laying a hand on Jinny's arm. "He came looking for you, didn't he? Quinn says he stayed until everyone knew you were safe."

"Then rode back to town without a word," Jinny bit out, resentment lacing her words.

"There must be a reason he hasn't come to see you."

"Aye, I'm sure there is, Emma. I'd just like to hear what it is. The not knowing is torture."

Sarah sat forward, clasping her hands together. "Perhaps we should go to town tomorrow and speak with Maggie. If Sam has said anything to Brodie, he'll have told her. You know he can't keep secrets from his wife."

"Nae. I'll not be putting Maggie in such a position with my brother. When Sam wants to talk, he'll find me."

"Well, there is the part about Deke being there with the search party. Maybe Sam heard about all the time you've spent with him. And the fact you were together when you were taken."

Emma summed up Jinny's thoughts in a few sentences. Sam had seen Deke hold her, kiss her face, whisper in her ear. None of it meant anything to Jinny, other than the joyful reaction of a friend who'd also been brutalized by the raiders. Sam didn't know her feelings toward Deke because he hadn't been here. He'd been back east, doing God knew what with whom, without a thought of her waiting thousands of miles away for word of his intentions.

Her brows scrunched together. Maybe she wasn't the one who should be stewing, wondering why he hadn't visited. Sam's the one who reined his horse around and took off without the briefest acknowledgment of her. The look on his face didn't reflect a man who didn't care. The pain and surprise indicated a man who cared very much, but hadn't the courage to confront her. The Sam who rode away wasn't the man she loved. Jinny wanted to find out why.

Sarah stood. Bending over, she gave Jinny an encouraging hug. "The trial is two days away. You're sure to see Sam there."

Jinny leaned back in the rocker. "Aye. Brodie thinks most of the town will be there. And they should be. Men like them should have to face judgment from the kind of people they threaten."

Emma tightened her coat for more warmth, then stood. "Quinn says if they're found guilty, the judge will send them to San Quentin for a good, long time."

Sarah nodded. "Colin said Brodie tried to find other warrants, anything to show they'd murdered others, stolen cattle, something to get a harsher sentence. At least going to prison will get them out of Conviction. We'll be able to rest easier knowing they're behind bars."

Joining Sarah by the steps, Emma faced Jinny. "You have two days to prepare yourself. For the trial and for confronting Sam." Emma lifted a brow. "You do plan to talk to him, don't you?"

"Aye. I'll be talking to *Mr. Covington*, and hope he'll be honest with me." She already knew he would, and that scared her the most. Jinny had never truly contemplated a life without Sam, and it was the last thing she wanted to consider now.

"Good. We'll be with you throughout the trial. Afterward, well....you'll have to face Sam on your own. Hope you have a good night, Jinny. Sarah and I will be by again tomorrow."

She didn't move from her spot on the porch, her brave front dissolving as she watched them leave. In two days, she'd face her kidnappers, and Sam. She didn't know which disturbed her more.

Sam had kept track of Nate all day—following him on his rounds, standing across the street when he stopped for lunch, keeping a good distance away as he disappeared into one of the shops in Chinatown. Leaning his shoulder against a storefront, he waited, finally sitting down on a bench outside one of the many markets. Nate had been inside for close to an hour, raising Sam's suspicions.

Most of those who inhabited this area of Conviction had worked in the mines. They'd brought their own customs with them, settling into quiet, unobtrusive neighborhoods in a few California towns. Markets, restaurants, herb stores, and laundries lined the boardwalk, and from what Sam knew, a man could find anything he wanted behind those doors. He had to wonder what Nate needed that kept him inside so long. Standing, he walked toward the building Nate had disappeared into, halting when his friend stumbled out the door and onto the boardwalk. If he hadn't grabbed the railing, he'd have landed in the street.

Rushing up to him, Sam gripped Nate's right arm, holding him upright. "What the..." His words drifted off as he studied his friend's face, noting the red eyes, slow movements, and lack of coordination. Nate's eyes closed, as if he were about to fall asleep. Sam shook him. "Nate, get ahold of yourself."

Blinking a few times, Nate raised his head. "What's wrong?" The two words were dragged out and slurred.

Mumbling a curse, Sam glanced around, glad they hadn't already drawn a crowd. Nate's horse stood a few feet away, while his was down the street. Placing two fingers in his mouth, he whistled. Pirate's head lifted, turning when Sam whistled again. The horse reared back, easily dislodging the reins tossed loosely over the rail, then trotted toward Sam.

Helping Nate onto his own horse's saddle, Sam mounted Pirate, holding both sets of reins, hoping his friend was lucid enough not to fall off. Riding toward the Gold Dust, he planned to settle Nate in his room, then talk to Brodie.

Sam's chest felt heavy, his spirits sinking at the news he had to convey. It hadn't taken long for him to understand what had troubled Brodie. Sam had seen the signs before in men and women who'd reached their limit with what a doctor could provide. Few worked themselves out of the hole Nate had fallen into, but as long as Sam had a breath, he'd do whatever it took to help his friend and keep him alive.

Brodie scrubbed his hands over his face, groaning. Lifting his chin, his gaze landed on Sam sitting across from him, his features still, his eyes distant.

"You're sure, lad?"

Sam nodded. "I've seen it before—more than once. Vickery or Tilden need to see him to confirm what I suspect." He looked away, unable to voice his fear over the possibility of losing Nate. For all Sam knew, they may have already lost him.

"If you're right, we'll need their help."

Sam stood, pacing to the stove. Lifting the coffee pot, he poured a cup, then held it toward Brodie, who shook his head. His hand shook as he held the cup to his lips. Without taking a drink, he threw it against the wall, sending the hot brew everywhere.

"Damn opium." Sam swore again, slamming his fist on top of Brodie's desk. "We've got a mess hiding in Chinatown. If Nate's using it, you can be sure there are others."

Brodie watched the anger grow on Sam's face. He'd never seen him so consumed by rage. Rarely seen him lose his temper. Brodie knew little about the drug, other than what he'd heard.

"Have you ever seen anyone get off it?"

"No. That doesn't mean he can't. Hell, Brodie, we have to make *sure* he gets off it."

Standing, Brodie walked to the front window and looked out. Darkness blanketed the street, the noise from the closest saloon pouring outside.

"Find one of the doctors and get him to the Gold Dust. Then find Jack and send him back here. I'll be taking Nate to Circle M tonight."

Chapter Twenty

Circle M Ranch

Brodie and Sam climbed out of the wagon they'd borrowed from Stein Tharaldson, lifted a shivering Nate out of the back, and carried him up the steps.

"Colin, open the door!"

A moment later, the door swung open. "Brodie MacLaren, what—" Kyla stopped, staring at what they carried. "Is that Nate Hollis?" Pulling the door wide, she stepped aside.

"Aye. He needs to stay here for a while, Aunt Kyla. Do you have room?"

She didn't question him. "Aye. The bedroom in the back is empty."

Following her down the hall, they laid Nate on the bed. Grabbing his stomach, he rolled to his side, drawing both knees to his chest on a deep moan.

"I'd have taken him to my ma's house, but I know they've no spare bedrooms."

Kyla closed the bedroom door, brushing Brodie aside to get a better look at Nate. "What happened?"

He looked at Sam. Most times, he had a ready answer. This time, he had no answers at all, except one his aunt might not accept.

"He's sick."

Crossing her arms, she tilted her head, sending him a withering look. "Don't be daft, lad. I can see he's sick."

Brodie didn't want to lie, knowing she'd figure it out anyway. "The lad, uh—"

The door burst open, slamming against the wall as Colin walked in, Blaine following. "What happened?" Colin rushed to the bed, his eyes narrowing. "Nate?" His worried gaze returned to Brodie.

"The lad, he..." Brodie sucked in a deep breath, then blew it out.

Kyla looked at Nate, then Sam, seeing his jaw clenched tight. "Opium." Her single word came out as a whisper.

Brodie's jaw dropped. "How did you know, Aunt Kyla?"

She didn't answer, letting her hand smooth down Nate's back in an attempt to calm him. Her actions stopped when Geneen walked into the room and gasped. Eyes widening, she stepped forward.

"Nate?"

Kyla didn't let her get any further. "Geneen, I need cool water and clean rags. Also a bottle of whiskey for later." When Geneen didn't move, Kyla walked to her, gently edging her away from the bed and into the hall. "I need your help, lass. Please, fetch what I asked."

Nodding, Geneen moved away in a daze. Her hands trembled as she reached for a basin on a kitchen shelf, filling it with water from a kettle on the stove. Grabbing rags, she returned to the bedroom.

She'd heard what Kyla said, knew of the drug, understood it was used for pain, the same as laudanum, only stronger. Geneen had also heard of opium dens, dangerous places where men and women lost their souls. Her legs trembled beneath her as she stopped outside the bedroom, willing herself to continue. Nudging the door open with her shoulder, she walked past the men, setting the bowl on a nearby table.

"Ah, thank you, lass." Kyla took the rags from her. "You don't have to stay."

"Yes, I do." Geneen's voice was stilted, cloaked in concern. Edging backward, she slowly lowered herself into a chair and stared at the bed—and the man she'd come to love.

Doubled over with nausea, Nate's red-rimmed eyes opened to slits, a tremor vibrating through him when he saw Geneen. Closing his eyes, shame wrapped around him. He had no excuses for the choices he'd made. Just as he had no future to offer the beautiful woman staring at him, compassion and pity clear in her features.

He'd never expected to become a prisoner to the drug he took for pain. Laudanum had stopped working months ago, forcing him to drink the ache away each night. When whiskey failed to lessen his agony, Nate turned to the only other remedy he knew. The fact opium was so easy to obtain in Chinatown made it both a blessing and a curse.

Each time he entered one of the three establishments offering the drug, he felt his self-respect slip further away. Regaining it became impossible as he continued to smoke the vile substance, forcing himself to think of it as a cure rather than a sickness of another kind.

Kyla turned to the four men standing at the foot of the bed. "The lad needs rest. It's best if you leave him here. I've a sense of what to do."

Colin shook his head. "Nae, Ma. One of us should stay with you and Nate."

"I'll stay." They turned toward Geneen, their faces showing different reactions. "I'd like to help."

Walking up to her, Kyla settled a hand on Geneen's arm. "You've no idea what the lad is going through. Watching him over the next few days will not be pleasant, lass. It will be a memory you'll not want haunting you the rest of your life."

Gently removing Kyla's hand, Geneen stood, walking to the edge of the bed. "No one wants him to live through this more than me." Her body tensed, eyes startled when a damp hand clamped around her wrist.

"You can't stay." The edge to Nate's voice made her cringe.

She didn't try to loosen his grip as she bent down. "I want to help you."

Closing his eyes, he shook his head. "You don't understand. I don't want you here." The cold, unrelenting tone shook Geneen.

"Nate, please, let me help."

Dropping his hold on her wrist, he lifted his gaze to Kyla. "Get her out of here."

Colin stepped up to her. "Come with me, lass. Sarah is with Emma and Jinny at Uncle Ewan's. I'll walk over with you."

Her heart sank when Nate refused to look at her. Staying wouldn't help, and he'd made it clear he didn't want her around.

"All right." Taking a deep breath, she made one more attempt to reach him. "Nate, I'm here if you change your mind." When he didn't respond, she turned away, leaving Kyla alone to watch after him.

"I don't know where Geneen could be. She told me she'd be walking down right after Emma and I left." Sarah turned from the front window.

"I'm sure she'll be here soon." Jinny set a tray down, then poured tea into cups and passed them out.

Ewan worked behind the closed doors of his den, while Lorna had disappeared into her sewing room, giving the young women a quiet place to talk.

"Tomorrow is the big day, Jinny. Are you ready?" Sarah sat down, adding milk to her tea.

"Aye. I want to get the trial behind me. Fletcher and Sean will have two wagons ready." Jinny sat next to Sarah, cradling her cup in her hands.

Emma took a sip of tea. "Quinn mentioned he and Caleb planned to stay here with a few others. With all that's happened, they don't want to leave the ranch unprotected."

Jinny opened her mouth to respond when the front door opened. Geneen walked inside, followed by Colin, Brodie, and Blaine. An instant later, Sam walked in, his gaze moving across the room until it landed on Jinny.

Seeing the distress on her sister's face, Sarah hurried to Geneen. "What's wrong?" When she didn't respond, Sarah looked at her husband. "Colin?"

He wrapped an arm around her shoulders, drawing her close. "It's Nate. Brodie and Sam brought him from town. Ma is taking care of him."

Emma stood, walking to the door. "I'll get Fletcher and Sean. They're in the barn with Bram."

Jinny watched Emma leave, unable to move from her spot. Sam hadn't taken his smoldering gaze off her, and although his features were neutral, his entire body tensed the longer he watched. Pushing up from her seat, she took a hesitant step forward. Removing his hat, Sam cleared his throat.

"Hello, Jinny. It's been a long time."

She nodded, not trusting her voice. Her heart squeezed, chest tightening so much she found it hard to draw a breath. He looked good, better than in her memories, and much better than when she'd seen him at Eplett's camp.

Looking down, he fingered the rim of his hat, unsure how to ask the question burning within him. He needed to hear it from her lips.

Jinny clasped her hands in front of her, shifting from one foot to the other. "I saw you at the camp."

"I'd gotten back to town the day before, had planned to ride out and see you. Then Nate told me you went missing." Running a hand through his hair, he looked away. "I almost went crazy with worry. When we found you, well...I wanted to kill every last one of them. Then, when it was over and you were safe..." His voice trailed off, remembering Jinny wrapped in Deke's arms. Lifting his eyes, he forced himself to look at her. "Well, I couldn't stay."

Capturing her lower lip between her teeth, she nodded. She wanted to go to him, throw her arms around his neck and never let go. Instead, Jinny found herself rooted in place. If he made the slightest move toward her, gave her any indication he still had feelings for her...but he didn't.

Turning away, she took a breath, wishing this wasn't so hard. "Did your trip east go well?"

She could hear him move closer, stopping right behind her. "My life isn't the same anymore, Jinny. So much has changed. It's good you've met someone else."

Whipping around, she fisted her hands at her sides, glaring at him. "Are you saying that because *you've* met someone else? Is that why I never heard from you, or that you were coming back?"

He raised his hands as she took a step closer. "Jinny..."

"Nae, Sam Covington. You'll not be dismissing me as if I were a child. Did you meet someone, fall in love...marry?" She choked the last word out, refusing to give in to the tears beginning to pool.

His eyes widened as he shook his head. "No. It's just there are things in my life you don't know about. I have responsibilities now, others to consider."

Jinny rubbed a finger against the ache in her temple. "Ach. You're making no sense. If you aren't married, then who do you have to consider? Tell me, Sam. I want to understand." Taking a step closer, she cupped his cheek with her hand. Leaning up, she kissed his chin, watching as he lowered his head, his lips hovering above hers. The front door banging open had them jumping apart.

"Sam?" Taking a breath, Sam turned to see Bram walking toward him, unaware of what he'd broken up. "We came to check on Nate. Quinn and Caleb were just walking outside, told us Aunt Kyla doesn't want us to bother him."

"He's in a bad way." Sam looked at Jinny, knowing she'd hear the story from Brodie.

"If anyone can help him, it's Aunt Kyla. This may not be the time, but Brodie mentioned you were looking for a horse. Is Pirate not working out for you?"

"You trained Pirate right, Bram. He's better than any horse I've ever owned."

"Well, then, that is good news. We've a few to show you, depending on what you're looking for. Is this one also for you?"

Sam shook his head. "No, not for me." This wasn't the time to talk about his reason for needing another horse. There were things he had to explain to Jinny first.

"I heard you brought your father back with you. Would it be for him?"

Sam felt Jinny stiffen beside him. "Uh...no. Not for my father."

Bram cocked his head to the side, scratching his chin. "Well, lad, who is the horse for then?"

Turning, Sam's gaze settled on Jinny. "It's for my son."

"His son. Sam has a son and he never told me." Jinny paced back and forth in the parlor, her arms flailing about as her anger grew. She stopped, glaring at Brodie, who'd decided to stay at the ranch overnight.

Right after he made the announcement, Sam had walked outside with Bram, as if the news of him having a son would have no impact on her. He didn't return to the house before riding back to town, leaving her confused and fuming.

"*No one* told me."

Brodie flinched under her scolding. "Lass, it wasn't my story to tell." He glanced at the stairs, thankful their parents had gone to bed long ago.

"So everyone stayed silent...for a week. I'm the only one who didn't know?" She glanced around the room, her gaze moving from Fletcher to Bram to Emma. Besides Brodie, they were the only ones who'd stayed. All three shook their heads.

"Almost no one knows about Robbie, Jinny." Brodie rubbed the back of his neck, trying to keep his patience. "August Fielder found them a house close to his. They'd barely moved in when you were taken. Since then, he took back his badge and worked on getting his family settled."

"His family?"

"Aye. His father and son." Standing, Brodie walked to a table. Picking up a decanter, he poured a measure of whiskey, tossing it back.

"What about his wife and mother?"

"His mother drowned when the steamer sank. As for the rest, you'll be needing to ask him." He set the glass down, then crossed his arms. "And what of the Arrington lad? Are you saying you've no feelings for him?"

Emma jumped up, coming to Jinny's aid. "Deke is her *friend*, Brodie."

His face softened at the belligerent look on her face. "She can answer for herself, lass."

Straightening her back, Jinny stuck out her chin. "Emma is right. Deke and I are friends, nothing more."

Brodie chuckled, his eyes crinkling at the corners.

Jinny walked up to him, poking her brother in the chest. "And why are you so amused?"

He glanced at Emma, then back at his sister. "Quinn and Emma were *friends*, too."

Waving her hands in the air, his sister turned, stomping away. "That was different."

"Jinny's right. It was *quite* different." Emma slipped her arm through Jinny's. "I believe Deke would agree that they're just friends. Besides, I think he may have his sights on someone else."

Stepping away, Jinny's eyes widened. "Who?"

"Since it's only a guess, I'm not saying."

"A MacLaren?" Brodie tilted his head.

"Well, yes. But, as I said, it's a guess. The important part is Deke doesn't feel the same way about Jinny as Sam does."

"Ach, Emma. Haven't you heard anything?" Jinny sat down, covering her face with her hands.

"Sam told me he has others to think of. He said it was good I'd met someone else." The room fell into a strained silence.

"It's late and I'm going to bed." Fletcher stood, moving in front of his sister. "Jinny, lass, you need to talk to Sam."

Bram stood up, too. "I've an early day tomorrow, so I'll be heading home. Fletch is right, lass. Sam is a reasonable and honest lad. You won't learn the answers to your questions until you ask." He turned to Emma. "I'll walk you to the house."

Kissing Jinny on the cheek, Emma followed Bram outside and up the path.

Waiting until they left, Brodie knelt in front of his sister, taking her hands in his. "Sam has been forced to deal with a great deal the last few months. I know how much his leaving hurt you, Jinny, and for that, I cannot make excuses for the lad. As Fletch and Bram said, you need to find room in your heart to talk to him."

She shook her head, a lone tear rolling down her cheek. "I don't understand about his family or why he never told me about his son."

"And that's why you must talk to him."

"What if he no longer wants me?"

Brodie offered her a grim smile. "It's a risk, lass. One you'll be needing to take. Whatever happens, you'll always have your family. You'll never be alone with your troubles."

She sniffled, her lips twisting into a wry grin. "Aye. No one is ever alone with this brood."

Standing, he helped her up. "Ah, now that's my Jinny. Tomorrow is the trial. We'll get through that, then worry about the rest afterward."

Settling his arm over her shoulders, he walked with her to their bedrooms. Stopping at her door, he kissed her check. "I promise you, lass. Everything will be all right."

Chapter Twenty-One

Conviction

"You did well, lass." Fletcher sat next to Jinny, squeezing her hand. Brodie sat on the other side, his face a mask. Their parents sat in chairs behind them, pride showing on their faces at Jinny's testimony. Several of the MacLarens who rescued Jinny testified before her, all doing well.

Jinny leaned toward Brodie. "Do you think Sarah or the others will have to testify?"

August Fielder had surprised all of them when they arrived that morning. He wanted all the women who'd been held hostage at Maloney's to be prepared to be a witness. She glanced at her cousins, hoping what she and Deke told the jury would be enough to find the three men guilty.

He turned to look behind him. Colin had his arm around Sarah. Quinn and Emma sat next to them, holding hands. Brodie's wife, Maggie, sat with Geneen, and the row behind them was filled with MacLarens. At the back, Sam leaned against a wall, his arms crossed, eyes locked on Jinny.

"I don't know, lass. Sometimes..." Brodie's voice trailed off when August Fielder stood.

"Your Honor, I believe the case against these three is quite solid. I have several more witnesses, women who were held hostage in the general store. If you'd like—"

The judge's gavel pounded on the table. "I believe the jury's heard enough, Mr. Fielder." He looked at the defense attorney, who shrugged, then the judge turned his attention to the twelve men sitting to one side of the room. "Would you like to listen to more testimony?"

They shook their heads, all turning to look at the foreman, who stood. "Nope. I think we're just fine, Judge."

"All right. You men head out back and talk this through. Tell Deputy Perkins when you've made a decision and he'll bring you back inside."

Jack stood next to the jury, his newly polished badge pinned against his dark shirt. "Come along with me, gentlemen." He ushered them outside while Sam and Brodie escorted the prisoners back to jail.

Jinny let out a deep sigh when the men disappeared outside, then turned to Fletcher. "I'm so glad the others didn't need to go up there." She stood when August walked up to them.

"You did wonderful, my dear, as did Mr. Arrington and the others."

"Thank you, Mr. Fielder. Do you think they'll be found guilty?"

He chuckled, glancing over his shoulder in the direction where the jury now discussed the fate of the prisoners. "Young lady, I'd be shocked if they weren't. Within a few days, those miscreants will be on their way to San Quentin. Well, I believe I'll go outside for some fresh air. This shouldn't take long."

"Come on, lass. It's best if we do the same."

Following Fletcher, she joined the other women, who were already deep in an animated discussion about the trial and what the jury would say. Jinny found herself distracted, her gaze moving down the street to the jail, hoping for another glimpse of Sam.

She'd been awake most of the night, thoughts of the trial warring with images of Sam for a place in her head. After several hours of tossing and turning, Jinny came to the conclusion the men were right. She needed to talk with Sam, wanting to do it soon.

"There's your man now, Jinny." Emma nudged her, nodding toward the jail. "He and Brodie just walked out. Hmmm. It looks like they're staying close by to watch the prisoners."

Jinny's shoulders sagged. She'd hoped to have a few minutes with Sam, enough to at least plan a time they could talk.

"The jury's made a decision."

Her attention turned to the steps behind her. A man shouted the announcement several times before going back inside. Stomach clenching, she moved with the crowd, returning to her place in front, praying for a guilty verdict.

Circle M Ranch

At least one of her prayers had been answered. The jury found the three men guilty, and the judge handed down long sentences at San Quentin. Monday, Jack would drive the wagon holding the prisoners while four guards rode alongside. It would leave Brodie and Sam as the only two lawmen in town for a few days, but it couldn't be helped. They needed to get Eplett and his men out of Conviction.

Deke begged off riding to the ranch on Saturday, telling her his uncle needed him in the saddlery. Business had picked up, making it more difficult to get days off. It had been a relief. She needed time to decide what to do about Sam, figure out if she loved him enough to put her heart out there for him to accept or reject.

The women gathered at Kyla's house to prepare Sunday supper. She'd heard Heather would be joining them. Jinny suspected the uncles had made a decision about the Evanston ranch, a topic sure to make the meal an exciting one.

"Did you see Sam at church this morning, Jinny?" Kyla set potatoes on the counter, picking up a small knife.

She and Quinn's mother, Audrey, had stayed behind to look after Nate. It had been three days since Sam had gotten him away from Chinatown. The older women took turns sitting with him, always two at a time, doing their best to help as his body trembled. At times, his anxiety and agitation would be so great, he'd jump out of bed and pace, mumbling to himself. Cold sweats would cause him to shake uncontrollably, and nausea kept him doubled over much of the time. The men made certain at least one of them stayed behind each day, which usually meant Fletcher, Bram, or Sean since they handled the horse breeding program centered around the barns and pastures of Circle M.

"Nae. He must have decided to stay home with his son and father."

By now, everyone in the family, and most of the townsfolk, knew of Sam's son, although few had seen him or Sam's father.

Maggie set down a basket of vegetables, turning to face Jinny. "Brodie told me Sam spends all his free time with his family."

Jinny's heart sank at the mention of *family*. She had so many questions with no opportunity to ask.

Lorna looked at Maggie. "Does anyone know anything about the boy's mother?"

She shrugged. "If Brodie knows, he's said nothing to me. I'm certain she isn't in Conviction."

The women continued to speak as if Jinny didn't stand a few feet away, her heart twisting. She wished they'd move on to another topic, but didn't interrupt, knowing there'd be no answers until she confronted Sam.

"Will Deke be joining us for supper, Jinny?"

At the mention of her name, she looked at Sarah, who bounced Grant on her lap.

"Nae. He's staying in town today."

"He did a good job at the trial, as did everyone." Kyla's hands stilled at the sound of something crashing down the hall. "Ach. Nate must be thrashing around again. I'll be back in a bit."

"I'll go with you." Geneen started to follow before Kyla turned, halting her progress.

"You know the lad doesn't want you to see him like this, lass. Once he's through the worst, I'm certain he'll feel differently."

"But I could—"

"Nae, lass." Kyla laid a hand on Geneen's arm. "You've got to respect the lad's wishes."

"I'll go with you, Kyla." Lorna clasped Geneen's shoulder. "Why don't you return to the kitchen, lass? The others can use your help."

Jinny walked up, gripping her arm to pull her toward the kitchen. "There's no sense arguing when Aunt Kyla has made up her mind. We'll work together. You can tell me about the new horse Bram is training for you."

Conviction

"Are you ready to visit the horses, Robbie?" Thomas sat on one side of the buggy seat, Sam on the other, Robbie in the middle. They were a mile from Circle M and Robbie had yet to sit still.

The boy's face lit up. "Yes, Grandfather. Papa says if I'm very good, I might be able to sit on one today."

"Only if Mr. MacLaren says it is all right, son." Sam thought of Bram, already knowing he'd be fine letting Robbie sit atop a horse—as long as one of them held the reins.

As they approached the entrance to the ranch, Sam inhaled a deep breath, willing away the nervous energy and trepidation of seeing

Jinny. He'd wanted to stay and talk with Jinny the night they'd brought Nate to the ranch. After looking at horses with Bram, the hour had grown late, forcing him to return home. Sam had promised Robbie he'd read him a story and tuck him into bed—a promise he meant to keep.

"Look, Papa." Robbie bounced in his seat, pointing to a corral with several horses.

Thomas leaned forward, adjusting his spectacles. "Are those some of the ones Bram is considering for Robbie?"

"I believe so. The one prancing about at the closest fence, sorrel color with the white blaze and white stockings, is one I looked at the other night. I'm not sure about the others." Pulling the lines, he drew the buggy to a stop near the fence, waving to Bram.

Helping Robbie down, Sam grabbed his hand. "Now, you must be quiet and not jump around. Can you do that?"

His head bobbed up and down, his eyes bright with excitement. "Yes, Papa."

"Good afternoon, Sam." Bram shook his outstretched hand.

"Bram, this is my father, Thomas Covington, and my son, Robbie."

After shaking Thomas's hand, Bram bent low to shake Robbie's. "Well, lad, you're much taller than I thought you'd be."

"I am?"

"Aye." Bram raised his hand a short distance above the ground. "I expected you to be about this tall." His hand came to Robbie's shoulders.

Giggling, he turned to his father. "I'm much taller than that."

Grinning, Sam nodded. "Much taller."

Straightening, Bram looked over his shoulder at the last house up the path. "The women are preparing supper up at Colin's. Would you like to look at the horses now or wait until after we eat?"

Robbie tugged on Sam's hand, his face turned up. "Can we look at horses now, Papa?"

He wanted to find Jinny, introduce her to his family, and try to explain all that had happened since he'd left. Seeing the hopeful look on Robbie's face, he decided talking with her would have to wait.

"Now would be fine, Bram."

Looking over Bram's shoulder, he spotted several MacLaren men walking their way, no doubt curious about the young boy and older man with him. They were a protective lot, probably more so knowing his feelings for Jinny. Sam braced himself, unsure of what to expect.

Brodie stuck out his hand first. "Glad you could make it today, Sam." He shook Thomas's hand, then greeted Robbie.

Colin, Quinn, Fletcher, Blaine, Sean, and Caleb walked up, waiting while Sam introduced them.

Sean knelt beside Robbie. "I hear you'd be looking for a horse, lad."

Robbie glanced at the other men, his gaze cautious. "Yes, sir."

"The lads here learned to ride when they were about your age. You're about seven, right?"

Giggling, Robbie shook his head. "I'm almost five."

"Five is it. Well, that's a fine age to learn. Why don't you, Bram, and I take a look at the horses while the others talk to your father?"

Gripping Sam's hand a little tighter, Robbie looked up.

"It's all right, son. Go ahead with Sean and Bram. I'll be over in a few minutes."

"Would you like me to go with them, Sam?" Thomas asked as he watched his grandson and the two men walk away.

"No, Father. I think the gentlemen have something to say and you might as well hear it." Sam crossed his arms, ready for the first of what he knew would be many questions.

Fletcher spoke first. A year younger than his sister, Jinny, he didn't have the same reservations about asking questions.

"Where's Robbie's ma?"

Sam appreciated how Fletcher got straight to the point. "She died not long after his birth."

"Why didn't you bring him with you when you first came to Conviction?"

His gaze didn't move from Fletcher's. "First, I was on assignment for Allan Pinkerton. Second, I didn't know about Robbie until a few months ago."

"You didn't marry the lass?" Quinn asked, his features unreadable.

"No." Sam glanced at Robbie, who seemed completely content with Bram and Sean. "It's complicated, but I assure you, I'll explain it all to Jinny."

Brodie took a step forward. "Now that you're back, what are your intentions toward her?"

"I'm in love with her, Brodie, but you already know that. I'd planned to ask her to marry me before I received word about Robbie and had to leave."

"And now?"

Sam stared at his friend and boss. "My situation has changed. I can't expect a young woman as wonderful as Jinny to accept what is now my life."

Fletcher crossed his arms, glaring at him. "You'll not be asking her to marry you?"

Pushing away the ball of dread in his gut, Sam shook his head. "Why would she want to be burdened with a son who isn't her own and have to move from the ranch she loves to live in town? It's too much to ask of her."

Brodie stepped forward, taking Sam's arm and pulling him several feet away. "Excuse us a moment, Mr. Covington, while we have a few private words with your son."

Thomas did his best not to grin. "Take as long as you need, gentlemen."

Escorting Sam about twenty feet away, the MacLarens formed a circle around him. Some crossed their arms and braced their feet. Others let their arms hang slack at their sides. All wore fierce expressions.

Glancing behind them, toward the porch, Sam saw Jinny with her hands on the rail, watching. Their eyes met and held for an instant before she spun around, heading back inside the house.

"You'll be asking my sister to marry you." Fletcher spat the words out.

"But—"

Quinn didn't let Sam finish. "Do you still love her?"

"Of course I do, Quinn. It isn't a question of love."

"Do you want her for your wife?" Colin asked, his gaze narrowing.

Sam nodded. "I've wanted her from the first moment we met."

"Do you think the lass no longer has feelings for you?" Blaine had stayed quiet to this point.

Sam shook his head. "I can't speak for Jinny."

Brodie shifted his weight from one leg to the other, his mouth forming a thin line. "The lass is in love with you, Sam. It'd be a grand idea if you reconsidered your position. Jinny's a grown woman with a big heart—that you broke. It's past time you made it right with her."

His jaw going slack, Sam turned in a circle, looking at each man. "After what you know, you still want me to ask her?" He'd felt certain the MacLaren men would prefer she marry Deke Arrington, or one of the other young men in town who didn't have the responsibilities of a son and elderly father.

The question brought various reactions from chuckles to heads nodding before they all broke into laughter. Sam had no idea what was happening, even as the tension in his shoulders began to relax.

Fletcher stepped forward, clasping Sam's shoulder. "Oh, you'll be asking her to marry. First, you'll be courting her for as long as needed to set things right with her."

"Courting..." Sam breathed out. He hadn't expected to have them support him, and he sure as heck hadn't expected they'd want him to court her.

Brodie nodded. "Aye. Have you never courted a woman before?"

Sam looked at Colin, then Quinn, and finally Brodie. "Did any of you *court* your wives?" He already knew the answer, feeling smug satisfaction as their smiles faded.

Brodie tugged on his earlobe, shaking his head. "It doesn't matter how we came to marry the lasses, Sam. You'll be courting Jinny, and there'll be no excuses. She deserves that much from you."

Sam couldn't argue. Jinny deserved much more than suppers, walks, and flowers. She deserved a man without the burdens he already carried. Looking at the MacLaren men, the way their gazes locked on him, he knew there wasn't a chance he'd walk away without her.

"All right. If Jinny's willing, I'll court her." He turned in a circle again, looking at each face, giving them notice. "Be warned. This won't be a long courtship. Jinny will be my wife sooner rather than later."

Chapter Twenty-Two

The sight of Sam at the ranch, surrounded by her family, sent Jinny's mind spinning. She hadn't expected to see him for a few more days when she went into town for supplies—where she meant to hunt him down and force him to explain himself. Sam's arrival with his son and father, plus Kyla's insistence on changing their normal seating arrangement, stripped away any time Jinny had to prepare.

Lightheaded and nervous, she sat next to him during supper. On the other side of Sam sat Robbie, Thomas next to him.

There'd been no time for Sam to do more than make brief introductions. It disappointed Jinny she had no time to talk with him, holding out hope he'd be open to speaking with her before they left to go back to town.

From his spot at the end of the table, Ewan looked at Robbie. "How old are you, lad?"

Sam saw his son stiffen. Two MacLarens were an imposing presence. An entire table of them seemed overwhelming to a small boy.

"It's all right, Robbie. Answer Mr. MacLaren."

Robbie glanced down the table at Ewan. "I'm almost five."

"Are you now? You see the young laddie at the other table?" Ewan looked at the table where the youngest MacLarens sat. "Davina is five and Bryce is six. Aiden is three, maybe a mite young for an older lad such as you. They were all born in America after we came from Scotland. Would you like to sit with them?"

Robbie looked at Sam. "Can I sit with them, Papa?"

The question surprised and pleased Sam. "Of course, son."

Kyla and Lorna moved chairs, settling Robbie between Sean's younger sister, Davina, and Quinn's youngest brother, Bryce. Within seconds, they were all talking and laughing.

Several minutes later, Ewan looked at Caleb, who sat across the table from Heather. Clearing his throat, he got everyone's attention.

"We've made a decision about the Evanston ranch. We've already spoken with several of you about this, so there should be no cause for argument. Caleb will become the foreman and Blaine will move with him. Heather has agreed to come back to Circle M to work with Colin and Quinn."

All eyes focused on Heather, but if she felt any distress, she covered it well. Caleb's face gave nothing away, not even the joy Jinny thought he must be feeling.

Heather was the first to speak. "Congratulations, Caleb. It's well deserved." The family couldn't have been more surprised if a tornado had blown through the ranch.

Seconds later, everyone joined her in congratulating him, letting Caleb know he had their support in whatever he needed. After a few minutes, conversation moved on to other topics, the Evanston ranch forgotten—at least for the time being.

Jinny leaned back in her chair, watching the children. "He's a beautiful lad, Sam. You must be proud of him."

Sam's heart squeezed at her kind words, as well as the hesitancy in her voice. After talking to the MacLaren men, he realized how much of a fool he'd been to keep the fact he had a son from her. It had been intentional at first, not knowing if he would be returning to Conviction. Once the decision had been made, all his efforts went into packing, booking passage, and getting letters off to Brodie and August Fielder, telling them of his return. Although his excuse now sounded weak, Sam knew why he hadn't written Jinny. Fear.

He'd never been a weak man, always trying his best to make the right decisions and do all he could to live honorably. Sam had failed Jinny on both counts, hurting her by the choices he'd made.

"Yes. I'm quite proud of him." Reaching over, he covered the hand in her lap with his, thankful the others at the table paid them no attention. To his surprise, she didn't pull away, placing her other hand on top of his. "We need to talk, Jinny. There's much I need to tell you."

"I'd like that, Sam."

The tension in his body relaxed, his relief at her response more than he deserved. "After supper, we'll take a walk. My father will be happy to watch Robbie."

Her eyes sparkled. "I doubt you'll have any trouble finding someone to watch over him." She nodded toward the table of children, then looked at Sarah, Geneen, and Emma. "Any of the lasses would be honored to take care of him while we talk."

The rest of the meal passed in a blur, each hurrying to finish, both accepting small portions of dessert. When finished, Sam leaned over to his father.

"I'd like to take Jinny for a walk. Are you all right watching Robbie?"

"Of course, son. Take as long as you need to convince that girl to give you another chance."

Nodding, Sam stood, pulling out Jinny's chair. "If you'll excuse us, Jinny and I will be outside."

Leaving the table, Sam placed a hand on the small of her back, missing the smiles of approval from those watching.

Sam told her everything, starting with when he'd met Vera, how he thought they'd been in love, then learning of her betrayal. Believing she supported the Northern cause as much as him, he'd unknowingly provided her with small details of one of his assignments. To anyone else, the information would've seemed worthless. As he learned later, Vera wasn't anyone else.

She was a spy for the South and had been before they met. Combining her information with what had been obtained by others, the Confederate Army planned an attack on Union forces. The attack could've been devastating if Sam hadn't followed her one night, learning of her betrayal. Reporting what he'd heard, Sam left Vera a brief note, then walked away, leaving her behind when Allan Pinkerton offered him another assignment. He never heard from her again.

Jinny had kept silent, the revulsion of Vera's actions clear on Sam's face. "Surely she must have tried to reach you when she learned she was pregnant."

Sam stood outside the corral, leaning his arms on the top rail, staring out at the horses. "According to her father, she refused to try and find me. Vera didn't want me in Robbie's life, even though she included my name on the birth certificate. After she died, they respected her wishes until their health began to fade. Mrs. Foster already suffered from lapses of memory, and Mr. Foster feared Robbie would be sent to a home if anything happened to him."

Jinny stood on the lowest rail next to Sam, resting her arms next to his. "They did what was right, Sam. You never should've been cut from Robbie's life." Leaning to her side, she rested her head on his shoulder, lifting her gaze to his. "And you made a wise decision bringing him here."

Turning, he placed his hands on her waist, settling her on the ground. With no intention of letting go, he stared down into her eyes. "Do you really think this was right?"

"Aye, I do." Jinny saw his head lower, his lips a breath away from hers. Heart pounding, she willed Sam to kiss her.

Desire pulsing through him, Sam lowered his head, capturing her mouth with his. It wasn't as tentative as their first kiss had been so many months ago. This one spoke of a man claiming what he wanted, letting her know she would belong to him.

His hands moved up her back, then down, settling on her hips, drawing her to him. The kiss deepened, waves of passion rushing through him as raw need caused his body to tighten. Breaking away, his lips trailed kisses across her cheek, along her jaw, and down the slender column of her neck.

"Ah, Jinny. I've dreamed of this."

Moaning, she tightened her grip on his shoulders. "So have I."

A loud cough from behind them had Sam pulling away, turning so his body shielded her.

Looking around him, Jinny spotted Brodie, Fletcher, Bram, and Blaine on the porch, staring in their direction. Letting out a sigh, she stepped around Sam.

"We've an audience." Resting her hands on her hips, she glared back at her brothers and cousins. "They've no business watching us."

Chuckling, Sam settled an arm around her waist. Placing a kiss on her temple, he turned her to face him.

"It's best they came out."

"Why? We did nothing wrong." She glanced over her shoulder, seeing the four still standing by the rail. "Ach. It seems the lads won't leave us alone."

Needing to draw her attention back to him, Sam whispered in her ear. "Jinny..."

"Hmmm?" She snuggled closer, ignoring her family.

"I want to marry you."

The statement caught her unaware. Eyes widening, a radiant smile broke out across her face.

"Yes, Sam. I love you. Of course I'll marry you."

Breathing a sigh of relief, he brushed a quick kiss across her lips.

"There's just one problem."

Her brows furrowed. "A problem?"

"Your family insists we court before you agree to marry me."

Storming into the house, Jinny pushed the door to the den open, seeing her father, uncle, and the rest of the MacLaren men enjoying whiskey. She glared at her father.

"What do you mean by insisting Sam court me before allowing us to marry?"

Ewan's face stilled, his brows drawing together. "I've no idea what you're talking about, lass."

Slowly, she turned to Brodie. "It was you, wasn't it?"

Swallowing the whiskey in his mouth, he nodded. "It's for your own good, Jinny." He glanced at Sam, who casually rested a shoulder against the door frame, arms crossed, eyes glinting in amusement. Getting no support from him, Brodie looked back at Jinny. "He has a son and his father living with him. You need time to be sure it's what you want. Make certain you know your own mind."

Eyes shooting sparks, she placed her hands on her brother's chest and pushed. "So you're telling me it's *only* the MacLaren *men* who know their own mind?" Shoving him again, her irritation grew. "You're saying MacLaren *women* are too weak to know what they want?"

Holding up his hands, Brodie stepped away, trying to move out of range of Jinny's rage. "Sam agreed to the courting."

"Oh, did he now?" She glanced over her shoulder at Sam, seeing amusement on his face, before turning back to Brodie. "And what if I don't agree?"

Fletcher stepped forward, keeping a slight distance between himself and Jinny. "Lass, you've not seen Sam in months. His life has changed. What if he's not who you want?"

Covering her face with her hands, she turned toward Ewan. "Da, do you agree with this?"

Ewan shook his head. "Sorry, lass. You'll have to explain what your brothers did."

"They made Sam agree that we must court before committing to marriage. All of you know I love him and he loves me. There's no reason to court." Stalking to a chair, she dropped into it, uncaring if her actions weren't that of a lady. "Besides, I've already agreed to marry him."

Brodie and Fletcher glared at Sam. "We had an agreement," Brodie said, unwilling to let it go. "Courting is important before marriage." He looked at Jinny.

"Ach. And tell me, Brodie, how much *courting* did you and Maggie do before you married?"

Brodie had the good sense to look away.

"And you, Quinn. How long did you court Emma before she agreed to marry you?"

Quinn stood from where he'd been sitting on the sofa. "Now, lass, courting is different for each couple." He backed up when Jinny stood and walked toward him.

Taking a deep breath, she turned to look at Sam, the warm expression on his face calming her. Remembering their passionate decision to marry, she swung back around.

"Aye, you're right, Quinn. And it means something else to Sam and me. Now, if you'll excuse us, we're going for ride." She walked up to

Sam, slipping her arm through his, then looked at the others, a smirk on her face. "To plan our wedding."

Epilogue

Two weeks later...

"You're a bonny bride, Jinny. It's still hard to believe your mother and aunts put this wedding together in such a short time." Emma stood beside her, holding a glass of punch, looking out at the guests to see Sam and Quinn talking. She and Jinny had been best friends for years. Now they were both married to men they loved.

"Sam refused to wait."

Emma's brow shot up. "Sam?"

Jinny felt her face heat, a grin lifting the corners of her mouth. "Aye, and I felt the same. If it had been possible, I'd have become Mrs. Covington the day after he proposed."

Maggie and Sarah joined them, each looking beautiful in new dresses.

"So it's done." Sarah held up her glass of punch, offering an informal toast. "I'm so happy for you and Sam."

Touching her glass to Sarah's, Jinny took a sip, then looked around. "Where's Geneen?"

Sarah nodded toward the porch where her sister sat alone, rocking back and forth, a plate of untouched food on her lap.

"How's the lass doing?"

Sarah shook her head. "Not good, Jinny. Nate rode out a week ago, leaving no word for her. He'd spoken to Kyla and your pa the night before, thanking them for all the family had done and vowing to repay us. None of that matters to Geneen. She wants the lad well. I'm afraid she loves him."

Jinny settled a hand on Sarah's arm. "Of course she does. The lass hasn't hidden her feelings about Nate. How was he when he left?"

"Kyla says the opium is out of his body, but fears it may take a long time to clear from his mind. Doc Tilden told her it can take years to get over the craving for the drug." Sarah let out a deep sigh. "I believe that's the reason Nate left town."

Emma's brows rose. "He quit his job?"

Maggie nodded. "According to Brodie, he packed his few belongings and rode out the instant Jack returned to town after delivering the prisoners to San Quentin."

Jinny shook her head. "Sam said nothing to me about Nate leaving."

"He didn't want to spoil your wedding," Maggie said. "Sam wanted this to be a special day for you. We all did. Besides, there's nothing you could've done. Nate needs time to clear his head of the opium and decide what he wants."

Sarah huffed out a breath, drawing their attention. "I like Nate, and I'm glad he's doing his best to get better."

"But?" Maggie asked, raising a brow.

"I think the way he left, without saying a word to Geneen, was cowardly. She didn't expect much, but a simple goodbye may have eased her pain."

"Does Brodie think he's coming back?" Emma looked at Geneen again, who continued to rock back and forth in the chair.

Shaking her head, Maggie sighed. "He doesn't know, but he is looking for a deputy to replace him." Glancing up, she smiled as Brodie walked toward them. Leaning down, he kissed her cheek, then turned to Jinny.

"I know this is your day, lass, but Maggie and I would like to make an announcement."

"An announcement?" Jinny's brows furrowed for an instant before his meaning became clear. Her attention swung to Maggie. "Oh, lass. Is it what I hope?"

Maggie settled a protective hand on her stomach and nodded.

Grabbing Maggie's hand, Brodie walked her to the porch steps. Settling an arm over her shoulders, he faced family and guests.

"If I can have your attention for a moment, I have an announcement." Everyone quieted. "I'm proud to share our news." A broad smile split his face. "Maggie is expecting a wee bairn."

As everyone cheered, offering toasts and congratulations, Sam made his way to Jinny, slipping an arm around her waist.

"That will be us one day, love." Kissing her lips, he smiled down at her.

"And how many lads and lasses would you be thinking of having, Mr. Covington?"

He thought a moment. "Two or three would be good."

"Ach. Two or three is only a start."

Chuckling, he pulled her tighter to his side. "Then tell me, Mrs. Covington. How many children are you thinking of?"

Her eyes twinkled in delight as she looked up at him. "At least a dozen...maybe more."

Sam's jaw dropped, the number making his head spin. Seeing the amusement on her face, he broke into a deep, rich laugh before lifting her into the air, spinning her around.

"Ah, Mrs. Covington. I can see we are going to have a grand time."

Thank you for taking the time to read Sam's Legacy. If you enjoyed it, please consider telling your friends or posting a short review. Word of mouth is an author's best friend and much appreciated.

Watch for the other books in the MacLarens of Boundary Mountain Historical Western Romance Series.

Please join my reader's group to be notified of my New Releases at: http://www.shirleendavies.com/contact-me.html

I care about quality, so if you find something in error, please contact me via email at shirleen@shirleendavies.com

About the Author

Shirleen Davies writes romance—historical, contemporary, and romantic suspense. She grew up in Southern California, attended Oregon State University, and has degrees from San Diego State University and the University of Maryland. During the day she provides consulting services to small and mid-sized businesses. But her real passion is writing emotionally charged stories of flawed people who find redemption through love and acceptance. She now lives with her husband in a beautiful town in northern Arizona.

I love to hear from my readers.

Send me an email: shirleen@shirleendavies.com
Visit my Website: www.shirleendavies.com
Sign up to be notified of New Releases:
www.shirleendavies.com
Check out all of my Books:
http://www.shirleendavies.com/books.html
Comment on my Blog:
http://www.shirleendavies.com/blog.html
Follow me on Amazon:
http://www.amazon.com/author/shirleendavies
Follow my on BookBub:
https://www.bookbub.com/authors/shirleen-davies

Other ways to connect with me:

Facebook Author Page:
http://www.facebook.com/shirleendaviesauthor
Twitter: www.twitter.com/shirleendavies
Pinterest: http://pinterest.com/shirleendavies
Instagram:
https://www.instagram.com/shirleendavies_author/

Books by Shirleen Davies

Historical Western Romance Series

MacLarens of Fire Mountain

Tougher than the Rest, Book One
Faster than the Rest, Book Two
Harder than the Rest, Book Three
Stronger than the Rest, Book Four
Deadlier than the Rest, Book Five
Wilder than the Rest, Book Six

Redemption Mountain

Redemption's Edge, Book One
Wildfire Creek, Book Two
Sunrise Ridge, Book Three
Dixie Moon, Book Four
Survivor Pass, Book Five
Promise Trail, Book Six
Deep River, Book Seven
Courage Canyon, Book Eight, Releasing 2017

MacLarens of Boundary Mountain

Colin's Quest, Book One,

Brodie's Gamble, Book Two
Quinn's Honor, Book Three
Sam's Legacy, Book Four, Releasing 2017

Contemporary Romance Series

MacLarens of Fire Mountain

Second Summer, Book One
Hard Landing, Book Two
One More Day, Book Three
All Your Nights, Book Four
Always Love You, Book Five
Hearts Don't Lie, Book Six
No Getting Over You, Book Seven
'Til the Sun Comes Up, Book Eight
Foolish Heart, Book Nine, Releasing 2017

Peregrine Bay

Reclaiming Love, Book One
Our Kind of Love, Book Two

Burnt River

Shane's Burden, Book One by Peggy Henderson
Thorn's Journey, Book Two by Shirleen Davies

Find all of my books at:
http://www.shirleendavies.com/books.html

Tougher than the Rest – Book One
MacLarens of Fire Mountain Historical Western Romance Series

"A passionate, fast-paced story set in the untamed western frontier by an exciting new voice in historical romance."

Niall MacLaren is the oldest of four brothers, and the undisputed leader of the family. A widower, and single father, his focus is on building the MacLaren ranch into the largest and most successful in northern Arizona. He is serious about two things—his responsibility to the family and his future marriage to the wealthy, well-connected widow who will secure his place in the territory's destiny.

Katherine is determined to live the life she's dreamed about. With a job waiting for her in the growing town of Los Angeles, California, the young teacher from Philadelphia begins a journey across the United States with only a couple of trunks and her spinster companion. Life is perfect for this adventurous, beautiful young woman, until an accident throws her into the arms of the one man who can destroy it all.

Fighting his growing attraction and strong desire for the beautiful stranger, Niall is more determined than ever to push emotions aside to focus on his goals of wealth and political gain. But looking into the clear, blue eyes of the woman who could ruin everything, Niall discovers he will have to harden his heart and be tougher than he's ever been in his life...Tougher than the Rest.

Faster than the Rest – Book Two
MacLarens of Fire Mountain Historical Western Romance Series

"Headstrong, brash, confident, and complex, the MacLarens of Fire Mountain will captivate you with strong characters set in the wild and rugged western frontier."

Handsome, ruthless, young U.S. Marshal Jamie MacLaren had lost everything—his parents, his family connections, and his childhood sweetheart—but now he's back in Fire Mountain and ready for another chance. Just as he successfully reconnects with his family and starts to rebuild his life, he gets the unexpected and unwanted assignment of rescuing the woman who broke his heart.

Beautiful, wealthy Victoria Wicklin chose money and power over love, but is now fighting for her life—or is she? Who has she become in the seven years since she left Fire Mountain to take up her life in San Francisco? Is she really as innocent as she says?

Marshal MacLaren struggles to learn the truth and do his job, but the past and present lead him in different directions as his heart and brain wage battle. Is Victoria a victim or a villain? Is life offering him another chance, or just another heartbreak?

As Jamie and Victoria struggle to uncover past secrets and come to grips with their shared passion, another danger arises. A life-altering danger that is out of their control and threatens to destroy any chance for a shared future.

Harder than the Rest – Book Three
MacLarens of Fire Mountain Historical Western Romance Series

"They are men you want on your side. Hard, confident, and loyal, the MacLarens of Fire Mountain will seize your attention from the first page."

Will MacLaren is a hardened, plain-speaking bounty hunter. His life centers on finding men guilty of horrendous crimes and making sure justice is done. There is no place in his world for the carefree attitude he carried years before when a tragic event destroyed his dreams.

Amanda is the daughter of a successful Colorado rancher. Determined and proud, she works hard to prove she is as capable as any man and worthy to be her father's heir. When a stranger arrives, her independent nature collides with the strong pull toward the handsome ranch hand. But is he what he seems and could his secrets endanger her as well as her family?

The last thing Will needs is to feel passion for another woman. But Amanda elicits feelings he thought were long buried. Can Will's desire for her change him? Or will the vengeance he seeks against the one man he wants to destroy—a dangerous opponent without a conscious—continue to control his life?

Stronger than the Rest – Book Four
MacLarens of Fire Mountain Historical Western Romance Series

"Smart, tough, and capable, the MacLarens protect their own no matter the odds. Set against America's rugged frontier, the stories of the men from Fire Mountain are complex, fast-paced, and a

must read for anyone who enjoys non-stop action and romance."

Drew MacLaren is focused and strong. He has achieved all of his goals except one—to return to the MacLaren ranch and build the best horse breeding program in the west. His successful career as an attorney is about to give way to his ranching roots when a bullet changes everything.

Tess Taylor is the quiet, serious daughter of a Colorado ranch family with dreams of her own. Her shy nature keeps her from developing friendships outside of her close-knit family until Drew enters her life. Their relationship grows. Then a bullet, meant for another, leaves him paralyzed and determined to distance himself from the one woman he's come to love.

Convinced he is no longer the man Tess needs, Drew focuses on regaining the use of his legs and recapturing a life he thought lost. But danger of another kind threatens those he cares about—including Tess—forcing him to rethink his future.

Can Drew overcome the barriers that stand between him, the safety of his friends and family, and a life with the woman he loves? To do it all, he has to be strong. Stronger than the Rest.

Deadlier than the Rest – Book Five
MacLarens of Fire Mountain Historical Western Romance Series

"A passionate, heartwarming story of the iconic MacLarens of Fire Mountain. This captivating historical western romance grabs your attention from the start with an engrossing story encompassing two romances set against the rugged backdrop of the burgeoning western frontier."

Connor MacLaren's search has already stolen eight years of his life. Now he is close to finding what he seeks—Meggie, his missing sister. His quest leads him to the growing city of Salt Lake and an encounter with the most captivating woman he has ever met.

Grace is the third wife of a Mormon farmer, forced into a life far different from what she'd have chosen. Her independent spirit longs for choices governed only by her own heart and mind. To achieve her dreams, she must hide behind secrets and half-truths, even as her heart pulls her towards the ruggedly handsome Connor.

Known as cool and uncompromising, Connor MacLaren lives by a few, firm rules that have served him well and kept him alive. However, danger stalks Connor, even to the front range of the beautiful Wasatch Mountains, threatening those he cares about and impacting his ability to find his sister.

Can Connor protect himself from those who seek his death? Will his eight-year search lead him to his sister while unlocking the secrets he knows are held tight within Grace, the woman who has captured his heart?

Read this heartening story of duty, honor, passion, and love in book five of the MacLarens of Fire Mountain series.

Wilder than the Rest – Book Six
MacLarens of Fire Mountain Historical Western Romance Series

"A captivating historical western romance set in the burgeoning and treacherous city of San Francisco. Go along for the ride in this gripping story that seizes your attention from the very first page."

"If you're a reader who wants to discover an entire family of characters you can fall in love with, this is the series for you." — Authors to Watch

Pierce is a rough man, but happy in his new life as a Special Agent. Tasked with defending the rights of the federal government, Pierce is a cunning gunslinger always ready to tackle the next job. That is, until he finds out that his new job involves Mollie Jamison.

Mollie can be a lot to handle. Headstrong and independent, Mollie has chosen a life of danger and intrigue guaranteed to prove her liquor-loving father wrong. She will make something of herself, and no one, not even arrogant Pierce MacLaren, will stand in her way.

A secret mission brings them together, but will their attraction to each other prove deadly in their hunt for justice? The payoff for success is high, much higher than any assignment either has taken before. But will the damage to their hearts and souls be too much to bear? Can Pierce and Mollie find a way to overcome their misgivings and work together as one?

Second Summer – Book One
MacLarens of Fire Mountain
Contemporary Romance Series

"In this passionate Contemporary Romance, author Shirleen Davies introduces her readers to the modern day MacLarens starting with Heath MacLaren, the head of the family."

The Chairman of both the MacLaren Cattle Co. and MacLaren Land Development, Heath MacLaren is a success professionally—his personal life is another matter.

Following a divorce after a long, loveless marriage, Heath spends his time with women who are beautiful and passionate, yet unable to provide what he longs for . . .

Heath has never experienced love even though he witnesses it every day between his younger brother, Jace, and wife, Caroline. He wants what they have, yet spends his time with women too young to understand what drives him and too focused on themselves to be true companions.

It's been two years since Annie's husband died, leaving her to build a new life. He was her soul

*mate and confidante. She has no desire to find a
replacement, yet longs for male friendship.*

Annie's closest friend in Fire Mountain, Caroline
MacLaren, is determined to see Annie come out
of her shell after almost two years of mourning. A
chance meeting with Heath turns into an offer to
be a part of the MacLaren Foundation Board and
an opportunity for a life outside her home
sanctuary which has also become her prison. The
platonic friendship that builds between Annie
and Heath points to a future where each may rely
on the other without the bonds a romance would
entail.

*However, without consciously seeking it, each
yearns for more . . .*

The MacLaren Development Company is
booming with Heath at the helm. His meetings at
a partner company with the young, beautiful
marketing director, who makes no secret of her
desire for him, are a temptation. But is she the
type of woman he truly wants?

Annie's acceptance of the deep, yet passionless,
friendship with Heath sustains her, lulling her to
believe it is all she needs. At least until Heath
drops a bombshell, forcing Annie to realize that

what she took for friendship is actually a deep, lasting love. One she doesn't want to lose.

Each must decide to settle—or fight for it all.

Hard Landing – Book Two
MacLarens of Fire Mountain
Contemporary Romance Series
Trey MacLaren is a confident, poised Navy pilot. He's focused, loyal, ethical, and a natural leader. He is also on his way to what he hopes will be a lasting relationship and marriage with fellow pilot, Jesse Evans.

Jesse has always been driven. Her graduation from the Naval Academy and acceptance into the pilot training program are all she thought she wanted—until she discovered love with Trey MacLaren

Trey and Jesse's lives are filled with fast flying, friends, and the demands of their military careers. Lives each has settled into with a passion. At least until the day Trey receives a letter that could change his and Jesse's lives forever.

It's been over two years since Trey has seen the woman in Pensacola. Her unexpected letter stuns him and pushes Jesse into a tailspin from which she might not pull back.

Each must make a choice. Will the choice Trey makes cause him to lose Jesse forever? Will she follow her heart or her head as she fights for a chance to save the love she's found? Will their independent decisions collide, forcing them to give up on a life together?

One More Day — Book Three
MacLarens of Fire Mountain
Contemporary Romance Series

Cameron "Cam" Sinclair is smart, driven, and dedicated, with an easygoing temperament that belies his strong will and the personal ambitions he holds close. Besides his family, his job as head of IT at the MacLaren Cattle Company and his position as a Search and Rescue volunteer are all he needs to make him happy. At least that's what he thinks until he meets, and is instantly drawn to, fellow SAR volunteer, Lainey Devlin.

Lainey is compassionate, independent, and ready to break away from her manipulative and controlling fiancé. Just as her decision is made, she's called into a major search and rescue effort, where once again, her path crosses with the intriguing, and much too handsome, Cam

Sinclair. But Lainey's plans are set. An opportunity to buy a flourishing preschool in northern Arizona is her chance to make a fresh start, and nothing, not even her fierce attraction to Cam Sinclair, will impede her plans.

As Lainey begins to settle into her new life, an unexpected danger arises —threats from an unknown assailant—someone who doesn't believe she belongs in Fire Mountain. The more Lainey begins to love her new home, the greater the danger becomes. Can she accept the help and protection Cam offers while ignoring her consuming desire for him?

Even if Lainey accepts her attraction to Cam, will he ever be able to come to terms with his own driving ambition and allow himself to consider a different life than the one he's always pictured? A life with the one woman who offers more than he'd ever hoped to find?

All Your Nights – Book Four
MacLarens of Fire Mountain
Contemporary Romance Series

"Romance, adventure, cowboys, suspense—everything you want in a contemporary western romance novel."

Kade Taylor likes living on the edge. As an undercover agent for the DEA and a former Special Ops team member, his current assignment seems tame—keep tabs on a bookish Ph.D. candidate the agency believes is connected to a ruthless drug cartel.

Brooke Sinclair is weeks away from obtaining her goal of a doctoral degree. She spends time finalizing her presentation and relaxing with another student who seems to want nothing more than her friendship. That's fine with Brooke. Her last serious relationship ended in a broken engagement.

Her future is set, safe and peaceful, just as she's always planned—until Agent Taylor informs her she's under suspicion for illegal drug activities.

Kade and his DEA team obtain evidence which exonerates Brooke while placing her in danger from those who sought to use her. As Kade races to take down the drug cartel while protecting Brooke, he must also find common ground with the former suspect—a woman he desires with increasing intensity.

At odds with her better judgment, Brooke finds the more time she spends with Kade, the more she's attracted to the complex, multi-faceted agent. But Kade holds secrets he knows Brooke will never understand or accept.

Can Kade keep Brooke safe while coming to terms with his past, or will he stay silent, ruining any future with the woman his heart can't let go?

Always Love You— Book Five
MacLarens of Fire Mountain
Contemporary Romance Series

"Romance, adventure, motorcycles, cowboys, suspense—everything you want in a contemporary western romance novel."

Eric Sinclair loves his bachelor status. His work at MacLaren Enterprises leaves him with plenty of time to ride his horse as well as his Harley...and date beautiful women without a thought to commitment.

Amber Anderson is the new person at MacLaren Enterprises. Her passion for marketing landed her what she believes to be the perfect job—until she steps into her first meeting to find the man she left, but still loves, sitting at the management table—his disdain for her clear.

Eric won't allow the past to taint his professional behavior, nor will he repeat his mistakes with

Amber, even though love for her pulses through him as strong as ever.

As they strive to mold a working relationship, unexpected danger confronts those close to them, pitting the MacLarens and Sinclairs against an evil who stalks one member but threatens them all.

Eric can't get the memories of their passionate past out of his mind, while Amber wrestles with feelings she thought long buried. Will they be able to put the past behind them to reclaim the love lost years before?

Hearts Don't Lie– Book Six
MacLarens of Fire Mountain
Contemporary Romance Series

Mitch MacLaren has reasons for avoiding relationships, and in his opinion, they're pretty darn good. As the new president of RTC Bucking Bulls, difficult challenges occur daily. He certainly doesn't need another one in the form of a fiery, blue-eyed, redhead.

Dana Ballard's new job forces her to work with the one MacLaren who can't seem to get over himself and lighten up. Their verbal sparring is second nature and entertaining until the night of

Mitch's departure when he surprises her with a dare she doesn't refuse.

With his assignment in Fire Mountain over, Mitch is free to return to Montana and run the business his father helped start. The glitch in his enthusiasm has to do with one irreversible mistake—the dare Dana didn't ignore. Now, for reasons that confound him, he just can't let it go.

Working together is a circumstance neither wants, but both must accept. As their attraction grows, so do the accidents and strange illnesses of the animals RTC depends on to stay in business. Mitch's total focus should be on finding the reasons and people behind the incidents. Instead, he finds himself torn between his unwanted desire for Dana and the business which is his life.

In his mind, a simple proposition can solve one problem. Will Dana make the smart move and walk away? Or take the gamble and expose her heart?

No Getting Over You— Book Seven
MacLarens of Fire Mountain
Contemporary Romance Series

Cassie MacLaren has come a long way since being dumped by her long-time boyfriend, a man she believed to be her future. Successful in her job at MacLaren Enterprises, dreaming of one day leading one of the divisions, she's moved on to start a new relationship, having little time to dwell on past mistakes.

Matt Garner loves his job as rodeo representative for Double Ace Bucking Stock. Busy days and constant travel leave no time for anything more than the occasional short-term relationship—which is just the way he likes it. He's come to accept the regret of leaving the woman he loved for the pro rodeo circuit.

The future is set for both, until a chance meeting ignites long buried emotions neither is willing to face.

Forced to work together, their attraction grows, even as multiple arson fires threaten Cassie's new home of Cold Creek, Colorado. Although Cassie believes the danger from the fires is remote, she knows the danger Matt poses to her heart is real.

While fighting his renewed feelings for Cassie, Matt focuses on a new and unexpected opportunity offered by MacLaren Enterprises—

an opportunity that will put him on a direct collision course with Cassie.

Will pride and self-preservation control their future? Or will one be strong enough to make the first move, risking everything, including their heart?

'Til the Sun Comes Up— Book Eight
MacLarens of Fire Mountain
Contemporary Romance Series

Skye MacLaren's life revolves around her family and the fierce bucking bull stock they provide to rodeos. She's competitive and competent, having no room in her life for a relationship—including one with a world champion rider and business competitor.

Gage Templeton's rodeo past and executive position with a national bucking stock supplier assures him of exciting work and nights with any woman he chooses. He'll let no one get close— until his company partners with a competitor, forcing him to work with the one woman who could turn his resolve upside down.

Knowing a relationship is the last thing either needs, both charge ahead, certain they can keep their explosive feelings for each other in check— and away from curious family and friends.

Continuing their secret encounters becomes even harder when outside forces threaten both their businesses and the people they care about.

As Gage works to discover the threat meant to cripple his company, Skye's doubts increase. She wants more from the most magnetic man she's ever known, but protecting her heart must come first.

Desire, distrust, fear, and the pain of the past cloud their minds, even as they work together to identify the danger. Can two strong, determined people conquer the perils to their lives as well as their hearts?

Redemption's Edge – Book One
Redemption Mountain – Historical Western Romance Series

"A heartwarming, passionate story of loss, forgiveness, and redemption set in the untamed frontier during the tumultuous years following the Civil War. Ms. Davies' engaging and complex characters draw you in from the start, creating an exciting introduction to this new historical western romance series."

"Redemption's Edge is a strong and engaging introduction to her new historical western romance series."

Dax Pelletier is ready for a new life, far away from the one he left behind in Savannah following the South's devastating defeat in the Civil War. The ex-Confederate general wants nothing more to do with commanding men and confronting the tough truths of leadership.

Rachel Davenport possesses skills unlike those of her Boston socialite peers—skills honed as a nurse in field hospitals during the Civil War. Eschewing her northeastern suitors and changed by the carnage she's seen, Rachel decides to accept her uncle's invitation to assist him at his clinic in the dangerous and wild frontier of Montana.

Now a Texas Ranger, a promise to a friend takes Dax and his brother, Luke, to the untamed territory of Montana. He'll fulfill his oath and return to Austin, at least that's what he believes.

The small town of Splendor is what Rachel needs after life in a large city. In a few short months, she's grown to love the people as well as the majestic beauty of the untamed frontier. She's settled into a life unlike any she has ever thought possible.

Thinking his battle days are over, he now faces dangers of a different kind—one by those from his past who seek vengeance, and another from Rachel, the woman who's captured his heart.

Wildfire Creek – Book Two
Redemption Mountain – Historical Western Romance Series

"A passionate story of rebuilding lives, working to find a place in the wild frontier, and building new lives in the years following the American Civil War. A rugged, heartwarming story of choices and love in the continuing saga of Redemption Mountain."

Luke Pelletier is settling into his new life as a rancher and occasional Pinkerton Agent, leaving his past as an ex-Confederate major and Texas Ranger far behind. He wants nothing more than to work the ranch, charm the ladies, and live a life of carefree bachelorhood.

Ginny Sorensen has accepted her responsibility as the sole provider for herself and her younger sister. The desire to continue their journey to Oregon is crushed when the need for food and shelter keeps them in the growing frontier town of Splendor, Montana, forcing Ginny to accept work as a server in the local saloon.

Luke has never met a woman as lovely and unspoiled as Ginny. He longs to know her, yet fears his wild ways and unsettled nature aren't what she deserves. She's a girl you marry, but that is nowhere in Luke's plans.

Complicating their tenuous friendship, a twist in circumstances forces Ginny closer to the man she most wants to avoid—the man who can destroy her dreams, and who's captured her heart.

Believing his bachelor status firm, Luke moves from danger to adventure, never dreaming each step he takes brings him closer to his true destiny and a life much different from what he imagines.

Sunrise Ridge – Book Three
Redemption Mountain – Historical Western Romance Series

"The author has a talent for bringing the historical west to life, realistically and vividly, and doesn't shy away from some of the harder aspects of frontier life, even though it's fiction. Recommended to readers who like sweeping western historical romances that are grounded with memorable, likeable characters and a strong sense of place."

Noah Brandt is a successful blacksmith and businessman in Splendor, Montana, with few ties to his past as an ex-Union Army major and sharpshooter. Quiet and hardworking, his biggest challenge is controlling his strong desire for a woman he believes is beyond his reach.

Abigail Tolbert is tired of being under her father's thumb while at the same time, being pushed away by the one man she desires. Determined to build a new life outside the control of her wealthy father, she finds work and sets out to shape a life on her own terms.

Noah has made too many mistakes with Abby to have any hope of getting her back. Even with the changes in her life, including the distance she's built with her father, he can't keep himself from believing he'll never be good enough to claim her.

Unexpected dangers, including a twist of fate for Abby, change both their lives, making the tentative steps they've taken to build a relationship a distant hope. As Noah battles his past as well as the threats to Abby, she fights for a future with the only man she will ever love.

Dixie Moon – Book Four
Redemption Mountain – Historical Western Romance Series

Gabe Evans is a man of his word with strong convictions and steadfast loyalty. As the sheriff of Splendor, Montana, the ex-Union Colonel and oldest of four boys from an affluent family, Gabe understands the meaning of responsibility. The last thing he wants is another commitment—especially of the female variety.

Until he meets Lena Campanel...

Lena's past is one she intends to keep buried. Overcoming a childhood of setbacks and obstacles, she and her friend, Nick, have succeeded in creating a life of financial success and devout loyalty to one another.

When an unexpected death leaves Gabe the sole heir of a considerable estate, partnering with Nick and Lena is a lucrative decision...forcing Gabe and Lena to work together. As their desire grows, Lena refuses to let down her guard, vowing to keep her past hidden—even from a perfect man like Gabe.

But secrets never stay buried...

When revealed, Gabe realizes Lena's secrets are deeper than he ever imagined. For a man of his character, deception and lies of omission aren't negotiable. Will he be able to forgive the deceit? Or is the damage too great to ever repair?

Survivor Pass – Book Five
Redemption Mountain – Historical Western Romance Series

He thought he'd found a quiet life...

Cash Coulter settled into a life far removed from his days of fighting for the South and crossing the country as a bounty hunter. Now a deputy sheriff, Cash wants nothing more than to buy some land, raise cattle, and build a simple life in the frontier town of Splendor, Montana. But his whole world shifts when his gaze lands on the most captivating woman he's ever seen. And the feeling appears to be mutual.

But nothing is as it seems...

Alison McGrath moved from her home in Kentucky to the rugged mountains of Montana for one reason—to find the man responsible for murdering her brother. Despite using a false identity to avoid any tie to her brother's name, the citizens of Splendor have no intention of sharing their knowledge about the bank robbery which killed her only sibling. Alison knows her circle of lies can't end well, and her growing for

Cash threatens to weaken the revenge which drives her.

And the troubles are mounting...

There is danger surrounding them both—men who seek vengeance as a way to silence the past...by any means necessary.

Promise Trail – Book Six
Redemption Mountain – Historical Western Romance Series

Bull Mason has built a life far away from his service in the Union Army and the ravages of the Civil War. He's achieved his dreams—loyal friends, work he enjoys, a home of his own, and a promise from the woman he loves to become his wife.

Lydia Rinehart can't believe how much her life has changed. Escaping captivity from a Crow village, she finds refuge and a home at the sprawling Redemption's Edge ranch...and love in the arms of Bull Mason, the ranch foreman. For the first time since her parents' death, she feels cherished and safe.

In an instant their dreams are crushed...

Bull is resolute in his determination to track down and rescue Lydia's brother, kidnapped during the celebration of their friend's wedding. He's made a promise—one he intends to keep. Picking the best men, they are ready to ride, until he's given an ultimatum.

Choices can seldom be undone...

As their journey continues, the trackers become the prey, finding their freedom and lives threatened.

And promises broken can rarely be reclaimed...

Can Bull and Lydia trust each other again and find their way to back to the dreams they once shared?

Deep River – Book Seven
Redemption Mountain – Historical Western Romance Series

Beauregard Davis, ex-Confederate Captain and bounty hunter, has put his past behind him to focus on his future. He's a lawman with a purpose and a dream—do his job to the best of his abilities, and build a life with the woman he loves. Beau believes his life couldn't be better...until the day she boards a stagecoach, leaving him behind.

Caroline Iverson has a dream she won't deny. Traveling west, she expects to experience adventure. Instead, Caro finds a good man and unanticipated love. She never imagines the difficult decision to leave him behind would come back to haunt her.

After months of burying his pain in alcohol, Beau emerges stronger, determined to concentrate on a future without Caro. Doing his best to forget the past, he focuses his energy on work and preparing to build a home.

He never expected her to return, looking to recapture the love the two once shared.

Adding to Beau's concerns, two threats hang over him—outlaws have targeted his town, and he's being tracked by unidentified foes.

Keeping the town, Caro, and himself safe are his main priorities. He'll do whatever it takes to protect them. Guarding his heart is another matter.

How does a man ignore an all-consuming love without exposing himself to a threat worse than the physical dangers he already faces?

Reclaiming Love – Book One
Peregrine Bay – Contemporary Romance Series

Adam Monroe has seen his share of setbacks. Now he's back in Peregrine Bay, looking for a new life and second chance.

Julia Kerrigan's life rebounded after the sudden betrayal of the one man she ever loved. As president of a success real estate company, she's built a new life and future, pushing the painful past behind her.

Adam's reason for accepting the job as the town's new Police Chief can be explained in one word—Julia. He wants her back and will do whatever is necessary to achieve his goal, even knowing his biggest hurdle is the woman he still loves.

As they begin to reconnect, a terrible scandal breaks loose with Julia and Adam at the center.

Will the threat to their lives and reputations destroy their fledgling romance? Can Adam identify and eliminate the danger to Julia before he's had a chance to reclaim her love?

Our Kind of Love – Book Two
Peregrine Bay – Contemporary Romance Series

Selena Kerrigan is content with a life filled with work and family, never feeling the need to take a chance on a relationship—until she steps into a social world inhabited by a man with dark hair and penetrating blue eyes. Eyes that are fixed on her.

Lincoln Caldwell is a man satisfied with his life. Transitioning from an enviable career as a Navy SEAL to becoming a successful entrepreneur, his days focus on growing his security firm, spending his nights with whomever he chooses. Committing to one woman isn't on the horizon— until a captivating woman with caramel eyes sends his personal life into a tailspin.

Believing her identity remains a secret, Selena returns to work, ready to forget about running away from the bed she never should have gone near. She's prepared to put the colossal error, as well as the man she'll never see again, behind her.

Too bad the object of her lapse in judgment doesn't feel the same.

Linc is good at tracking his targets, and Selena is now at the top of his list. It's amazing how a pair of sandals and only a first name can say so much.

As he pursues the woman he can't rid from his mind, a series of cyber-attacks hit his business, threatening its hard-won success. Worse, and unbeknownst to most, Linc harbors a secret—one with the potential to alter his life, along with those he's close to, in ways he could never imagine.

Our Kind of Love, Book Two in the Peregrine Bay Contemporary Romance series, is a full-length novel with an HEA and no cliffhanger.

Colin's Quest – Book One
MacLarens of Boundary Mountain – Historical Western Romance Series

For An Undying Love...

When Colin MacLaren headed west on a wagon train, he hoped to find adventure and perhaps a little danger in untamed California. He never expected to meet the girl he would love forever. He also never expected her to be the daughter of his family's age-old enemy, but Sarah was a MacGregor and the anger he anticipated soon became a reality. Her father would not be swayed, vehemently refusing to allow marriage to a MacLaren.

Time Has No Effect...

Forced apart for five years, Sarah never forgot Colin—nor did she give up on his promise to come for her. Carrying the brooch he gave her as proof of their secret betrothal, she scans the trail from California, waiting for Colin to claim her. Unfortunately, her father has other plans.

And Enemies Hold No Power.

Nothing can stop Colin from locating Sarah. Not outlaws, runaways, or miles of difficult trails. However, reuniting is only the beginning. Together they must find the courage to fight the men who would keep them apart—and conquer the challenge of uniting two independent hearts.

Brodie's Gamble – Book Two
MacLarens of Boundary Mountain – Historical Western Romance Series

Brodie MacLaren has a dream. He yearns to wear the star—bring the guilty to justice and protect those who are innocent. In his mind, guilty means guilty, even when it includes a beautiful woman who sets his body on edge.

Maggie King lives a nightmare, wanting nothing more than to survive each day and recapture the life stolen from her. Each day she wakes and prays for escape. Taking the one chance she may ever have, Maggie lashes out, unprepared for the rising panic as the man people believe to be her husband lies motionless at her feet.

Deciding innocence and guilt isn't his job.

Brodie's orderly, black and white world spins as her story of kidnapping and abuse unfold. The fact nothing adds up as well as his growing attraction to Maggie cause doubts the stoic lawman can't afford to embrace.

Can a lifetime of believing in absolute right and wrong change in a heartbeat?

Maggie has traded one form of captivity for another. Thoughts of escape consume her, even as feelings for the handsome, unyielding lawman grow.

As events unfold, Brodie must fight more than his attraction. Someone is after Maggie—a real threat who is out to silence her.

He's challenged on all fronts—until he takes a gamble that could change his life or destroy his heart.

Quinn's Honor – Book Three
MacLarens of Boundary Mountain – Historical Western Romance Series

Quinn MacLaren has one true love...Circle M, the family ranch. He makes it a habit of working hard and playing harder, spending time with experienced women who know he wants nothing more than their company. He buries the love he feels for one woman deep inside, knowing he'll never be the man she needs.

Emma Pearce is a true ranch woman, working long hours to help keep the family ranch thriving. Feisty, funny, and reliable, she's the girl all the single young men want—after they've sewn their wild oats. Few know Emma has her heart set on one man. A man who may never grow up enough to walk away from his wild ways and settle down.

When tragedy strikes, Quinn's right where he doesn't want to be—as temporary foreman of the Pearce ranch. Stepping in to fill Big Jim Pearce's shoes isn't easy. Neither is keeping his feelings for Emma hidden and his hands to himself. Honor-bound to do what is right, Quinn meets the challenge, losing Emma's friendship in the process.

Adding to Quinn's worries, something sinister is working its way through the thriving town of Conviction. Unforeseen forces are at work. Debt builds, families lose their ranches, and newcomers threaten to divide not only the land, but the people—including the Pearce family.

As events unfold, Quinn faces the difficult challenge of keeping his feelings for Emma hidden and his honor intact. Doing what he believes is right couldn't feel more wrong.

After all, what's a man without honor?

Sam' Legacy – Book Four
MacLarens of Boundary Mountain – Historical Western Romance Series

Samuel Covington, ex-Pinkerton agent and deputy in the frontier town of Conviction, has come a long way from his upbringing in Baltimore. His job, and a particular woman, occupy his time and thoughts. His future is assured—until a message from home tears it all apart.

Jinny MacLaren loves the ranch, her family, and one particular deputy. Even though Sam's never said the words, she's certain of his feelings, envisioning a future as his wife—until the day he announces he's leaving without a promise to return.

His future no longer belongs to him. Sam never anticipated the news awaiting him, or the consequences of a past he'd left far behind.

Shoving painful thoughts of Sam aside, Jinny focuses on a life without him, allowing a friendship to grow with someone else. He's handsome, smart, and caring, yet in Jinny's heart, he'll never be Sam.

As both face an uncertain future without the other, neither anticipates the dangers stalking them.

Protecting what's his is Sam's calling. Reclaiming what he left behind may prove to be the biggest challenge of his life.

Find all of my books at:
http://www.shirleendavies.com/books.html

Avalanche Ranch Press, LLC
PO Box 12618
Prescott, AZ 86304

Made in the USA
Middletown, DE
24 July 2021